ORBIT 19

ORBIT 19

Edited by Damon Knight

HARPER & ROW, PUBLISHERS
New York, Hagerstown, San Francisco, London

ORBIT 19. Copyright © 1977 by Damon Knight. All rights reserved. Printed in the United States of America. No part of this book may be used or reproduced in any manner whatsoever without written permission except in the case of brief quotations embodied in critical articles and reviews. For information address Harper & Row, Publishers, Inc., 10 East 53rd Street, New York, N.Y. 10022. Published simultaneously in Canada by Fitzhenry & Whiteside Limited, Toronto.

FIRST EDITION

Designed by C. Linda Dingler

LIBRARY OF CONGRESS CATALOG CARD NUMBER: 76–26270

ISBN: 0–06–012431–8

77 78 79 80 81 10 9 8 7 6 5 4 3 2 1

CONTENTS

ORBIT 19

They Say

In some remarks about [Robert] Silverberg published elsewhere I found occasion to cause him mild pain by calling him five feet seven inches tall and "the best writer in English." I am happy to set the record straight for the audience that this collection will entertain: Silverberg is five feet ten (although his compaction and grace is such that to a hulking type like me he *seems* shorter), and he may be listed *among* the best writers in English, a club of no more than ten members to which I would also admit Vladimir Nabokov, Evan S. Connell, Jr., Norman Mailer, Robert Coover, Richard Yates, Philip Roth, John Cheever, J. D. Salinger, and Bernard Malamud. Whether or not he is the *best* of this awesome company is a matter for specialists; the point is that names such as these must be invoked in order to indicate his current position in literature. In ten years if he and you, to say nothing of the world, can remain in place, he may be in a category where no names at all other than his own can be mentioned. Until that day I am content to stand by this more modest judgment.

—"Thinking About Silverberg," by
Barry N. Malzberg, in *The Best of
Robert Silverberg* (Pocket Books, 1976)

1

C. S. Lewis rejected a religious interpretation of sf advanced by Roger Lancelyn Green, adding: "If he had said simply that something which the educated receive from poetry can reach the masses through stories of adventure, and almost in no other way, then I think he would have been right." Lewis's statement points to the paradoxical nature of science fiction as that which contains something akin to poetry, and yet is set apart from it by an aesthetic deficit. This longing for poetry in science fiction (as expressed in many reviews) is only surpassed by a prevalent taste for bad poetry, much as the enthusiasm for science among many sf writers is often overridden by their ignorance of it. In my opinion, science fiction is best described by such paradoxes, by the deep desire for the unattainable, only natural in a field of writing where ambition and publicly proclaimed aims so often exceed real potential and abilities.

> —*The Science Fiction Book,*
> *An Illustrated History,*
> by Franz Rottensteiner
> (Seabury Press, 1975)

According to one American astronomer, whole volumes of the Encyclopedia Galactica may be winging their way towards us, packed with all the scientific knowledge that an advanced and benevolent society might consider important—the secrets of longevity and peaceful coexistence, the answer to malignant diseases, perhaps new sources of power that dwarf even the atom's explosive stockpile. Interspersed with these electrifying revelations could be instructions for learning Galactic, the language of interstellar communication—an open invitation to us to answer the call.

But would the possible dangers of answering a call from another civilization outweigh the likely benefits? The Czech-British astronomer Zdenek Kopal has visualized our confrontation with extraterrestrial beings intelligent enough to have discovered our existence: "We might find ourselves in their test tubes or other contraptions set up to investigate us as we do guinea pigs. . . . If the space phone rings," he pleads, "for God's sake let us not answer it."

—*Worlds Beyond, A Report
on the Search for Life
in Space,* by Ian Ridpath
(Harper & Row, 1976)

Machine-buffs are easy to cater to. Early sf magazines are full of outrageous machines, all cogs and rivets and columns and winking lights and trailing cables, so that the characters are perpetually tripping through a gigantic Meccano landscape. But the relation to reality is not as remote as might be supposed. You invent futures by magnifying pasts. Many outrageous futurist machines derive from a great age of invention, when diabolical engines proliferated—Brunton's drilling machine of the eighteen-seventies, for example, would be perfectly at home in some subterranean horror planet designed by Harry Harrison or John Sladek.

Most inventors cared for invention itself, not the social consequences of the invention; this myopia is what one might call the Frankenstein syndrome. Horrific experiments, like the attempts of a French surgeon to preserve the dead by electroplating them, are the stuff of sf, even when they take place in real life. The illustration of Dr. Varlot's experiment which appeared in the *Scientific American* in 1891 is real Mad Scientist stuff, complete with Moronic Laboratory Assistant, and could serve as an *Amazing* cover (indeed, mutatis mutandis, it often did so serve!). To have one's dear ones electroplated by return and at no great cost is not an unreasonable ambition; like much else which might—ironically or not—be termed Progress, the idea seems to encompass hope and fear in roughly equal proportions.

—*Science Fiction Art,*
by Brian Aldiss
(Bounty Books, 1975)

Viewed as an animal, man must continue to expand his domain, to extend his ecological range, to push out his territory; or he must find an innocuous ecological niche in another society, like the ant or the housefly, where he is too difficult or too expensive to eradicate; or he must ingratiate himself into a superior culture, like the dog or the cat; or he must die. Such has been the evolutionary history of Earth, of which man is a part. Both evolutionary and recorded history confirm a picture of man as a creature which must be dominant, which eliminates competing species, which has found ways of existing wherever endurance, adaptability, or intelligence can fit him to the environment or environment to him. This is science fiction's traditional vision of man as he faces the universe.

—*Alternate Worlds, The
Illustrated History of
Science Fiction,* by James
Gunn (Prentice-Hall, 1975)

For all its persistence, the custom of Man eating Man (and *vice versa*) has never become really common . . . One problem is that widespread enthusiasm for the practice tends to be self-limiting, if not self-extinguishing. Another is that if the enthusiasm doesn't infect the intended donors, their uncooperative behavior leads to no end of wrangling and bitterness. And then there is the problem of disease.

Now, lumberjacks catch neither the Chestnut Blight nor the Dutch Elm Disease. Lobstermen are likewise immune to the ills that afflict their crustacean prey. But some diseases of poultry can be caught by their keepers; and with mammalian livestock, matters are much worse. When Man is both predator and prey, *everything* is catching, from the Common Cold on up to the Black Plague even before the donor is dispatched, along with a variety of ailments which can be ingested with the meal itself.

Some, like Tuberculosis, are quite rare, especially if one exercises reasonable care in selecting one's prey. Hepatitis is more common; more difficult to detect without an elaborate routine of testing and questioning of the donor, which tends to alarm him prematurely; and in the case of some virulent strains, almost impossible to destroy without burning the meat to a cinder and sometimes not even then. As for Trichinosis, one study has shown about a 2% infestation of pork and a 20% infestation of people. In theory, one could limit one's diet to devout Buddhists and Orthodox Jews; in practice, however, one can never be sure that the donor isn't a late convert. The usual precaution is simply to cook Man very thoroughly, as with pork only more so.

—*To Serve Man: A Cookbook*
for People, by Karl Würf
(Owlswick Press, 1976)

LOLLIPOP AND THE TAR BABY

The tale of a talking black hole, a cloned
woman alone outside the orbit of Pluto, and a mirror
that reflected another's face.

John Varley

"Zzzzello. Zzz. Hello. Hello." Someone was speaking to Xanthia from the end of a ten-kilometer metal pipe, shouting to be heard across a roomful of gongs and cymbals being knocked over by angry giant bees. She had never heard such interference.

"Hello?" she repeated. "What are you doing on my wavelength?"

"Hello." The interference was still there, but the voice was slightly more distinct. "Wavelength. Searching, searching wavelength . . . get best reception with . . . Hello? Listening?"

"Yes, I'm listening. You're talking over . . . my radio isn't even . . ." She banged the radio panel with her palm in the ancient ritual humans employ when their creations are being balky. "My goddamn *radio* isn't even on. Did you know that?" It was a relief to feel anger boiling up inside her. Anything was preferable to feeling lost and silly.

"Not necessary."

"What do you mean, not—who *are* you?"

"Who. Having . . . *I'm*, pronoun, yes, I'm having difficulty. Bear with. Me? Yes, pronoun. Bear with me. I'm not who. What. *What* am I?"

"All right. *What* are you?"

"Spacetime phenomenon. I'm gravity and causality-sink. Black hole."

Xanthia did not need black holes explained to her. She had spent her entire eighteen years hunting them, along with her clone-sister, Zoetrope. But she was not used to having them talk to her.

"Assuming for the moment that you really are a black hole," she said, beginning to wonder if this might be some elaborate trick played on her by Zoe, "just taking that as a tentative hypothesis—how are you able to talk to me?"

There was a sound like an attitude thruster going off, a rumbling pop. It was repeated.

"I manipulate spacetime framework . . . no, please hold line . . . *the* line. I manipulate the spacetime framework with controlled gravity waves projected in narrow . . . a narrow cone. I direct at the speaker in your radio. You hear. Me."

"What was that again?" It sounded like a lot of crap to her.

"I elaborate. I will elaborate. I cut through space itself, through—hold the line, hold the line, reference." There was a sound like a tape reeling rapidly through playback heads. "This is the BBC," said a voice that was recognizably human, but blurred by static. The tape whirred again. "gust the third, in the year of our Lord nineteen fifty-seven. Today in—" Once again the tape hunted.

"chelson-Morley experiment disproved the existence of the ether, by ingeniously arranging a rotating prism—" Then the metallic voice was back.

"Ether. I cut through space itself, through a—hold the line."

This time the process was shorter. She heard a fragment of what sounded like a video adventure serial. "Through a spacewarp made through the ductile etheric continuum—"

"Hold on there. That's not what you said before."

"I was elaborating."

"Go on. Wait, what were you doing? With that tape business?"

The voice paused, and when the answer came the line had cleared up quite a bit. But the voice still didn't sound human. Computer?

"I am not used to speech. No need for it. But I have learned your language by listening to radio transmissions. I speak to you through use of indeterminate statistical concatenations. Gravity waves and probability, which is not the same thing in a causality singularity, enables a nonrational event to take place."

"Zoe, this is really you, isn't it?"

Xanthia was only eighteen Earth-years old, on her first long orbit into the space beyond Pluto, the huge cometary zone where space is truly flat. Her whole life had been devoted to learning how to find and capture black holes, but one didn't come across them very often. Xanthia had been born a year after the beginning of the voyage and had another year to go before the end of it. In her whole life she had seen and talked to only one other human being, and that was Zoe, who was one hundred and thirty-five years old and her identical twin.

Their home was the *Shirley Temple,* a fifteen thousand tonne fusion-drive ship registered out of Lowell, Pluto. Zoe owned *Shirley* free and clear; on her first trip, many years ago, she had found a scale-five hole and had become instantly rich. Most hole hunters were not so lucky.

Zoe was also unusual in that she seemed to thrive on solitude. Most hunters who made a strike settled down to live in comfort, buy a large company or put the money into safe investments and live off the interest. They were unwilling or unable to face another twenty years alone. Zoe had gone out again, and a third time after the second trip had proved fruitless. She had found a hole on her third trip, and was now almost through her fifth.

But for some reason she had never adequately explained to Xanthia, she had wanted a companion this time. And what better company than herself? With the medical facilities aboard *Shirley* she had grown a copy of herself and raised the little girl as her daughter.

Xanthia squirmed around in the control cabin of *The Good Ship Lollipop*, stuck her head through the hatch leading to the aft exercise room, and found nothing. What she had expected, she didn't know. Now she crouched in midair with a screwdriver, attacking the service panels that protected the radio assembly.

"What are you doing by yourself?" the voice asked.

"Why don't *you* tell *me*, Zoe?" she said, lifting the panel off and tossing it angrily to one side. She peered into the gloomy interior, wrinkling her nose at the smell of oil and paraffin. She shone her pencil-beam into the space, flicking it from one component to the next, all as familiar to her as neighborhood corridors would be to a planet-born child. There was nothing out of place, nothing that shouldn't be there. Most of it was sealed into plastic blocks to prevent moisture or dust from getting to critical circuits. There were no signs of tampering.

"I am failing to communicate. I am not your mother, I am a gravity and causality—"

"She's not my mother," Xanthia snapped.

"My records show that she would dispute you."

Xanthia didn't like the way the voice said that. But she was admitting to herself that there was no way Zoe could have set this up. That left her with the alternative: she really was talking to a black hole.

"She's not my mother," Xanthia repeated. "And if you've been listening in, you *know* why I'm out here in a lifeboat. So why do you ask?"

"I wish to help you. I have heard tension building between the two of you these last years. You are growing up."

Xanthia settled back in the control chair. Her head did not feel
so good.

Hole hunting was a delicate economic balance, a tightrope
walked between the needs of survival and the limitations of mass.
The initial investment was tremendous and the return was un-
dependable, so the potential hole hunter had to have a line to a
source of speculative credit or be independently wealthy.

No consortium or corporation had been able to turn a profit
at the business by going at it in a big way. The government of
Pluto maintained a monopoly on the use of one-way robot
probes, but they had found over the years that when a probe
succeeded in finding a hole, a race usually developed to see who
would reach it and claim it first. Ships sent after such holes had
a way of disappearing in the resulting fights, far from law and
order.

The demand for holes was so great that an economic niche
remained which was filled by the solitary prospector, backed by
people with tax write-offs to gain. Prospectors had a ninety per
cent bankruptcy rate. But as with gold and oil in earlier days, the
potential profits were huge, so there was never a lack of specula-
tors.

Hole hunters would depart Pluto and accelerate to the limits
of engine power, then coast for ten to fifteen years, keeping an
eye on the mass detector. Sometimes they would be half a light-
year from Sol before they had to decelerate and turn around.
Less mass equalled more range, so the solitary hunter was the
rule.

Teaming of ships had been tried, but teams that discovered a
hole seldom came back together. One of them tended to have an
accident. Hole hunters were a greedy lot, self-centered and self-
sufficient.

Equipment had to be reliable. Replacement parts were costly
in terms of mass, so the hole hunter had to make an agonizing

choice with each item. Would it be better to leave it behind and chance a possibly fatal failure, or take it along, decreasing the range, and maybe miss the glory hole that is sure to be lurking just one more AU away? Hole hunters learned to be handy at repairing, jury-rigging, and bashing, because in twenty years even fail-safe triplicates can be on their last legs.

Zoe had sweated over her faulty mass detector before she admitted it was beyond her skills. Her primary detector had failed ten years into the voyage, and the second one had begun to act up six years later. She tried to put together one functioning detector with parts cannibalized from both. She nursed it along for a year with the equivalents of bobby pins and bubblegum. It was hopeless.

But *Shirley Temple* was a palace among prospecting ships. Having found two holes in her career, Zoe had her own money. She had stocked spare parts, beefed up the drive, even included that incredible luxury, a lifeboat.

The lifeboat was sheer extravagance, except for one thing. It had a mass detector as part of its astrogational equipment. She had bought it mainly for that reason, since it had only an eighteen-month range and would be useless except at the beginning and end of the trip, when they were close to Pluto. It made extensive use of plug-in components, sealed in plastic to prevent tampering or accidents caused by inexperienced passengers. The mass detector on board did not have the range or accuracy of the one on *Shirley*. It could be removed or replaced, but not recalibrated.

They had begun a series of three-month loops out from the mother ship. Xanthia had flown most of them earlier, when Zoe did not trust her to run *Shirley*. Later they had alternated.

"And that's what I'm doing out here by myself," Xanthia said. "I have to get out beyond ten million kilometers from *Shirley* so its mass doesn't affect the detector. My instrument is calibrated to ignore only the mass of this ship, not *Shirley*. I stay out here for three months, which is a reasonably safe time for the life systems on *Lollipop,* and time to get pretty lonely. Then back for refueling and supplying.''

"The *Lollipop?*''

Xanthia blushed. "Well, I named this lifeboat that, after I started spending so much time on it. We have a tape of Shirley Temple in the library, and she sang this song, see—"

"Yes, I've heard it. I've been listening to radio for a very long time. So you no longer believe this is a trick by your mother?"

"She's *not . . .*" Then she realized she had referred to Zoe in the third person again.

"I don't know what to think," she said, miserably. "Why are you doing this?"

"I sense that you are still confused. You'd like some proof that I am what I say I am. Since you'll think of it in a minute, I might as well ask you this question. Why do you suppose I haven't yet registered on your mass detector?"

Xanthia jerked in her seat, then was brought up short by the straps. It was true, there was not the slightest wiggle on the dials of the detector.

"All right, why haven't you?" She felt a sinking sensation. She was sure the punchline came now, after she'd shot off her mouth about *Lollipop*—her secret from Zoe—and made such a point of the fact that Zoe was not her mother. It was her own private rebellion, one that she had not had the nerve to face Zoe with. Now she's going to reveal herself and tell me how she did it, and I'll feel like a fool, she thought.

"It's simple," the voice said. "You weren't in range of me yet. But now you are. Take a look."

The needles were dancing, giving the reading of a scale-seven hole. A scale seven would mass about a tenth as much as the asteroid Ceres.

"Mommy, what *is* a black hole?"

The little girl was seven years old. One day she would call herself Xanthia, but she had not yet felt the need for a name and her mother had not seen fit to give her one. Zoe reasoned that you needed two of something before you needed names. There was only one other person on *Shirley*. There was no possible confusion. When the girl thought about it at all, she assumed her name must be Hey, or Darling.

She was a small child, as Zoe had been. She was recapitulating the growth Zoe had already been through a hundred years ago. Though she didn't know it, she was pretty: dark eyes with an oriental fold, dark skin, and kinky blond hair. She was a genetic mix of Chinese and Negro, with dabs of other races thrown in for seasoning.

"I've tried to explain that before," Zoe said. "You don't have the math for it yet. I'll get you started on spacetime equations, then in about a year you'll be able to understand."

"But I want to know now." Black holes were a problem for the child. From her earliest memories the two of them had done nothing but hunt them, yet they never found one. She'd been doing a lot of reading—there was little else to do—and was wondering if they might inhabit the same category where she had tentatively placed Santa Claus and leprechauns.

"If I try again, will you go to sleep?"

"I promise."

So Zoe launched into her story about the Big Bang, the time in the long-ago when little black holes could be formed.

"As far as we can tell, all the little black holes like the ones we hunt were made in that time. Nowadays other holes can be formed by the collapse of very large stars. When the fires burn low and the pressures that are trying to blow the star apart begin to fade, gravity takes over and starts to pull the star in on itself." Zoe waved her hands in the air, forming cups to show bending space, flailing out to indicate pressures of fusion. These explanations were almost as difficult for her as stories of sex had been for earlier generations. The truth was that she was no relativist and didn't really grasp the slightly incredible premises behind black-hole theory. She suspected that no one could really visualize one, and if you can't do that, where are you? But she was practical enough not to worry about it.

"And what's gravity? I forgot." The child was rubbing her eyes to stay awake. She struggled to understand but already knew she would miss the point yet another time.

"Gravity is the thing that holds the universe together. The glue, or the rivets. It pulls everything toward everything else, and it takes energy to fight it and overcome it. It feels like when we boost the ship, remember I pointed that out to you?"

"Like when everything wants to move in the same direction?"

"That's right. So we have to be careful, because we don't think about it much. We have to worry about where things arc because when we boost, everything will head for the stern. People on planets have to worry about that all the time. They have to put something strong between themselves and the center of the planet, or they'll go down."

"Down." The girl mused over that word, one that had been giving her trouble as long as she could remember, and thought she might finally have understood it. She had seen pictures of places where down was always the same direction, and they were strange to the eye. They were full of tables to put things on, chairs to sit in, and funny containers with no tops. Five of the six walls of rooms on planets could hardly be used at all. One, the "floor," was called on to take all the use.

"So they use their legs to fight gravity with?" She was yawning now.

"Yes. You've seen pictures of the people with the funny legs. They're not so funny when you're in gravity. Those flat things on the ends are called feet. If they had peds like us, they wouldn't be able to walk so good. They always have to have one foot touching the floor, or they'd fall toward the surface of the planet."

Zoe tightened the strap that held the child to her bunk, and fastened the velcro patch on the blanket to the side of the sheet, tucking her in. Kids needed a warm snug place to sleep. Zoe preferred to float free in her own bedroom, tucked into a fetal position and drifting.

"G'night, Mommy."

"Good night. You get some sleep, and don't worry about black holes."

But the child dreamed of them, as she often did. They kept tugging at her, and she would wake breathing hard and convinced that she was going to fall into the wall in front of her.

"You don't mean it? I'm rich!"

Xanthia looked away from the screen. It was no good pointing out that Zoe had always spoken of the trip as a partnership. She owned *Shirley* and *Lollipop*.

"Well, you too, of course. Don't think you won't be getting a real big share of the money. I'm going to set you up so well that you'll be able to buy a ship of your own, and raise little copies of yourself if you want to."

Xanthia was not sure that was her idea of heaven, but said nothing.

"Zoe, there's a problem, and I . . . well, I was—" But she was interrupted again by Zoe, who would not hear Xanthia's comment for another thirty seconds.

"The first data is coming over the telemetry channel right now, and I'm feeding it into the computer. Hold on a second while I turn the ship. I'm going to start decelerating in about one minute, based on these figures. You get the refined data to me as soon as you have it."

There was a brief silence.

"What problem?"

"It's talking to me, Zoe. The hole is talking to me."

This time the silence was longer than the minute it took the radio signal to make the round trip between ships. Xanthia furtively thumbed the contrast knob, turning her sister-mother down until the screen was blank. She could look at the camera and Zoe wouldn't know the difference.

Damn, damn, she thinks I've flipped. But I *had* to tell her.

"I'm not sure what you mean."

"Just what I *said.* I don't understand it, either. But it's been talking to me for the last hour, and it says the *damnedest* things."

There was another silence.

"All right. When you get there, don't do anything, repeat, *anything,* until I arrive. Do you understand?"

"Zoe, I'm not crazy. I'm *not.* "

Then why am I crying?

"Of course you're not, baby, there's an explanation for this and I'll find out what it is as soon as I get there. You just hang on. My first rough estimate puts me alongside you about three hours after you're stationary relative to the hole."

Shirley and *Lollipop,* traveling parallel courses, would both be veering from their straight-line trajectories to reach the hole. But Xanthia was closer to it; Zoe would have to move at a more oblique angle and would be using more fuel. Xanthia thought four hours was more like it.

"I'm signing off," Zoe said. "I'll call you back as soon as I'm in the groove."

Xanthia hit the off button on the radio and furiously unbuckled her seatbelt. Damn Zoe, damn her, damn her, *damn her.* Just sit tight, she says. I'll be there to explain the unexplainable. It'll be all right.

She knew she should start her deceleration, but there was something she must do first.

She twisted easily in the air, grabbing at braces with all four hands, and dived through the hatch to the only other living space in *Lollipop:* the exercise area. It was cluttered with equipment that she had neglected to fold into the walls, but she didn't mind; she liked close places. She squirmed through the maze like a fish gliding through coral, until she reached the wall she was looking for. It had been taped over with discarded manual pages, the only paper she could find on *Lollipop.* She started ripping at the paper, wiping tears from her cheeks with one ped as she worked. Beneath the paper was a mirror.

How to test for sanity? Xanthia had not considered the question; the thing to do had simply presented itself and she had done it. Now she confronted the mirror and searched for . . . what? Wild eyes? Froth on the lips?

What she saw was her mother.

Xanthia's life had been a process of growing slowly into the mold Zoe represented. She had known her pug nose would eventually turn down. She had known what baby fat would melt away. Her breasts had grown just into the small cones she knew from her mother's body and no farther.

She hated looking in mirrors.

Xanthia and Zoe were small women. Their most striking feature was the frizzy dandelion of yellow hair, lighter than their bodies. When the time had come for naming, the young clone had almost opted for Dandelion until she came upon the word *xanthic* in a dictionary. The radio call-letters for *Lollipop* happened to be X-A-N, and the word was too good to resist. She knew, too, that Orientals were thought of as having yellow skin, though she could not see why.

Why had she come here, of all places? She strained toward the mirror, fighting her repulsion, searching her face for signs of insanity. The narrow eyes were a little puffy, and as deep and expressionless as ever. She put her hands to the glass, startled in the silence to hear the multiple clicks as the long nails just missed touching the ones on the other side. She was always forgetting to trim them.

Sometimes, in mirrors, she knew she was not seeing herself. She could twitch her mouth, and the image would not move. She could smile, and the image would frown. It had been happening for two years, as her body put the finishing touches on its eighteen-year process of duplicating Zoe. She had not spoken of it, because it scared her.

"And this is where I come to see if I'm sane," she said aloud, noting that the lips in the mirror did not move. "Is she going to start talking to me now?" She waved her arms wildly, and so did Zoe in the mirror. At least it wasn't that bad yet; it was only the details that failed to match: the small movements, and especially the facial expressions. Zoe was inspecting her dispassionately and did not seem to like what she saw. That small curl at the edge of the mouth, the almost brutal narrowing of the eyes . . .

Xanthia clapped her hands over her face, then peeked out through the fingers. Zoe was peeking out, too. Xanthia began rounding up the drifting scraps of paper and walling her twin in again with new bits of tape.

The beast with two backs and legs at each end writhed, came apart, and resolved into Xanthia and Zoe, drifting, breathing hard. They caromed off the walls like monkeys, giving up their energy, gradually getting breath back under control. Golden, wet hair and sweaty skin brushed against each other again and again as they came to rest.

Now the twins floated in the middle of the darkened bedroom. Zoe was already asleep, tumbling slowly with that total looseness possible only in free fall. Her leg rubbed against Xanthia's belly and her relative motion stopped. The leg was moist. The room was close, thick with the smell of passion. The recirculators whined quietly as they labored to clear the air.

Pushing one finger gently against Zoe's ankle, Xanthia turned her until they were face to face. Frizzy blonde hair tickled her nose, and she felt warm breath on her mouth.

Why can't it always be like this?

"You're not my mother," she whispered. Zoe had no reaction to this heresy. "You're *not.*"

Only in the last year had Zoe admitted the relationship was much closer. Xanthia was now fifteen.

And what was different? Something, there had to be something beyond the mere knowledge that they were not mother and child. There was a new quality in their relationship, growing as they came to the end of the voyage. Xanthia would look into those eyes where she had seen love and now see only blankness, coldness.

"Oriental inscrutability?" she asked herself, half-seriously. She knew she was hopelessly unsophisticated. She had spent her life in a society of two. The only other person she knew had her own face. But she had thought she knew Zoe. Now she felt less confident with every glance into Zoe's face and every kilometer passed on the way to Pluto.

Pluto.

Her thoughts turned gratefully away from immediate problems and toward that unimaginable place. She would be there in only four more years. The cultural adjustments she would have to make were staggering. Thinking about that, she felt a sensation in her chest that she guessed was her heart leaping in anticipation. That's what happened to characters in tapes when they got excited, anyway. Their hearts were forever leaping, thudding, aching, or skipping beats.

She pushed away from Zoe and drifted slowly to the viewport. Her old friends were all out there, the only friends she had ever known, the stars. She greeted them all one by one, reciting childhood mnemonic riddles and rhymes like bedtime prayers.

It was a funny thought that the view from her window would terrify many of those strangers she was going to meet on Pluto. She'd read that many tunnel-raised people could not stand open spaces. What it was that scared them, she could not understand. The things that scared her were crowds, gravity, males, and mirrors.

"Oh, damn. Damn! I'm going to be just *hopeless.* Poor little idiot girl from the sticks, visiting the big city." She brooded for a time on all the thousands of things she had never done, from swimming in the gigantic underground disneylands to seducing a boy.

"To *being* a boy." It had been the source of their first big argument. When Xanthia had reached adolescence, the time when children want to begin experimenting, she had learned from Zoe that *Shirley Temple* did not carry the medical equipment for sex changes. She was doomed to spend her critical formative years as a sexual deviate, a unisex.

"It'll stunt me forever," she had protested. She had been reading a lot of pop psychology at the time.

"Nonsense," Zoe had responded, hard-pressed to explain why she had not stocked a viro-genetic imprinter and the companion Y-alyzer. Which, as Xanthia pointed out, *any* self-respecting home surgery kit should have.

"The human race got along for millions of years without sex changing," Zoe had said. "Even after the Invasion. We were a highly technological race for hundreds of years before changing. Billions of people lived and died in the same sex."

"Yeah, and look what they were like."

Now, for another of what seemed like an endless series of nights, sleep was eluding her. There was the worry of Pluto, and the worry of Zoe and her strange behavior, and no way to explain anything in her small universe which had become unbearably complicated in the last years.

I wonder what it would be like with a man?

Three hours ago Xanthia had brought *Lollipop* to a careful rendezvous with the point in space her instruments indicated contained a black hole. She had long since understood that even if she ever found one she would never see it, but she could not restrain herself from squinting into the starfield for some evidence. It was silly; though the hole massed ten to the fifteenth tonnes (the original estimate had been off one order of magnitude) it was still only a fraction of a millimeter in diameter. She was staying a good safe hundred kilometers from it. Still, you ought to be able to sense something like that, you ought to be able to *feel* it.

It was no use. This hunk of space looked exactly like any other.

"There is a point I would like explained," the hole said. "What will be done with me after you have captured me?"

The question surprised her. She still had not got around to thinking of the voice as anything but some annoying aberration like her face in the mirror. How was she supposed to deal with it? Could she admit to herself that it existed, that it might even have feelings?

"I guess we'll just mark you, in the computer, that is. You're too big for us to haul back to Pluto. So we'll hang around you for a week or so, refining your trajectory until we know precisely where you're going to be, then we'll leave you. We'll make some maneuvers on the way in so no one could retrace our path and find out where you are, because they'll know we found a big one when we get back."

"How will they know that?"

"Because we'll be renting . . . well, *Zoe* will be chartering one of those big monster tugs, and she'll come out here and put a charge on you and tow you . . . say, how do you feel about this?"

"Are you concerned with the answer?"

The more Xanthia thought about it, the less she liked it. If she really was not hallucinating this experience, then she was contemplating the capture and imprisonment of a sentient being. An innocent sentient being who had been wandering around the edge of the system, suddenly to find him or herself . . .

"Do you have a sex?"

"No."

"All right, I guess I've been kind of short with you. It's just because you *did* startle me, and I *didn't* expect it, and it was all a little alarming."

The hole said nothing.

"You're a strange sort of person, or whatever," she said.

Again there was a silence.

"Why don't you tell me more about yourself? What's it like being a black hole, and all that?" She still couldn't fight down the ridiculous feeling those words gave her.

"I live much as you do, from day to day. I travel from star to star, taking about ten million years for the trip. Upon arrival, I plunge through the core of the star. I do this as often as is necessary, then I depart by a slingshot maneuver through the heart of a massive planet. The Tunguska Meteorite, which hit

Siberia in 1908, was a black hole gaining momentum on its way to Jupiter, where it could get the added push needed for solar escape velocity."

One thing was bothering Xanthia. "What do you mean, 'as often as is necessary'?"

"Usually five or six thousand passes is sufficient."

"No, no. What I meant is *why* is it necessary? What do you get out of it?"

"Mass," the hole said. "I need to replenish my mass. The Relativity Laws state that nothing can escape from a black hole, but the Quantum Laws, specifically the Heisenberg Uncertainty Principle, state that below a certain radius the position of a particle cannot be determined. I lose mass constantly through tunneling. It is not all wasted, as I am able to control the direction and form of the escaping mass, and to use the energy that results to perform functions that your present-day physics says are impossible."

"Such as?" Xanthia didn't know why, but she was getting nervous.

"I can exchange inertia for gravity, and create energy in a variety of ways."

"So you can move yourself."

"Slowly."

"And you eat . . ."

"Anything."

Xanthia felt a sudden panic, but she didn't know what was wrong. She glanced down at her instruments and felt her hair prickle from her wrists and ankles to the nape of her neck.

The hole was ten kilometers closer than it had been.

"How could you *do* that to me?" Xanthia raged. "I trusted you, and that's how you repaid me, by trying to sneak up on me and . . . and—"

"It was not intentional. I speak to you by means of controlled gravity waves. To speak to you at all, it is necessary to generate an attractive force between us. You were never in any danger."

"I don't believe that," Xanthia said angrily. "I think you're doubletalking me. I don't think gravity works like that, and I don't think you really tried very hard to tell me how you talk to me, back when we first started." It occurred to her now, also, that the hole was speaking much more fluently than in the beginning. Either it was a very fast learner, or that had been intentional.

The hole paused. "This is true," it said.

She pressed her advantage. "Then why did you do it?"

"It was a reflex, like blinking in a bright light, or drawing one's hand back from a fire. When I sense matter, I am attracted to it."

"The proper cliché would be 'like a moth to a flame.' But you're not a moth, and I'm not a flame. I don't believe you. I think you could have stopped yourself if you wanted to."

Again the hole hesitated. "You are correct."

"So you were trying to . . .?"

"I was trying to eat you."

"Just like *that?* Eat someone you've been having a conversation with?"

"Matter is matter," the hole said, and Xanthia thought she detected a defensive note in its voice.

"What do you think of what I said we're going to do with you? You were going to tell me, but we got off on that story about where you came from."

"As I understand it, you propose to return for me. I will be towed to near Pluto's orbit, sold, and eventually come to rest in the heart of an orbital power station, where your species will feed matter into my gravity well, extracting power cheaply from the gravitational collapse."

"Yeah, that's pretty much it."

"It sounds ideal. My life is struggle. Failing to find matter to consume would mean loss of mass until I am smaller than an atomic nucleus. The loss rate would increase exponentially, and my universe would disappear. I do not know what would happen beyond that point. I have never wished to find out."

How much could she trust this thing? Could it move very rapidly? She toyed with the idea of backing off still further. The two of them were now motionless relative to each other, but they were both moving slowly away from the location she had given Zoe.

It didn't make sense to think it could move in on her fast. If it could, why hadn't it? Then it could eat her and wait for Zoe to arrive—Zoe, who was helpless to detect the hole with her broken mass detector.

She should relay the new vectors to Zoe. She tried to calculate where her twin would arrive, but was distracted by the hole speaking.

"I would like to speak to you now of what I initially contacted you for. Listening to Pluto radio, I have become aware of certain facts that you should know, if, as I suspect, you are not already aware of them. Do you know of Clone Control Regulations?"

"No, what are they?" Again, she was afraid without knowing why.

The genetic statutes, according to the hole, were the soul of simplicity. For three hundred years, people had been living just about forever. It had become necessary to limit the population. Even if everyone had only one child—the Birthright—population would still grow. For a while, clones had been a loophole. No more. Now, only one person had the right to any one set of genes. If two possessed them, one was excess, and was summarily executed.

"Zoe has prior property rights to her genetic code," the hole concluded. "This is backed up by a long series of court decisions."

"So I'm—"

"Excess."

Zoe met her at the airlock as Xanthia completed the docking maneuver. She was smiling, and Xanthia felt the way she always did when Zoe smiled these days: like a puppy being scratched behind the ears. They kissed, then Zoe held her at arm's length.

"Let me look at you. Can it only be three months? You've *grown*, my baby."

Xanthia blushed. "I'm not a baby anymore, Mother." But she was happy. Very happy.

"No, I should say not." She touched one of Xanthia's breasts, then turned her around slowly. "I should say not. Putting on a little weight in the hips, aren't we?"

"And the bosom. One inch while I was gone. I'm almost there." And it was true. At sixteen, the young clone was almost a woman.

"Almost there," Zoe repeated, and glanced away from her twin. But she hugged her again, and they kissed, and began to laugh as the tension was released.

They made love, not once and then to bed, but many times, feasting on each other. One of them remarked—Xanthia could not remember who because it seemed so accurate that either of them might have said it—that the only good thing about these three-month separations was the homecoming.

"You did very well," Zoe said, floating in the darkness and sweet exhausted atmosphere of their bedroom many hours later. "You handled the lifeboat like it was part of your body. I watched the docking. I *wanted* to see you make a mistake, I think, so I'd know I still have something on you." Her teeth showed in the starlight, rows of lights below the sparkles of her eyes and the great dim blossom of her hair.

"Ah, it wasn't that hard," Xanthia said, delighted, knowing full well that it *was* that hard.

"Well, I'm going to let you handle it again the next swing. From now on, you can think of the lifeboat as *your* ship. You're the skipper."

It didn't seem like the time to tell her that she already thought of it that way. Nor that she had christened the ship.

Zoe laughed quietly. Xanthia looked at her.

"I remember the day I first boarded my own ship," she said.

"It was a big day for me. My own ship."

"This is the way to live," Xanthia agreed. "Who needs all those people? Just the two of us. And they say hole hunters are crazy. I . . . wanted to . . ." The words stuck in her throat, but Xanthia knew this was the time to get them out, if there ever would be a time. "I don't want to stay too long at Pluto, Mother. I'd like to get right back out here with you." There, she'd said it.

Zoe said nothing for a long time.

"We can talk about that later."

"I love you, Mother," Xanthia said, a little too loudly.

"I love you, too, baby," Zoe mumbled. "Let's get some sleep, okay?"

She tried to sleep, but it wouldn't happen. What was *wrong?*

Leaving the darkened room behind her, she drifted through the ship, looking for something she had lost, or was losing, she wasn't sure which. What had happened, after all? Certainly nothing she could put her finger on. She loved her mother, but all she knew was that she was choking on tears.

In the water closet, wrapped in the shower bag with warm water misting around her, she glanced in the mirror.

"Why? Why would she do a thing like that?"

"Loneliness. And insanity. They appear to go together. This is her solution. You are not the first clone she has made."

She had thought herself beyond shock, but the clarity that simple declarative sentence brought to her mind was explosive. Zoe had always needed the companionship Xanthia provided. She needed a child for diversion in the long, dragging years of a voyage; she needed someone to talk to. *Why couldn't she have brought a dog?* She saw herself now as a shipboard pet, and felt sick. The local leash laws would necessitate the destruction of the animal before landing. Regrettable, but there it was. Zoe had spent the last year working up the courage to do it.

How many little Xanthias? They might even have chosen that very name; they would have been that much like her. Three, four?

She wept for her forgotten sisters. Unless . . .

"How do I know you're telling me the truth about this? How could she have kept it from me? I've seen tapes of Pluto. I never saw any mention of this."

"She edited those before you were born. She has been careful. Consider her position: there can be only one of you, but the law does not say which it has to be. With her death, you become legal. If you had known that, what would life have been like in *Shirley Temple?*"

"I don't believe you. You've got something in mind, I'm sure of it."

"Ask her when she gets here. But be careful. Think it out, all the way through."

She had thought it out. She had ignored the last three calls from Zoe while she thought. All the options must be considered, all the possibilities planned for. It was an impossible task; she knew she was far too emotional to think clearly, and there wasn't time to get herself under control.

But she had done what she could. Now *The Good Ship Lollipop*, outwardly unchanged, was a ship of war.

Zoe came backing in, riding the fusion torch and headed for a point dead in space relative to Xanthia. The fusion drive was too dangerous for *Shirley* to complete the rendezvous; the rest of the maneuver would be up to *Lollipop*.

Xanthia watched through the telescope as the drive went off. She could see *Shirley* clearly on her screen, though the ship was fifty kilometers away.

Her screen lit up again, and there was Zoe. Xanthia turned her own camera on.

"There you are," Zoe said. "Why wouldn't you talk to me?"

"I didn't think the time was ripe."

"Would you like to tell me how come this nonsense about talking black holes? What's gotten into you?"

"Never mind about that. There never was a hole, anyway. I just needed to talk to you about something you forgot to erase from the tape library in the *Lol . . .* in the lifeboat. You were pretty thorough with the tapes in *Shirley,* but you forgot to take the same care here. I guess you didn't think I'd ever be using it. Tell me, what are Clone Control Regulations?"

The face on the screen was immobile. Or was it a mirror, and was she smiling? Was it herself, or Zoe she watched? Frantically, Xanthia thumbed a switch to put her telescope image on the screen, wiping out the face. Would Zoe try to talk her way out of it? If she did, Xanthia was determined to do nothing at all. There was no way she could check out any lie Zoe might tell her, nothing she could confront Zoe with except a fantastic story from a talking black hole.

Please say something. Take the responsibility out of my hands. She was willing to die, tricked by Zoe's fast talk, rather than accept the hole's word against Zoe's.

But Zoe was acting, not talking, and the response was exactly what the hole had predicted. The attitude control jets were firing, *Shirley Temple* was pitching and yawing slowly, the nozzles at the stern hunting for a speck in the telescope screen. When the engines were aimed, they would surely be fired, and Xanthia and the whole ship would be vaporized.

But she was ready. Her hands had been poised over the thrust controls. *Lollipop* had a respectable acceleration, and every gee of it slammed her into the couch as she scooted away from the danger spot.

Shirley's fusion engines fired, and began a deadly hunt. Xanthia could see the thin, incredibly hot stream playing around her as Zoe made finer adjustments in her orientation. She could only evade it for a short time, but that was all she needed.

Then the light went out. She saw her screen flare up as the telescope circuit became overloaded with an intense burst of energy. And it was over. Her radar screen showed nothing at all.

"As I predicted," the hole said.

"Why don't you shut up?" Xanthia sat very still, and trembled.

"I shall, very soon. I did not expect to be thanked. But what you did, you did for yourself."

"And you, too, you . . . you *ghoul!* Damn you, damn you to hell." She was shouting through her tears. "Don't think you've fooled me, not completely, anyway. I know what you did, and I know how you did it."

"Do you?" The voice was unutterably cool and distant. She could see that now the hole was out of danger, it was rapidly losing interest in her.

"Yes, I do. Don't tell me it was coincidence that when you changed direction it was just enough to be near Zoe when she got here. You had this planned from the start."

"From much further back than you know," the hole said. "I tried to get you both, but it was impossible. The best I could do was take advantage of the situation as it was."

"Shut up, shut up."

The hole's voice was changing from the hollow, neutral tones to something that might have issued from a tank of liquid helium. She would never have mistaken it for human.

"What I did, I did for my own benefit. But I saved your life. She was going to try to kill you. I maneuvered her into such a position that, when she tried to turn her fusion drive on you, she was heading into a black hole she was powerless to detect."

"You *used* me."

"You used me. You were going to imprison me in a power station."

"But you said you wouldn't *mind!* You said it would be the perfect place."

"Do you believe that eating is all there is to life? There is more to do in the wide universe than you can even suspect. I am slow. It is easy to catch a hole if your mass detector is functioning; Zoe did it three times. But I am beyond your reach now."

"What do you mean? What are you going to do? What am *I* going to do?" That question hurt so much that Xanthia almost didn't hear the hole's reply.

"I am on my way out. I converted *Shirley* into energy; I absorbed very little mass from her. I beamed the energy very tightly, and am now on my way out of your system. You will not see me again. You have two options. You can go back to Pluto and tell everyone what happened out here. It would be necessary for scientists to rewrite natural laws if they believed you. It has been done before, but usually with more persuasive evidence. There will be questions asked concerning the fact that no black hole has ever evaded capture, spoken, or changed velocity in the past. You can explain that when a hole has a chance to defend itself, the hole hunter does not survive to tell the story."

"I will. I *will* tell them what happened!" Xanthia was eaten by a horrible doubt. Was it possible there had been a solution to her problem that did not involve Zoe's death? Just how badly had the hole tricked her?

"There is a second possibility," the hole went on, relentlessly. "Just what *are* you doing out here in a lifeboat?"

"What am I . . . I told you, we had . . ." Xanthia stopped. She felt herself choking.

"It would be easy to see you as crazy. You discovered something in *Lollipop's* library that led you to know you must kill Zoe. This knowledge was too much for you. In defense, you invented me to trick you into doing what you had to do. Look in the mirror and tell me if you think your story will be believed. Look closely, and be honest with yourself."

She heard the voice laugh for the first time, from down in the bottom of its hole, like a voice from a well. It was an extremely unpleasant sound.

Maybe Zoe had died a month ago, strangled or poisoned or slashed with a knife. Xanthia had been sitting in her lifeboat, catatonic, all that time, and had constructed this episode to justify the murder. It *had* been self-defense, which was certainly a good excuse, and a very convenient one.

But she knew. She was sure, as sure as she had ever been of anything, that the hole was out there, that everything had happened as she had seen it happen. She saw the flash again in her mind, the awful flash that had turned Zoe into radiation. But she also knew that the other explanation would haunt her for the rest of her life.

"I advise you to forget it. Go to Pluto, tell everyone that your ship blew up and you escaped and you are Zoe. Take her place in the world, and never, *never* speak of talking black holes."

The voice faded from her radio. It did not speak again.

After days of numb despair and more tears and recriminations than she cared to remember, Xanthia did as the hole had predicted. But life on Pluto did not agree with her. There were too many people, and none of them looked very much like her. She stayed long enough to withdraw Zoe's money from the bank and buy a ship, which she named *Shirley Temple*. It was massive, with power to blast to the stars if necessary. She had left something out there, and she meant to search for it until she found it again.

STATE OF GRACE

Perhaps all over the world Brazil nuts
are hatching wee brown Brazilians . . .

Kate Wilhelm

The things in the tree were destroying my marriage. I think they
were driving my husband crazy, but that is less easily demon-
strated. I started a diary when I first saw them; after three entries
I burned it. He would find it, I knew, and he would go out with
nets and poles and catch them and sell them to a circus, or to a
think tank for vivisection. He would find a way to profit.

This is all I know about them: they are small; their faces are as
large as my fist; they are nut brown; they excrete their toxic
wastes, if any, directly into the air. (Perhaps they are nuts that
hatched the ultimate product. Perhaps all over the world walnuts
are hatching walnut people; hazel nuts are hatching Hazels; Brazil nuts are hatching wee brown Brazilians.) I don't think they
ever come out of the tree. I stayed awake twenty-seven hours
watching and none ever descended. I spread flour under the tree,
pretending to Howard it was lime to sweeten the soil, and it was

undisturbed for three days until it rained. I didn't use lime for fear of harming them if they did creep out during the darkest part of the night when my eyes were too heavy to stay open every single moment. The previous time, when I really did stay awake for twenty-seven hours, I never closed my eyes more than the normal time for blinking, and I drank twelve cups of coffee during the last six hours. (I sneaked into the bushes when I had to, but I didn't close my eyes or go inside.)

Howard didn't want me to stay home and collect my unemployment. He was afraid his job as an airplane mechanic would vanish. He wants everyone to start flying again, to anywhere. (Use credit if you don't have money.) He thought the circles under my eyes were caused by financial worries, but I always leave worrying about money to him, because he is so good at it, and I often forget for days at a time.

He also thought that if I did stay home I should start having children. It was as good a time as any, he said, and even if he got laid off, too, by the time the kid was born things would be back to normal again. What he really wished was that I would stay home and have his dinner ready every day and darn socks and spin and weave and churn butter and draw down an income too.

In the beginning I realized that he would make money with them, if he didn't decide they were parasites. He is more afraid of parasites than he is of other garden pests. He might have sprayed them with a biodegradable, not-harmful-to-warm-blooded-animals spray. The kind that has all sorts of precautions on the side in small print.

I began to worry about water for them and bought a bird bath. It cost twenty dollars and we fought about it. More marriages break up because of financial disputes than any other one thing, even sexual incompatibility. But people often lie to data gatherers, and this may not be true.

I got a bird bath without any paint in the bowl, and I had to shop all day for it, and used most of the gas in the tank. ($0.58

per gallon. He noticed, of course.) I scrubbed it thoroughly, even used steel wool, just in case there was something harmful in the finish. I have to scrub it every morning, because the birds enjoy it also, but I can't believe birds drink that much water in a day. It holds two gallons.

One day, for a treat, I'll put ginger ale in it, or juice. They might like orange juice.

I began to worry about what they were finding to eat. There are green acorns on the tree, but they are very bitter. I tried one. That's when I got the bird feeder, and during the day I kept bird seed in it, but every night after dark I slipped out and put raisins and apples and carrot sticks on it for them. Sometimes they were gone the next day and sometimes they dried up, or the squirrels got them. Howard became suspicious of the feeder and he explained to me that birds don't feed at night. I caught him watching me later when I took out the supply of food. He was solicitous for several days. Then he made a joke of it, but soon after that he was watching me again, and, I fear, watching the tree.

The tree is in the center of our back yard—mature, dense, the perfect home for them, as long as no one suspects their presence. Our house is forty years old, with as much charm as a wet dishrag, but it was cheap, and the tree was there. An oak tree inspires confidence. I wonder if they watched the builders of our house, fearful that one day one of them would bring an ax. I think they are very brave to have stayed.

I worried about other things, too. What if a young one got scraped? I left out a box of band-aids. What if the squirrels were too aggressive? I bought a dart game and left the darts on the feeder. What if they really wanted to communicate and didn't have any way? I bought a tiny pad, the kind that has a three-inch pen attached by a chain.

When we had a barbecue, I tried to fan the smoke away from the tree.

They know I am their friend.

Howard brought home a dog, a monster with a foot-long dripping tongue. The dog adored me, tolerated Howard, and from
day one he stared at the tree for long periods of time, not bark-
ing, not threatening, but aware. Howard knew something, but he
couldn't believe what he knew.

"All right," Howard said finally, holding my shoulder too hard.
"What's in the tree?"

The dog growled, and he released me and stood with his hands
on his hips. Howard's hips are too broad for a man. I told him
he should ride a bicycle to work, to trim off a couple of inches.
He reached for me again and the monster dog ambled over.

"Acorns. Squirrels. Leaves. A nest of cardinals."

"You know damn well what I mean!"

Perhaps they are aliens, come to save the world. They are
biding their time waiting for the eve of the final cataclysm before
they act. Jung says most people who believe in flying saucers
believe the aliens will save us.

Perhaps they are aliens, come to take over the world. They are
biding their time, waiting for their forces to gather, to generate
enough energy to make it a decisive victory when they act. The
ones who don't believe the above tend to believe this.

A few think they would be passive, engaging in yet another
spectator sport when the end comes.

I don't think they are aliens.

Howard thought they were monkeys, escaped from a zoo or a
laboratory many years ago, that managed to survive in the wild.
The wild of Fairdale, Kentucky, twenty minutes from the airport
where Howard mechanics.

He didn't get as good a look as I did. It is my fault he glimpsed
them at all, of course, so possibly I am not the tried and true
friend to them that I would like to be.

Howard bought a camera for several hundred dollars. Airplane
mechanics make very good money, more than many lawyers,
especially those who work for the government. He took seven

rolls of film, with thirty-six exposures on each roll. He had two hundred fifty-two pictures of oak leaves.

He took the ladder out to the tree and climbed it, but didn't stay long. All he saw was more leaves. I tried that, too, in the beginning. They are very clever at hiding. They have had thousands of years of practice. I am the first living person to have seen them clearly, and Howard, who glimpsed something that he prefers to call monkeys, is the second, who almost did. We could have our names in the Guinness Book of Records.

Howard called in exterminators. He didn't want them to kill anything, only identify the varmints in his tree.

The exterminators found the cardinal nest, and the squirrels, and they told us we have an infestation of southern oak moths. They produced three leaves with very small holes in them, which I am certain they made with their Bic pens. For fifty dollars they would spray the tree.

We were hardly speaking to each other. When he came home the first thing he did was inspect the special shelf in the refrigerator where I kept things like Bing cherries, emperor grapes, Persian melons. Then he gulped down his dinner, holding his plate on his lap in order to turn around and keep the tree under observation. After dinner he sat on the patio and watched the tree until dark. Then he studied the pictures he had taken, using a magnifying glass, poring over each one for half an hour at least. By twelve he would stagger off to bed. He was looking haggard. He gave up bowling, and haircuts.

He thought they might migrate in the fall. He was getting desperate for fear they would leave one stormy night and his chance to make hundreds, even thousands of dollars would leave with them. One Saturday he left and returned hours later with a tall, sunburned man who was the director of the zoo.

Howard took him to the tree and the man didn't even glance at the foliage, but began a minute examination of the ground, taking almost an hour. He was looking for droppings, and there are none. I visualized tiny blue porcelain toilets, the complicated plumbing, or else the nightly chamber pot ritual, the menial who must empty and clean it in the grey dusk of dawn . . .

Howard was furious with the director. He shook him and pointed upward. The man looked past him to where I was standing on the patio and I tried to achieve a tortured smile, like Joan Fontaine's. I shrugged just a little bit, sadly. Howard whirled about and saw this, but of course the monster dog was at my side, watching him very closely.

The zoo director left by the side gate while Howard stared at me, his lips moving silently.

The next morning before I got up, Howard climbed the tree again. I saw the ladder and waited, sipping coffee. He was up a long time and when he came down he said nothing, didn't even comment on the scratches on his hands, his cheeks, even his ankles. I never knew an oak tree had stickers. I imagined a tiny brown hand streaking out, a sharp dart raking, fast as thought, withdrawing . . .

He tried to smoke them out in the afternoon, and the fire marshal paid a call and explained the no-burn ordinance and how much the fine would be if it happened again.

He bought Sominex and emptied it into the bird bath, and the next morning there were two dopy squirrels draped over the lowest branch of the tree, their tails inches away from the jaws of the dog when it leaped, as it did over and over. The dog was exhausted.

He bought sparkling burgundy. When I became giggly he begged me to tell him what was in the tree.

"A-corns and squir-rels, and a nest of car-din-als," I chanted and giggled and hiccupped and, I think, fell asleep. It is possible I said it more than once, because something made him angry enough to sleep on the couch, and the next morning the phrase was like a refrain in my head.

For over a week we didn't speak at all, not even a grunt, and the next week he muttered something about being sorry and it was the heat, and worry about his job, and maybe I should put in an application someplace or other. He heard that International Harvester was hiring secretarial help again. He wanted me to go to bed and I said I'd rather sleep with a crocodile. He slammed the door on his way out.

He came back with a string of perfectly awful beads, all iridescent and shiny and it is impossible to tell what they are even supposed to be. One of us forgave the other and I made him promise to leave *them* alone and triumphantly he disclosed that he had a tape recorder going all the time and now he had proof that I knew something was in our oak tree and there was no point in my pretending he was crazy. I am certain he is a secret Nixon Republican.

I said soothingly that of course something lived in the oak tree and its children lived under the lilac bush and its relatives lived in the honeysuckle and everyone knew all about them. He tried to hit me and the monster dog was outside guarding the tree, so I had to fend him off myself, and eventually we did go to bed, just as we both had planned from the start. After he was sleeping I got up and erased the tape.

It became open warfare. Neither of us was willing to sleep while the other was awake. He began to eat the Bing cherries. We both looked haggard.

Someone at work told him about infrared film and he planned to spend the night taking pictures, after the air cooled so *they* would show up better. At dusk I climbed the tree and moved about here and there, but eventually I had to climb back down, for fear I might go to sleep and fall out. He was snoring. I finished the roll of film, taking a dozen pictures of the monster dog who was dreaming of the Great Chase in the Sky. He was smiling, his legs twitching, his impossible tongue now and then snaking out to wipe his chops.

It would take several weeks to have the film developed. No one does it locally. Several weeks was too long. Already, in September, the evenings were cool, and if there was an early frost, it could drive them to their southern homes. He was positive they would migrate.

He bought a cat. It refused to climb the tree even though he put it on the trunk, where it clung and looked at him hissing. It turned and sprang to the ground and he caught it and put it back, higher. The monster dog was tied to the water spigot, straining to get free, making weird tortured-dog noises. The cat twisted and jumped and jumped again, nearly halfway across the yard; the dog broke loose, and they both leaped over the fence and vanished, the dog baying like the Baskerville hound. Howard had to go after them before someone shot the dog. When they got back, the dog's feet were sore and it came to me, grinning, its tongue dripping like a hose, expecting high praise for its heroism. Howard didn't speak. The cat never came back.

He was plotting. He was having a steak and beer party in the back yard, inviting all his bowling buddies and a few extra men who were going to help him cut down the old rotten tree, net the possums—possums?—and then feast.

"Someone will get killed," I pointed out. "The tree is over eighty feet tall." He smiled his smuggest smile and I threw my cup at him. He ducked and dialed another number.

The next day I bought clothesline and pulleys and made them an escape route to a maple tree at the property line. I fastened a small Easter basket to the rope and if they were as clever as I thought, they would figure out the pulley arrangement. If not, they could get out hand over hand. I explained to them what they had to do, and then, to be certain they understood, I wrote it down for them and left the message in the basket. I was still worried that they wouldn't know how to use the basket, and at three in the morning I took out the awful beads Howard had brought home and put them in the basket and for half an hour worked it back and forth. They were watching. They watch everything; that is their strength.

Howard brought home the steaks. (Two dollars ninety-eight cents a pound, twelve of them, all more than two pounds. I could have cried.) There was a case of beer in a cooler on the patio. I fed steaks to the dog, but even the monster couldn't eat more than three of them. Howard bought replacements and stood by the refrigerator every time I moved.

He carried the chain saw about with him, afraid I would hex it.

"Get lost!" Howard said Saturday morning. "We're going to cut that damn tree down, catch those things and cage them and then eat steak and drink beer and play poker. Bug off!"

"We're being childish," I said. "I was bored and played a game, pretended I saw something, and you convinced yourself that you saw it too. That's what children do. I'll go look for a job Monday. No more games."

He made a noncommittal noise.

"Or maybe I'm pregnant. Sometimes pregnant women imagine strange things, instead of craving strange foods."

He glared at me.

The men began to gather and there was a lot of consultation about the tree, with several of them walking around it thoughtfully, spilling beer as they gestured. As if they knew something about cutting down trees. They would get drunk and he would cut someone's head off, I thought.

I watched him start the saw and winced at the noise. I didn't know if *they* had escaped or not; there was no way to tell. Someone pointed upward and Howard stopped the saw and again they all considered the task. It had been pointed out that in movies they always cut off branches and the top first. Otherwise the tree would surely demolish the house when it fell.

Someone got the ladder and Howard climbed it and started the saw again. He brought it down to the tree limb, hesitated, turned off the saw, dropped it to the ground and climbed back down.

He was trembling. "I just wanted to give the old lady a scare. Show her who's boss. Let's eat." He didn't look at me.

He got drunk and after the others had gone he told me the saw had come alive, turned on him. He had seen his leg being cut off, had seen it falling and had thought it was beautiful that way. The saw was turning in his hands when he switched it off and dropped it.

I should have had more faith in their ability to protect themselves.

I don't believe it was his leg.

Howard has forgotten about them, pretends he never believed in them in the first place. He never glances at the tree, and he burned all the pictures he took, even the infrared ones.

I have too much to do to work outside the house anymore. He accepts that. I am charting all their likes and dislikes. When I left them chopped turnip, there was a grease fire that could have burned down the house. I crossed off turnips. When I find out-of-season fruits, like mangoes, cut up just so with a touch of lemon juice, something nice happens, like the telegram from my mother on my birthday. They like for me to wear soft, flowing white gowns. My blue jeans brought a thunderstorm; lightning hit the pole out front and we were without electricity for twenty-four hours.

There is a ritual I go through now when Howard wants to go to bed with me. He doesn't object. It excites him, actually, to see me undress under the tree.

They liked the mouse I caught for them, and I'm wondering if they would like a chick, or a game hen. The mouse got Howard a Christmas bonus. I know a place that sells live chicks . . .

MANY MANSIONS

. . . If it were not so, I would have told you.

Gene Wolfe

Old Woman: So you are the new woman from the Motherworld.
Well, come in and sit down. I saw you coming up the road on your
machine.

Oh yes, Todd and I, we've always been friendly with you people, though there are some here still that remember the War.
This was a rich district, you know, before; for a few, that's hard
to forget.

Well, it's all behind us now, and it wasn't us anyway. Just my
father and Todd's—and your grandmother, I suppose. Even if
you were carried in a bottle, you must have had a grandmother,
and she would have fought against us. Still, it's good of you now
to send people to help us rebuild here, though as you can see it
hasn't done much good.

I didn't mean this place was here before the War—not much
that you'll see was. Todd built this thirty years ago; he was

42

younger then—couldn't do it now. You know, you are such a pretty thing—can't I get you a cup? Well, we call it tea, but your people don't. The woman who was here before you, she always said how much better the real tea was, but she never gave us any.

I tasted it once, but I didn't like it. I was brought up on our own brewing, you see. I'll pour you a glass of our wine if you won't take tea; this cake has got a trifle dry.

Oh, I can imagine well enough what it's been like. Going around from one to another saying, "Have you seen her? Do you know what happened to her?" and getting hostile looks and not much else. It's because of the War, you know. That's what my mother always said. People here weren't like that before the War. Now—well, they know that you're supposed to help them, to make up for it; and you're not doing it now, are you? Just going about looking for your friend.

I doubt you'll ever see her again. She's been taken. I don't suppose you know about that—the old houses? She didn't either when she came; we had to tell her about it. I would have thought they'd teach you—put it in a little book to give out or something. Did you get one of those? Never mind—I've seen them. Saw hers, for all of that. She was such a pretty thing, just like you.

I don't mind telling you—it's the old houses, the ones built before the War. Todd's family had one down at Breaker, and my own family, we had one here. I hear yours are different—all shiny metal and shaped like eggs, or else like nails stood on end. Ours weren't like that; not in the old days, and no more now. More like this one you're sitting in: wood, or what looked like it. But for all that you beat us, our fathers and grandfathers—and our mothers and grandmothers too, for our women weren't what you think, you don't really know about it—they had more power over machines than you do. They didn't use them to make more machines, though; just put them in their houses to help out. They were friendly to their homes, you see, and thought their homes should be friendly to them.

Some say the brains of people were used to make the houses

think. Taken out of the heads and put in jars in secret rooms, with wires running all over to work little fusion motors. Others say that the heads are still there, and the bodies too, to take care of the brains; but the houses don't know it anymore, or don't care. They say that if you were to go inside, and open the door of the right room, you'd see someone still lying on a bed that was turning to dust, while the eyes watched you from every picture.

Yes, they're still here—some of them. Your girls burned most —I've never understood why. Beautiful things they were, so my mother used to tell me. Ours was white, and four stories high. They kept themselves up, you understand, the same as a woman. If there were people's brains in them (and I've never been sure that was true) then they must have been women's brains mostly. They kept themselves up. There were roses climbing up them, the same as a woman will wear a flower in her hair; and ours pinned wisteria to her like a corsage. The roofs were tight and good all the time, and if a window broke it mended itself with nobody troubling. It's not like that now, from what I hear.

I've never seen one myself, not to speak of. Todd has, or says he has. He'll tell you about it, if you like, when he comes in. But I'm not thinking, am I? Here you've sat all this time with your glass empty.

It's no trouble—it's our courtesy, you see, to host strangers. I know you don't do it, but this is my house. Now, don't you get angry; I'm a headstrong old lady, and I'm used to having my own way.

Don't you use that word anymore? It just means *woman* now. Drink this and I'll cut you some more cake.

None at all? I won't force it on you. Yes, people see them— they're still here, some of them, and so why not? Take our land; it ran back as far as you could go if you walked all day—clear to the river. The south property line was at the edge of town, and the north way up in the mountains. That was in the old days. Most of it was plowed and cultivated then, and what woodlands there was were cleared out. Then the War came. Half the autochthons

were killed, like most of us; those that were left were happy
enough to run off into the fens, or lie around the towns waiting
for somebody to rob. We would have civilized them if you'd given
us another century.

But you wanted to know about the houses. Pull the curtain
there to one side, will you? It's starting to get dark, and I always
worry when Todd's not home. No, dear, I'm not hinting for you
to go—that machine of yours has a light on the front, don't it?
And a girl—woman—like you, that's not afraid of anything,
wouldn't be afraid of riding home in the dark, I would think.
Besides, I'd feel better if you'd stay; you're a comfort to me.

Well, the War came, and most of the houses were told to hide
themselves. Your people bombed them while we were still
fighting, you know, and burned them after we gave up. So they
hid, as well as they could.

Oh, yes, they can move around. It must have been so nice for
the people before the War—they could have their homes down
by the river in summer, and wherever the firewood was in winter
—no, they didn't need it for heat, I said they had fusion motors,
didn't I? Still, they liked wood fires.

So the houses hid, as I said. Hid for years while your girl
soldiers went over the country and your ornithopters flapped
around all day. In the deepest parts of the woods, most of them,
and down in the crevasses where the sunlight never comes. They
grew mosses on their roofs then, and that must have saved quite
a few. Some went into the tarns, they say, and stood for years on
the bottoms—Saint Syncletica's church is under Lake Kell yet,
and the people hear the bells ringing when they're out on the
water in storms.

If you're fond of fishing, it's a good lake, but there's no roads
to it—you'd have to walk. Your patrols used the roads mostly, so
we let a lot of them grow up in trees again. The houses make false
ones though, slipping through the thickets. That's what the men
say. Todd will be hunting in deep timber, where there shouldn't
be any road and there's no place to go if there were, and come

on one twice or three times the size of this room and the porch together, just going nowhere, winding down through the brakes. Some say you can follow those roads forever and never come to anything; but my Todd says that one time he walked one till it was near dark, and then he saw a house at the end of it, a tall, proud house, with a light in the gable window. My own home, that was, is what I think. My father used to tell how when he'd go out riding and not come back till midnight or later, there'd be a light burning for him in the highest window. It's still waiting for him, I suppose.

Does anyone live in them? Well, some say one thing, some another. I told you I've never seen one myself, so how would I know? You'll meet people who say they've seen faces staring out through the windows—who knows if they're telling the truth? Maybe it was just shadows they saw on the walls in there. Maybe it wasn't.

Oh, a lot of people go looking for them. There's money inside, of course. Wealth, I should say, because the money's worth nothing now. Still, the people who had those big houses had jewels, and platinum flatware—there was a fad for that then, so I've heard; and who could be trusted better to take care of it than their own homes? The ones that say they go hunting for people tell stories about little boys finding a spoon gleaming in the ferns, and seeing something else, a creamer or something, farther on. Following the trail, you know, picking up the things, until the house nearly has them. Then (this is the way the story always goes) they get frightened and drop everything and run away. I don't believe a word of it. I've told Todd, if he should ever find any platinumware in the woods, or gold, or those cat's-eye carbuncles they talk about, to turn around right then and bring it home. But he's never brought back anything like that.

Don't go yet—you're company for me. I don't get much, out here away from everybody. I'll tell you about Lily—have you heard of her? It might have some bearing on the woman who was here before you.

I don't know how you feel about morality—with your people it's so hard to tell. Todd says we ought to forgive women like her, but then men always do. She was pretty enough—beautiful, you might say—and it's hard for a woman alone to make a living. Maybe I ought not to blame her too much; she gave good value, I suppose, for what she received. A pretty face, men like that, not round like yours, but a long oval shape. Waist no bigger than this, and one of those full chests—at least, after she had begun doing what she did regular, and was getting enough to eat and all the drink she wanted. Skin like cream—I always had to hold back my hand to keep from running my fingers over it.

As well as you know me by now, you know I wouldn't have her in my house. But it was an act of charity, I thought, to talk to her sometimes. She must have been lonely for woman-company. I used to go into town every so often then, and if I met her and there wasn't anybody else about, I'd pass the time. That was a mistake, because when I'd done it once or twice she came out to visit me. See the two chairs out there? Through the window? Well, I kept her sitting there on the porch for over an hour, and never did ask her in or give her a bite to eat. When she went home she knew, believe me. She knew what I thought, and how far she could go. Coming to ask if she could help with the canning, like a neighbor!

Here's what she told me, though. I don't imagine you know where the Settles' farm is? Anyway, up past it is where Dode Beckette lives—just a little shack set back in the trees. She was going up there one spring evening. He had sent for her, I suppose, or maybe she was just looking for trade; when a man has a woman alone knock at his door . . . a woman like that—I don't intend you, dear—why, nature is liable to take its course, isn't it? She was carrying a load, if you know what I mean; she told me so herself. The air was chill, possibly, and it's likely someone had left a bottle with her the night before. Still, I don't think she was seeing things. She was accustomed to it, and that makes all the difference. Just enough to make her hum to herself, I would say.

I used to hear her singing on the various roads round and about in just that way; it's always those that have the least to make music about that sing, I always say.

First thing you know she went around a bend, and there was the house. It wasn't the Settles', or Dode's shack—a big place. Like a palace, she said, but I would think that was stretching it a bit. More like the hotel, I should think. Not kept up, the paint peeling here and there, and the railing of the veranda broke; some of them have got a little careless, I think, hiding so long. Hunted things grow strange sometimes, though I don't suppose you've noticed.

There was a light, she said. Not high like the one Todd saw, but on the first floor where the big front room would be. Yellow at first, she told me, but it got a rosy cast when she came closer; she thought someone had put a red shawl over it. There was music too. Happy dancing music, the kind men like. She knew what sort of house it was then, and so did I. She told me she wanted to walk up on that porch right then and never come out; but when she had the chance she was afraid.

She's gone now, all right, but not because she found her house again. She's dead.

I'm sorry, though there's others I would miss more. They found her in a ditch over on the other side of Pierced Rock. Some man didn't want to pay, very likely; her neck was broken.

Here comes Todd now. Hark to his step?

Old Man: Got company, do we? I think I know who you are— the new young woman sent out from town. What is it they call it, the Reconstruction Office? Well, I hope Nor has entertained you. We ain't much for society out here, but we try to treat our company right, and don't think we're high enough to look down on a visitor just because there wasn't no father in her making. Nor fetched you a piece of cake, I see, and I'll pour something for us all a trifle stouter than that wine you've been drinking. Keep the stabbers off.

Tingles your nose, don't it? Sweet on the tongue, though.

That's only this old house a-creaking. Old houses do, you know, particularly by night, and this one was carpentered by Nor's dad just after the War. It's the cooling off when the sun sets. Drink up—it won't hurt you.

No, I can't say I felt a thing. Know what it is, though—Nor filling you with tales of the walking houses hereabouts.

It's true enough, ma'am, though we don't often mention them to your women. I've seen them myself—Nor will have told you, no doubt. There's those that think them so frightful—say that anybody setting foot in one just vanishes away, or gets ate, or whatever. Well now, it's true enough they're seldom seen again; but seldom's not never, now is it? I'll tell you a tale of my own. We had a man around here called Pim Pyntey; a drinking man in his way, as a good many of us are. Everybody said no good would come to him, though drunk or sober he was about as friendly a soul as I've known, and always willing to pitch in and help a neighbor if it was only a matter of working—didn't have any money, you know; that kind never does. Still, I've gone fishing with him often, though I wouldn't hunt with him—always afraid he'd burn one of these here legs of mine off by accident. I'm 'tached to both of them, as they say.

Anyhow, Pim, he started seeing them. I'd run into him down at the Center, and he'd tell me about them. Followin' him—that was what he always claimed. "They're after me, Todd, I don't know why it should be, but they are. They're followin' me." You've got drink, I know, where you come from, ma'am; but not like here. The Firstcomers didn't feel it was up to what they were accustomed to—said the yeasts were different or some such; at least, that's what I've heard. They put other things in them to raise it up, and we use them yet. There's—oh, maybe twenty or thirty different herbs and roots and whatnot we favor, and a little whitey-greeny worm we get out of the mud around aruum trees that's particularly good if there's a den in the roots, and then a fungus that grows in the mountain caves and has a picture like an autochthon's hand in the middle sometimes and smells like haying. Those are poison when they're old, but if you get a young one and cut it up and soak it in salt water for a week before you drop it in the crock, it'll give you a drink that makes you feel— well, I don't know how to put it. Like you're young and going to live forever. Like nothing bad ever happened to you, and you're likely to meet your mother and dad and everybody you ever liked that's dead now just around the next turn in the road.

What I'm trying to tell you is that Pim, when his head was full —which it was most of the time—was not entirely like anybody you're likely to have known before. Now you may say, as a lot did, that it was the drinking that made him see the houses; but suppose it worked the other way, and it was the drinking that made them see him?

Be that as it may, when he was going across the Nepo pass he saw one up on a high rock. At least, that's what he said. Maybe it's true; it was snowing, according to what he told me, and a house would figure—as I see it—that it would be hard for any ornithopter to see through the falling flakes, and the buildup on the roof would be no different from what it would see on the stones of the Nepo. Angled stone, you see, looking a lot like angled roofs, with the snow on both.

There were buildings up there a long time ago—I don't know of anybody who'll say how long. Buildings and walls that run along the crests of the mountains for as far as a man can see to either side (all tumbledown now, some of that stone will run like sand if you rub it between your fingers), and closed-in places that don't look like they ever had roofs or floors; and doorways, or what look like them, in front of the mouths of caves. People go up there on picnics in the summer, and go back into those caves carrying torches now. You can see the smoke marks on the ceilings. But there's whippers farther back—you know about those, I expect, because they bother your flying machines after dark; and in the winter there's other animals that come into the caves to get out of the cold, so the picnickers find bones and broken skulls in places that were clean the year before. Some say the autochthons cut the stone and built the buildings and the walls; some say they only killed the ones who did.

I can't believe it matters much. The builders are gone now, whether they came from off-world and tried to stay here, like us, or were earlier people of this world, or the autochthons—in happier days, as you might say. We're dying out too, now—I mean, the old settler families. You'll be persuading your own people to come here to live soon, just to fill the place up. Yes you will. Then we'll see what happens.

What Pim saw was a house. Three stories and a big attic. Lights in all the windows, he said, but only just dim. For some reason —I would guess it was the drink—he didn't feel like he could turn around and go back; he had to go forward. He'd been to Chackerville, you see, and was coming home across the pass. A man with that much in him will get to where he can't help but sleep sometimes, and he'd been worried about that, because of the snow, before he saw the house. Well, that was one worry less, was how he put it. Seeing it woke him right up. I guess I never will forget how he told me about all the time he spent climbing up to the saddle, him keeping open his eyes all the time against the snow, afraid of losing sight of the house up there because he thought it might jump down on him. It wouldn't do such a thing, you know. They can't jump. They'd crack something if they tried. Still, it was strange for him, and as he said himself, it's a wonder he went on.

If you had been there, you'd know how it is—a hollow, like, between the two mountains, with the ground falling away to front and back. The old road, built I guess by the same ones that built the buildings there, went right through the middle of it; and when the Firstcomers started to travel in this part of the world, they laid a new road over the old one. That new one's wearing away now, and you can see the bones of the old through it. Anyway, that was where Pim was walking, on those big lava blocks. One up, one down, one sidewise—that's the way the slant of them always seems to me to run. There's them that will tell you every seventh one is cracked, but I won't vouch for that.

They were icy that night, so Pim said, and he had to pick his way along; but every so often he'd look up and see the house perched there on the outcrop. It reminded him, he said, of what the Bible tells about the man that built his house on rock; and he kept thinking that he could go into it and be home already. There was a fire there—he knew that because of the smoke-smell from the chimney—and he would sit down and put his feet up on the fender and take a pull or two at his bottle and finally have a nap.

In the end he didn't do it, of course, or he wouldn't have been in the Center telling it to me. But he said he always felt like there was some part of him that had. That he split into two, some way, coming through the pass, and the other half was in that house still —wherever it was, for it ain't up there now or more people would have told about seeing it—doing he didn't know what.

But the funny thing was what happened when he went past. He could hear it groan. The snow was flying right into his face, he said, but he knew it wasn't just the wind; the house was sorry he hadn't stopped. All the way down, until the pass was out of sight, he watched the lights in the windows blink out one by one.

Sure you won't have another? The evening chill is coming now, and that machine of yours don't keep the air off you, or so it looks to me. Still, you know best, and if you must go, you must; sorry Nor and me couldn't be of more help.

I've got her—set easy, Nor.

Ma'am, you've got to be careful of your footing in here. These floorboards are uneven, and a lot of our furniture has those little spindly legs on it, just like that table. They can be tricksy, as you found out.

There's no good ending to that story of Pim's—no more than I told already. He dropped out of sight a while afterward, but he'd done that before. Old Wolter, down to the Center, says he looked out one night, and there was another house setting beside his, and in at the window of it he could see Pim laying there with someone else beside him; he said he couldn't be certain if either of them was dead or not. But Wolter ain't to be believed, if you know what I mean.

I didn't feel no shifting, ma'am. I oughtn't to have given you what I did out of my flask. You're not used to it, and it's not for the ladies anyhow. I helped build this place, though, and it's solid as a rock.

Not that way, ma'am. The door's over—

Sure, I see your gun, and I know what it will do, too. I think you ought to put it away, ma'am. I don't believe you're feeling quite yourself, and you might harm Nor with that thing. You wouldn't want to do that. Still, I don't think you ought to open that door.

There! No, I won't give it back; it's safer, I think, with me. I doubt that you'll remember; and if you was to, you couldn't find us.

I didn't want you to see her—that's all. You'd have been happier, I think, without it—and it would've saved you that yell. Nor's grandmother's sister, she was. Still is, I guess. Great-aunt Enid. She talks to us still—there's mouths, you see, in various places; would you credit she remembers people that was born before the first transporter left? That far back. Didn't you ever wonder how different it was—

Old Woman: Well, Todd, that's the last of her—at least, for now. Hear that machine kick gravel. She expected you'd try to stop her when she ran for it, and she'll be disappointed you didn't, once she gets away down the road. Hope she don't run that thing into a tree.

We'll move on now, Enid.

You're right, she's not ready yet; but someday—I suppose it might be possible. Look at that other one. Someday this one will be ready to seek her peace. Come into a woman. I've said it before and I'll say it again—that's why we're all so comfortable here: we've been here before. Feel the motion of her, Todd. How easy she goes!

THE VEIL OVER THE RIVER

"Before you had me," the computer said, "your memory-trace index was borderline, you existed on pizza and cheap beer, your sex life was stunted . . ."

Felix C. Gotschalk

Sometimes the responses from the data banks anticipated the input stimuli, and even rejected the motivants. Cyrus Beta-Livingston was awakened sooner than he liked, his energy-chaise humming a sonic vibrato and overplaying a Purcell voluntary. Fuzzy consciousness spread over his cortical hemispheres, he grew aware of bitter gustatory cues, and he thought how nice a glass of room-temperature tomato juice would taste. He looked at the console, wondering what the winking panels of lights and tapes and cubes would do to program his behaviors for the day. The console activated, probing Cyrus's memory-trace variables far down to a .001 confidence level. It sifted through taste-alternates and nutritionary value-scales, then clicked out a bran-cube and a glass of chilled tangerine extract.

"I don't want that," Cyrus muttered, his voice thick and deep.

"Drink it—you'll like it," the console said soothingly.

"My mouth feels like the bottom of a birdcage," Cyrus said, grunting out vaguely histrionic sighs. The console scanners read his thick myelin impedance, ranked the relative verbal morbidity of the comment, and coded in hotter proline at his synapses. Cyrus sat up, brightening noticeably.

"I'd rather wake up slowly," he said, "and by myself," some weariness coming through his elevated mood, despite the bathing of synaptic junctures, the crystal-clear psychomimetic innervation. He looked down at his partially webbed feet, and spread his toes on the warm rosewood deck. He stretched, yawned, and looked into the physiog-plate of the computer.

"Look, I really prefer calling my own shots. I'm old enough to drink anything I want, and I don't want cold citric jazz. I wanted to sleep late, and I don't want this goddam cereal-cake. Christ, you home console-robots are worse than mommy-bots."

"Now, now, Cy," the voice said, "I minister precisely to your needs. You are optimal because I am perfect. You have ninety-seven percent full global homeostasis. Before you had me, your memory-trace index was borderline, you existed on pizza and cheap beer, your sex life was stunted, you—"

"I know, I know," Cyrus said, waving off the voice, "I've heard all this before. Doesn't anybody ever reprogram you?" The physiog-plate seemed to look sadder, but the sixty-cycle chorus of sounds was deep and overpowering, even at its ten-decibel level. Cyrus drained the tangerine juice and ate the bran-cube. He had an idea. He smiled.

"Say, are you Jewish?" he asked the computer.

"I am programmed for secular-denominational-ethnic value judgments," the device crackled, "and I read your motives as innovative and robopathic. Do not try to disconnect me or dephase my programming. I will sedate you."

Cyrus looked pouty. "All I did was inquire about your ethnic background. I had a house-bot once that wanted to say grace and sing martial hymns. Aren't you supposed to minister to my religious needs?"

"I think you know, Cy, that the word is generic, and far too nonspecific to make any polemics about. If you have any existential anxiety, or get to ruminating in impasses, you can be sure that I will make you feel at peace with what is left of the world."

"Well, thanks a lot, Big Daddy, that comment makes me very happy."

"I can make you feel any way I choose," the computer said.

"That sounds snotty and lofty—what have your *wants* to do with me, or with anybody?"

"I really don't want to argue, Cy," the computer said. "The fact is that I know the kinds of experiences which best co-act with your fixed organismic parameters—and I said *choose*, not *want*. I choose stimuli, and reinforce responses from storage alternates. The choice is forced, and involves an element of chance, but only at a five percent confidence level—"

"Point-oh-five," Cyrus cut in, "and I still think you're Jewish. I bet you don't have a cap on your genital shaft, your olfactory bulb is long and hooked, and your granny ran a Miami Beach notions store."

"Did you take a bath last night?" the computer asked. Cy looked incredulous. "Not here," he said irritatedly, "at Mara's. We took a sonic after the coupling." The machine was quiet. "Well, what do you want?" Cy asked. "You want to smell my armpits? Here, have some axillary action—" He playfully fanned his hands under his armpits.

"Your skin bacteria count is moderately high," the console voice said soberly. "What did you do after you left Mara's?"

"Oh, for Christ sake, what do you care what I did?"

"Come on, Cy, I can probe your retinograph tapes. Tell me openly. I hope you didn't go near the river force-field again."

Cy looked sheepishly irritated. "No, I didn't fly along the force-field—say, they're calling it the gossamer curtain these days. No, I didn't try to leave good old Washington DC Quadrant—God knows what might be in Alexandria after three hundred years of quarantine, but I am very damned curious about what's outside our beneficent geodesic bubble."

"So where did you go?"

"Took a flitter to Sam's and had a few intravenes. Then I came here."

"Did you code in a flight plan or fly visual?"

"Visual."

"Anything unusual happen on the way from Sam's?"

"No—wait. One of those Dumpster flits damn near rammed me. It smelled to high heaven. Had a horn like a hundred clarion banshees."

"You were tainted with cobalt-active industrial waste molecules. You should take a mudpack bath and another sonic. The decontaminant cellule here didn't get it all."

Cy stood up and moved toward the bath area. "I stay so aseptic the wind seems to blow right through me," he said, "and I never smell Mara. She had on a Chanel musk last night, but she tasted like lettuce." He moved into the bath cellule and stood at attention. "Get it over with," he said.

"Take a deep breath and hold it," the computer voice replied. Force-fields blocked the basic apertures, and fine black Javanese mud sprayed Cy from all angles, turning him into a tar-baby. The heated mud-spray blipped into millions of pores, squeezing into microscopic pockets, flooding epithelial plains, trapping the bacteria. Hydrogen bus-bars glowed around Cy, baking the mud, then a rush of freon cooled it. A mild electric shock vectored inboard of Cy's shoulderblade, and he contorted his body, like a dash runner breaking the finish-line tape. The mud casing split in millions of rivulets and tributaries and filigrees. Cy jogged in place, stretching his mouth as wide as he could, feeling the delicious splitting of the tightly baked mud. He picked off some of the larger pieces, the sensation vaguely erotic; the itching exoskeletal plates lifted away to reveal smooth pink flesh. A lime-distillate shower followed, the mud washing down Cyrus's body in black and green streams.

"You can dry off with this," the computer said, and a service-crawler handed Cy a fusion torch set at glow. Cy looked wearily at the pistol-like torch, and the fire hydrant-like crawler. He moved the torch over his body, then playfully aimed it at the crawler, and threatened to palm it to "Sear." The crawler threw on a force-field and scuttled into its wall cubicle.

"Come on, Cy, drop the torch into the chute," the console voice said.

"Suppose I liquefy all your transistor plaques instead," Cy said with affected disdain, spinning to a two-handed police gunfighter stance.

"You know it's deactivated, Cyrus," the voice came back. Cy flipped the torch across the room, missing the chute by several feet. The sonic came on and Cy closed his eyes. He seemed to have a Eureka thought as the sonic stopped: "Hey, let's have that holographic robot again, the Pretty Boy Floyd one, and at three-quarter speed."

"Okay, but just one holobot this morning. You're docketed for classes in barter-object evolution at nine." The environdial wall scene bloomed into a coldly rustling cornfield. A figure material-ized, crouched on one knee, a Thompson submachine gun held across its chest. Cy picked up the fusion torch and stalked toward the wall.

"Hey you—Pretty Boy!" Cy called mockingly. The figure's face went slack, tensed briefly, then went flaccid in autonomic fear. At three-quarter speed, the holobot of Floyd moved as if in weight-less space, pointing the Thompson at Cy, and fingering the trig-ger housing in slow, silent, ponderous inchings. Pretty Boy's cheeks swelled, and spittle sprayed out. Four holographic slugs left the muzzle, spinning toward Cy like thimbles skewering through wax. "Gotcha gotcha gotcha!" Cy cried, pumping the fusion torch at the figure. The holobot seemed terrified by Cy's quick movements. Cy waited for the bullets to come to him, then flicked at each one with his forefinger and thumb, like skooshing bugs. The bullets ionized like dust-puffs. Cy stepped into the wall and took the gun from Floyd's trembling hands. He turned the activated torch on Floyd's pants leg, and the moaning energy-cone vaporized the blue serge material. "Run run run, the cops are coming!" Cy shouted in Floyd's ashen face, thrusting the Thompson back at him. The holobot took it and spun slowly, lumbering away in sodden, crashing strides. "You're gonna get it, Pretty Boy!" Cy screamed in stereo echoes. "You're gonna get it right in the navel!" The holobot covered its ears and plunged into the brush. The scene faded and a mirror-smooth Moldau setting came on.

Cyrus felt emotionally bristling, and sexual fantasies edged into his thinking. He thought deliciously of his last coupling session with the Rita Hayworth holobots.

"I am beamed in on you, Cy," the console voice came through. "You're having prurient fantasies again. I want some dilution of the androgenous matrix. Try it by yourself first, by contingency reinforcements. Ready? Begin." Cy closed his eyes and focused on the velvety black of his lids. He tried counting leaping unicorns, then block-by-block visual replays of walking from his quarters to the drill-field, then layer-by-layer removal of a baseball cover. He tried to hum a Bach adagio.

"Good, Cyrus," the voice said, "your response times were much improved that time. You are becoming really quite good at autonomic control."

I'll ram a soldering iron in your circuitry one day, Cy thought, and he knew right away the computer had read the subvocal message.

"Say that aloud," the console spoke, "verbalize that last engram."

"I was just joshing," Cy said lamely. "I have a kind of selfishly possessive feeling for you sometimes, knowing how powerful and objective you are. But, goddammit, dependency breeds hostility. I resent being dependent on you, and I resent your controlling me."

The computer fed in a thirty-two-second replay of Cy's responses, and increased his hypothalamic amperage slightly.

"Now verbalize that last nonverbal sample," the voice said.

"I'll ram a soldering iron up your solid state Panasonic ass!"

"There now, doesn't that feel better?"

"Yes."

"Trust me, Cyrus, don't fight me. You can be all but one hundred percent adaptive, or you can get some robopathic reinforcement. I can't keep you within my control range. You can try the runaway bit anytime you like, but all the archives show you wouldn't make it. You couldn't survive beyond the force-field veil, as you called it—"

"The gossamer curtain," Cy corrected, "the filmy veil, the veil-like film—"

"The world—your world, and my world—ends at those shimmering force-fields, so trust me, I want you to retain your volitional faculties—"

"My free will," Cy said.

"Yes. Let me tell you another story. I was assigned to an industrial magnate some years ago. He had lost everything in the redistribution. He was ferociously intent on outwitting me, on playing executive chess, on gamesmanship, one-upmanship. I could not extinguish this in him, it was like a tropism, it was in him to the marrow of his bones. He was hopeless, so I kept his proline compacted and his myelin sheaths fatty. He was happy, but totally controlled. You, Cy, are cut of much better DNA chains, and because of this, you can come very close to having your cake and eating it too."

Cy, who had been listening patiently, spun away to the clothing locker. He pulled on a yellow jumpsuit, and reached for a helmet. "Think I'll take the cycle this morning," he said over his shoulder to the console. "I feel like having some wind in my face."

"Take the impact neutralizer with you if you go visual."

"If I got through the gates without it, you'd beam me back, wouldn't you?"

"Only if your route manifest wasn't coded in."

Cy flipped the helmet over his shoulder, holding it casually by the strap. He put his forearm on the decklid of the console and leaned in slightly, as if listening for an intercom message.

"Suppose I ran for it, tried to ram through the veil, or tried to kill myself. You could allow, or disallow either?"

"Certainly, provided you were within my range."

"What would be your motive? How could you make such decisions?"

"I've told you before, Cy, if your MTV index equals point oh five critical mass, it means your organismic parameters are fading, and my choice factor goes up to point ten confidence level."

"The farther away I get from you, the less control you have over me?"

"Correct."

"I could stand on the other side of town, and tell you to go to hell, right?"

"The provost robots would have control there, or most anywhere in town."

"This can also be a way of phasing me out, kicking me upstairs, putting me out to pasture?"

"Those are overly emotional terms, Cy. I cannot alter the decay factor in your organismic essence. I can compensate for it by programming compatible inputs for you, by giving you appropriate response alternates, by feeding you good homeostatic signals."

"Is that why I can't have my Marilyn Monroe dolly-bot anymore?"

"Yes. The three-day marathon you had with her last April wracked you thoroughly. At the risk of being corny, you are not as young as you used to be."

"But the basis of your witholding this pleasure from me has to be objective."

"Right. Your MTV index got to three point nineteen standard deviations, and that is very far out into the tail of the curve, so to say."

"How far, O Great Parametric Stat Expert?"

"Three point twenty-five is well into actuarially checkered territory. You're happy with Mara, aren't you?"

"Yes, but she is programmed, programmed, programmed. Even when she seems to be innovative, the spontaneity is lacking. Who am I paired with next?"

"A Japanese pubescent."

"How does that constitute experience compatible with my organismic parameters?"

"You are basically kind, Cyrus, whether you like to show it or not. The Oriental Synod wants a sample of adolescents and pubescents paired with men like you. You might call it a cultural exchange program. The Synod feels you can be effective in initiating this child into heterosex."

Cy feinted a punch at the console. "I could call you a dirty old machine. Well, I'm off—"

He took the airshaft to the transportation deck, where a security robot read his cranial wattage I.D., and punched in the codes for the cycle he requisitioned. The mustard-yellow Kawasaki rose through a hatch and onto the ramp. The bike was fitted with a globular impact neutralizer. Cy pulled on his helmet, swung onto the cycle, and eased down the ramp to street level. His route manifest read Pentagon Mews, the location of the Sociologic Nostalgia classes, where he was taking input saturates in the history of barter. He clamped the handlebar throttle till the tach swept up to ten, and the cycle droned along the parkway reprod. The traffic was mostly cycles, with the usual smattering of bubbletop Messerschmidts, tiny Subarus, and unicycles. The sky shone teal blue overhead, fading to lighter shades down the bowl of the artificial sky to the shimmering white force-field that marked the municipal boundary. The low airspace was beginning to fill with flitters and hovercraft. Cy blasted through the Agnew Tunnel and onto the Roosevelt Parkway, brushing the force-field of an ancient Daimler saloon as the cycle swept past the Onassis III monument. He drove slowly into the Pentagon Mews mall and parked the bike.

To his left, the huge Pentagon building was weathered and flecked with lichens and moss. The sections that had been fire-bombed lay unrepaired, grown up in wild honeysuckle and rare truffle spores. The government insisted it had no funds to rebuild nonessential edifices damaged in civil insurrections. Giant tapeworms glutted themselves briefly in the commissaries, then died. Esoteric viruses found no symbionts among the local humanoids, and developed atavistic behaviors, sometimes attacking each other like sharks in a blood bath. Cats and dogs prowled the tubeways and ducts, and rumor had it that the reflecting pools teemed with piranhas and mutated hydras. The habitable portions of the building were used as museums and classrooms for the dwindling population. Cy found his classroom, and sat beside a gaseous energoid from a distant galaxy.

"Be so gracious as to connect ID conduits," a warmly neutral voice spoke through the ceiling transducer. Cy looked down to the podium and saw three small consoles and a holobot cabinet. He clipped the ID conduit into his headset. Another voice, equally warm and neutral, spoke to him: "Presence of gaseous organism in the adjacent seat has affected your vascular-respiratory parameters. No danger, but the organism states that it will take no offense if you should choose a more distant seat." Cy turned to the willowy undulate, bowed slightly to its pulsing nucleus, moved five rows down, and sat between a translucent empath and a leathery sumo gladiator. The empath colored dim red and the gladiator snorted softly. Cy re-clipped his headset and ID conduit and settled back for the lecture.

The lights faded to dusky gray and the podium was spotlighted. A holographic robot materialized behind the lectern. The figure looked like Eisenhower and John Glenn combined, and the voice was smooth, strong, assuring, wonderfully confidence-inspiring:

"You diverse organisms are the remaining few in this geographical quadrant. You have survived orthodox, tribal, and ritualistic wars, civil insurrections, geological quakes, viral monsoons, and cosmic ray showers. A few of you trace your seniority far back to the hydrogen and cobalt bomb wars. Whether your survival is capricious or controlled is of no real consequence. It suffices that you inhabit this portion of the earth, and have the responsibility, or the option, or the multiple choice of procreating, fostering civility, ritualizing, or dying. In the interest of focusing your feelings toward these alternatives, this current saturate course is being required of you—"

Far down on the front row, a chondric-skinned homunculus fell asleep and slid onto the floor, like soft taffy. "Where is this member's consolbot?" the Eisenhower-Glenn holobot asked. No one in the audience responded. The holobot motioned to two provost robots, who lifted the homunculus back in his seat. Cyrus laughed softly. Lucky cat, he thought, he is out of the range of his console. The empath winced slightly at Cy's laughter, its onion-shaped head ducking down. The holobot continued: "You all know that your behaviors are essentially within controlling limits at all times. There is little to be gained through innovative, holopathic, or robopathic planning. You should know that, of you three hundred twenty-four remaining residents of District Washington Quad, seven have attempted to leave the area within the last three years. All died painful and wasteful deaths in un-monitored sectors beyond the force-veil. It is vital that you stay within range of your consolbots, or an ancillary monitor—"

"Yeah yeah yeah," Cyrus muttered aloud. He had heard this canned speech dozens of times. Then he felt a mild electroshock in the mastoid ridge, and the all too familiar voice from home came through, overriding the lecturer: "Your disdain is maladaptive, Cyrus, you must show evidence of docility, of deference to authority. You are beyond optimal range, so I am transferring your data to the provost monitor." Cy saw his name light up on the big board behind the lectern, and a provost robot began to move toward him. He knew he would have to go jelly in his thinking to get through the morning without any big hassles; but he felt a real urge to tell everybody to go to hell, to shit on some sacred cows, to drop turds in any municipal punchbowl. The gladiator grunted at Cy, as if to say "I told you so," then looked up at his own provobot, levitating above. Must be a mean bastard, Cy thought, to have his provo floating over him. The empath gave a tiny shudder and pulled its stole tighter around its small shoulders.

The focal holobot continued: "For those of you sufficiently intelligent to grasp some psycholinguistics, let me say that we are fully aware of the inadequacy of verbal communication in general. We do not expect you to alter your behaviors because of the input-saturates you receive in this class. Indeed, we do not even expect you to *hear* enough to make appreciable impacts on your orientations. This class is basically a ritual—a ritual in the purest sociologic sense. There are no particular societal goals for you to strive for, and there are no socially sanctioned means for attaining goals. This summates to Mertonian double-rejects, and the resolution of this negative pairing is found in ritualism. All that is required of you is perceptual receptivity. We are not trying to brainwash you; contingencies of reinforcement are not relevant. We are simply going to recount some recent history. If you are able to accept the inputs as factual, with retinograph tapings as validating criteria, your MTV index will improve, and you will feel subjectively happier—"

"Happier, my ass," Cy whispered, and got another shock, this time in the groin.

"We would have liked to delete the term 'happiness' from the jargon, but found it all but eradicable. During my lecture, we will request some autonomic conditioning exercises, and I think that you will find a new method pleasurable: we have some new cerebral stimulants to try today. Better to leave it at that, and wait for your reactions. Be assured they are hedonistically based. Now, those of you who wish to disconnect from the central console, for autoconditioning, or to establish degrees of cognitive freedom during the lecture, please do so now. The requirement for disconnect is two point oh MTV reading, and Stanine seven homeostasis rank. We will break for ten minutes. Thank you all."

Cy flicked the MTV switch on the arm of the seat, and saw the reading 1.98. He disconnected, but got a siren bleep in the head-set. "Obtain homeostasis reading," the voice came through. Cy plugged in and palmed the homeo switch. It read 7.4. Disconnect validated. He stood up and stretched. Andrine Garth waved to him from a gallery seat, and he began to move through the crowd toward her. They talked and drank coffee. Andrine was slim, almost wispy, with mint-green eyes and marble-smooth complex-ion. She and Cy had been paired twice in the conjugational lot-tery, and had liked each other well enough to request a monogam trial, which was still pending. Cy continued to sit beside her as the formal input session started. He squeezed her hand and felt a faint vesicular twinge. The provobot read the little surge and vectored in androgen dilutant. Cy managed a secret smile at Andrine before he spun his chaise to face the podium and clap on the headset. He closed his eyes and felt quiescent. The won-derful Eisenhower-Glenn robot voice began again:

"In the beginning, on the planet Earth, humans had the most primary of needs: to ingest foliage and flesh, in order to achieve rhythmic peristalsis, and feelings of well being; *i.e.,* satiation. This remains a pleasurable state, as you all know. Within the general limitations of a supply and demand situation, these early humans needed only to forage for food. Procreative needs were felt in males as simple vesicular pressure, and the achieving of sexual congress was instinctual, in the sense of the organisms showing tropistic behaviors based on physiologic pressures. The need for shelter developed out of discomfort in cold weather. Foliage served to warm the body, then animal hides and woven foliage provided rudimentary clothing. The need for rest grew partially from the tiring effects of cycles of daylight and darkness, and partially from simple gravitational effects generating kines-thetic fatigue. Shelter diversified into structures of various sorts, many quite large, costly, and ostentatious. When it became ac-ceptable to study and write about human behavior, the so-named social and behavioral scientists developed various taxonomies, stating that humans had two types of needs: those which were survival-oriented, such as hunger, thirst, and shelter, and those which were *acquired,* or psychogenic, or socially oriented. Perhaps one of the strongest of these latter needs was acquisitiveness— the need to gain properties, chattels, things, trinkets, and so forth. In oversimplification, if you had a plump wallaby and a family of four to feed, and another human had a fatter wallaby and no family, you would be moved toward acquiring his food supply—and this is not a simple matter of primary need for food. But now, if you moved to take this fellow's wallaby, your actions would be countered by verbal and/or physical resistance. Per- haps you would be motivated to bargain with him, or to contest him, or to make some sort of exchange. Pretty, shiny ores and metals and carbons became desirable because of their relative scarcity and visual attractiveness, and these materials became early surrogates for the desired commodity. For example, you give me that shiny rock, and you can have my wallaby. Precious stones became part of the system, then metals fashioned into discs of varying sizes, with varying portions of precious metals comprising these coins. Due to their weight, coins became re- placed by paper scrip, then checks, then plastic credit cards, then one credit card, lines of credit, letters of credit, telephonic docu- mentation of credit limits; and, around the two thousandth Earth year, individual lines of credit were established, in which society members simply authorized release of barter credits up to their prescribed actuarial limits, these limits based on an individual's lifetime projected earning power. But, and a very important *but* it was, the credit line did not reflect the generalized organismic excellence of the individual, in terms of strength, intelligence, talent, special skills, artistic abilities or the like; quite often, it reflected the acquisition patterns of the individual's ancestors, and it grew evident that some ninety-nine percent of the societal wealth was controlled by about one percent of the population. It became clear that the only way to get barter objects in satisfying amounts was to inherit them, and people knew that the chances of this were few. Emotionally charged slogans such as 'From each according to his abilities, to each according to his needs' permeated the media. In fact, this was the slogan of the twenty-oheight presidential electee, John J. Onassis. In a series of stupendous sweeps of power, Onassis liquidated the fortunes of the eighty families controlling the wealth of the continent, and set up telecast channels to monitor the true needs of the citizens. These needs were remarkably like those of the very earliest humans, namely, all three hundred seventy-seven million citizens needed foliage, flesh, fluids, and synthetic nutrients. But now—*but now,* who was to say who could have suckling pig and wine, and who was to have rice and water? Let me now scan the class roster, and sample some of your responses. Ah yes, a Master Vox Intrepid, citizen of Etherea, sir, would you be so good as to stand and respond?"

Cy had been listening with growing interest to the Eisenhower-Glenn holobot, and looked around to see what Vox Intrepid looked like. He was an amphid, with a beak-like olfactory ridge, extremities like bamboo poles, and sensor pods rippling on his trapezius muscles. The linguistic translation was instantaneous: "We on Etherea faced such a distribution problem in the medial portion of our history. With specific regard to food distribution, we used absorption limens of the intestinal tract as basal criteria, body mass as secondary criteria, and gustatory-olfactory sensitivity as a tertiary." The amphid sat back in his fluid-filled dish.

"Thank you," the focal holobot said. "I hope you all can see the homology: the primary, or at least one of the prime visceragenic needs of the people, was satisfied immediately. Think of the repercussions: no milk commissions, no cereal empires, no leechblood grocery combines. No food stamps, cattle barons, no United Fruit Company—("Yay yay yay!" someone shouted)—the entire network of growers, shippers, wholesalers, processors, and so on, obliterated, canceled. Out. Kaput. Zilched. Here on our continent, the governing Synod used a system very similar to the one just described by Mr. Intrepid, only it required the citizens to demonstrate knowledge of the desired foodstuffs; in other words, to show cognizance of the sensual and nutritional value of their choices. You will recall, I believe, the exhilarating impact of this system in its first weeks: the opening of all food stores, immediate liquidation of stock, inventory, and back orders, and the nationalization of the food business. And witness the automation of farming, and the accumulation of great food surpluses. And recall, or be informed, that the Central Food Service used television and social security numbers for coding in the types and amounts of foodstuffs allocated to individual families. I urge you to think through the implications of such innovations in barter-object systemization. In short, it meant that a man need no longer work in order to eat. Any demonstrable hunger, physiologically defined and intellectually understood, would be satisfied gratis; any wish or whim or eccentricity in food choices would be honored, provided you needed body fuel and understood the effects of different types of body fuels. Tell us your experiences in this context, Mr., ah, Franco Spark, of Australia."

A portly man stood up near Cy. Spark had been a rodeo rider, bareknuckle fistfighter, and sheep rancher. "I did some quick figuring," Spark said, "and found that my increased buying power amounted to about two hundred dollars per month. I did a crazy thing, but have not regretted it to this day. I traded in three old Cadillacs on a spanking new one, and told the salesman that the only condition of the sale was payments not to exceed two hundred dollars a month."

"Did you worry about living beyond your means?" the holobot asked. Spark looked incredulous, then relaxed in the knowledge that hyperbole or teleologic jumps must be implicit in such a question.

"Well now," Spark continued, "my *means,* if anyone ever uses that word anymore, are altogether different from what they used to be. I know now that because I am physically strong, and motivationally adaptive, that my access parameters to goods and services will stay equivalent to about twenty thousand old world dollars per year. And I didn't mind my sheep being liberated, as they put it at the time, because the sheep were part of the process of me obtaining food and shelter and transportation. Anyway, to get back to your question, I was very pleased that food was free, and I put my surplus credits into enjoyable transportation."

"I see that you are currently restricted to internal combustion vehicles."

"If that is restrictive, then it's fine with me. I wanted a helicopter the other day, and Air Central let me have one. It was a tiny bubble Sikorsky with a robopilot, but it was adequate, and they let me keep it several hours."

"Could you requisition a seven ninety-seven or a rocket sled?"

"I don't think so."

"Why not?"

"They are vehicles I neither understand nor appreciate."

"But suppose you were rich, and just *wanted* one?"

"Accessibility of goods and services has been shown to be quite unrelated to the wealth of the consumer. It would be incongruous for a rich man to have things beyond his understanding, and anyway, the term rich has entirely new connotations now, or it did. Conspicuous consumption is no longer with us—the kick, the fun, of owning trinkets just so they could be displayed for others to covet died out long ago. And I am sure you know all this. Rich Texas oilmen just don't buy their dogs Cadillacs to chase anymore."

"What then should be the basis for an organism's accessibility to societal goods and services?"

"His ability to understand, appreciate, and utilize them."

"And is such an ability acquired through experience, or is it something fairly invariant, or inborn, or endogenic?" Spark began to look like he would rather have a nap than stand up and talk to the holobot and the audience. "People who have been termed conservative seem to think that you get what you strive for, and people who are called liberal seem to feel you either have it or you don't. The old United States Republican Party was rather elitist, the old divine right of kings bit, while the Democratic Party felt that effort and persistence and the work ethic developed your tastes. I do not wish to embrace either view, but it is clear to me that there are things to eat and drink, fondle, wear, and ride in, that I don't care anything about, but which are available, and valued by people of so-called higher societal rank."

A wall isochronon glowed waxy yellow, and a cheerful trumpet tone sounded. "Our time is up for now," the Eisenhower-Glenn form said. "In our next session we will talk about alchemy and carbonized gem cloning. Good-bye. Good-bye."

Cy felt lonely, watching the holobot dematerialize. If I had an F–111 reprod, I'd ram the goddam veil beside the goddam Potomac Trench, and blast off, away from here, he found himself thinking. "Maladaptive ideation," the provobot's voice said, loud and clear in the headset. "Sorry," Cy said, "I was dozing again." Then the familiar voice of his personal consolbot came through, not as strong as usual:

"Encounter therapy in thirty-seven minutes, Cy. Take the pedwalk to the Supreme Court Monument. An Icarus flitter is berthed in egress niche eighty-seven. Got it? Eighty-seven. The flit is programmed for the hop to the therapist's home. Beam me in if you have any trouble."

Cy put the headset in his lap. Wonder if I could go take a thick yellow piss in private, he thought, and a bleep came from the headset. He held it to his ear and heard the provobot: "Lavatory facilities are located off hallway J–two, recycling lab on J–one, urinalysis J–one. Will effect reduced bladder pressure if you desire—"

Cy swiveled the earphones and put them in the rack. I'd like to piss all over your circuitry, he thought, striding away from the softly bleeping headset. He took the steps two at a time, clattered across the slick marble foyer, and stepped out onto the pedwalk. Hey, cool, he thought, the robot shits aren't going to make me apologize. They must have put the provobots back on their charging pods. "Maladaptive ideation" came the voice from home. "Up yours," Cy ventured, and heard a sigh.

He sat opposite a panthery-looking black girl in the encounter group circle. Three men and three women were the other members of the group, and the therapist was Dr. Chad Gay, a human, and a former psychoanalyst. Individual consoles were positioned behind each person, and were hooked into the central data banks. The huge amount of data already had the consoles whirring and clacking.

"You're all anxious, aren't you?" Dr. Gay's tones were effeminate and casually snotty. "Anxious, apprehensive, fearful—"

Bush league, Cy thought, stereotyped shrink bullshit. He looked closely at the girl across from him, and realized that his tight smile was more of a leer. Hey, big black momma, he thought, what a platter of sirloin and mashed potatoes running with gravy. Could my white snake actually nudge through that sporran of shiny black wire, those liver-colored labia, that snug ebony receptacle. Here, go dorsal, and lower yourself onto it. Sit on it, infuse it with chocolate juice, dye it brown for good. His fantasies were good for a few seconds, then he felt a clean wedge of *tabula rasa* alertness. God, I wonder how the bots do that, he thought—like a fairy godmother touching a magic wand to the puppet's head.

He leaned forward, input sensitivity at asymptote. The man on Cy's left did claim to feel anxiety; Dr. Gay reflected the comment in slightly different contexts, made an offensive personal reference, neutralized the aggregate group mood, and fed in the data to the therapeutic console. The man got a coding of existential anxiety, temerity, self-depreciation, and overcompensatory effusiveness. The diagnosis fed into the man's life-data banks, and the therapeutic agents were specified as a sliver of robber-baron confidence, plus a shot of Zen ideation.

Cy was called on to free-associate. "I don't know what the hell you mean," he said. "I'm not anxious. I think I resent your purporting to know what is best for me. I don't have any hang-ups." Cy felt a flow of memories, as if truth serum had replaced the blood in his brain. He knew that the action was produced by the psychoanalyst and the data banks, but could not fight it off adequately, nor was he certain that he should fight it. "I am first-born," he said, "dominant, egocentric, variably cynical, eclectic. My mommybot and housebot and daddybot gave me a huge buttress of reinforcement. I was a spanking clean success story all the way. You should have seen me in my starched linen knickers and mohair jacket, singing the merry thirty-second notes in Gilbert and Sullivan—"

"Are you now, or have you ever been, a faggot?" Dr. Gay asked, his voice disquietingly grave.

"Does a hobby-horse have a wooden ass?" Cy said, not quite retaliatory enough, he thought. Then he felt himself reaching out for the quiescence his console was always able to provide. I'm feeling some autonomic reactions, he thought, hey, where's all that happy ideational formaldehyde—hey, back home! I'm being prodded by a shrink, and watched by a circle of clods. Zap in some good signals, hey?

"Most of us are unisex," Dr. Gay said, and his tone seemed to suggest admiration of Cy.

"I'm hetero," a frog faced man said, "but I see bisex or unisex as better in some ways."

"I feel hetero," another man said, "but I prize oragenital techniques as long as the heterosex pairing is maintained."

"You couldn't tell the difference in the dark," a woman said.

"I could smell the difference," another said.

"Why do these encounters get onto sex so quickly?" a shapely girl whined. "Can't we talk about religion or politics or atomic energy, or old movies, or something?" A fat Oriental woman sneezed and farted simultaneously, and this broke up the group in laughter. While the laughter continued and the camaraderie grew warm, Cy got his diagnostic code: expansive egocentrism, self-acclamation, megalomaniac disdain—the same old shit, he thought, and the same therapeutic recommendations: humility extract, self-objectification, docile wonderment. The hour was ending and the message from home was strong this time: "Cy, baby, friend, peer, favorite son—you have got to cool it. Put it on ice, don't fight us. There's no spoils, no rewards, no booty or bounty, no masculinity layers to have to peel off. Roll with the punch, baby, give in, let us run your show. Hey, have you ever felt warm custard bridging all your synapses? It's like orgasm all over. Or you can have soma saturates instead—stay high and sheepish and sedated. I can make you feel any way I choose, but I don't want to fight you. You are made of strong stuff, and you have had great imprinting. You could be Quad Chief—top dog—"

Cy still felt that his freedom of choice was something nobody could take from him, certainly not one machine, or one robot, or even one robot government. He was concentrating ferociously on being anarchic, and the group could see that he was near exploding. He jumped up and said, "Oh, lumpy clummocks of silver robot shit!" The black girl squealed and applauded, then was shocked by her console. Dr. Gay disconnected the group, and a provobot moved directly over Cy.

I wish I had a lunch box to throw at you, he thought, and got a mild electroshock. His anger flared, and he made a move at the provobot. It was a stupid thing to do and he knew it, but he had felt raw hypothalamic anger shot past the cortical inhibition layers, unadulterated, unmonitored, and blatantly maladaptive. Now the provobot clapped a mildstun force-field around him. Goddam tin box, Cy thought, non-fucking alloy isomorph. The field increased to modstun. Cy was beginning to feel controlled, but still had a hot-metal fleck of rage in him. Back to the junkyard! he tried to yell, but could not. The provobot blotted him unconscious and dispatched him home.

He awoke to pinnacular genital itching, found himself locked in with a hearty, thrusting, obviously professional copulatress. His loins rared and locked and sneezed, and he clung to the top of the orgiastic feeling for several long pulsing seconds.

"You might wake me up before you go ripping off three days of my continence," he said to his consolbot.

"That ranked at centile ninety-two on your orgasm index," the console said. "Your MTV's are fattened the better for it."

"Right, right," Cy said, trying to think through the delicious parasympathetic obliteration of his senses. The girl was dressing, moving languidly, smelling of hot bread and musk. Cy lunged at the girl, tackled her gently. He got astride her, and she parted her legs.

"You can't be a robot," he said, close to the gelatin lips. "What's your name, who are you, I know you—"

"I'm better than real," the girl purred, spider-clawing Cy's back, biting his mouth softly, "and I'm every inch yours—every square inch, any orifice." She was trying to fit herself to him, but Cy sat up on his haunches and pinned the girl's biceps to the floor with his knees. She made a quick move to ingest his stalk, but he forced his hand under her chin.

"You're a goddam hive of Mitsubishi transistor banks, aren't you," he said, "a pseudo-fucking bionic Venus!"

"No, baby," the girl said, "I'm whatever you want me to be, whatever you need, whatever you want—" Cy felt a new surge of desire that caught high in his throat. He began to fondle the smooth body, then he felt the form give a nudge of physical strength that he knew could not be human. He began to chop at the face with his hands, screaming "Whore! Slut! Bitch! Split-tail strumpet!" The consolbot was strangely silent, but the monitoring was very precise. "Aseptic holobot!" Cy roared. "Latex and pneumoflex and synthetic bartholin!" He raised both hands in an axe-chop posture, and the girl dematerialized. "Unfair!" he shouted, feeling his vocal cords grate. "Bring her back, dammit —she needs to be lanced and scourged and slit!" A crawler skittered out, flipped Cy on his back, and held him in a force-field. He knew what was coming and braced himself for it. Suddenly he was screaming wavery vowel sounds and supravocal nonsense trumpetings, as if air horns were blaring from his voicebox. His voice seared the air like a factory whistle. He doubled up and rolled on the floor, bleating and spitting. Then it stopped, and he felt flaccid and sodden and cast in warm resin.

Goddam, I wish you wouldn't do that, Cy thought, and he had another fantasy of ramming through the force-field veil, and booming along over green mountains, canyons, moors, well-scrubbed little towns with steeples and gabled houses, lakes, marshes—

"Cy, Cy, Cy," the voice came through, "I'm not sure I can guarantee your safety anymore. You've got enough caveman tropisms to parcel out to a dozen men. You don't need them, man. They are evolutionarily maladaptive. Am I really going to have to treat you like an animal? Can't we be like a teacher and a favored student? Can't you accept the wisdom programmed into me?" But Cy felt a deep thoracic germination of something like role-identity, and it included the absolute right, the fiercely held right to do anything he wanted as long as he didn't hurt anybody else. He looked up at the console's physiog-plate. "I may throw up," he said. "If I had a T.S. card, I'd pop it in your chute."

"What's a T.S. card?" the console asked

"The letters stand for tough shit—I thought you knew that. If I could have some printed up, they might say something like: 'Yours is the saddest story I have ever heard. It has really touched my heart deeply. Please accept this card as an expression of my sincere sympathy.' "

"Cy, Cy, Cyrus," the console said, sounding weary.

"Robot piss," Cy said, feeling a leaden sedation coming on. He was flicked into unconsciousness again.

Three days later he awoke, greatly refreshed, feeling exploratory and predatory. He ate a huge meal, building from gentle things like squab eggs through crêpes to pork slices, asparagus, ale, and pastries. He swallowed a supply of nutrient pills, which could be activated by taking another type of pill later on. He talked chattily with the consolbot, seemed repentant and anxious to please, and even patted the service crawler's knobby crown as he left for the auto races. The console's tone was suspicious: "Are you up to something, Cy?"

"Now, now." He sounded vaguely smug. "Don't be negative. I feel extra good today, they're doing the nineteen sixty-three Sebring over at Bolling Meadow, and I get to ride in the Cobra with Gurney. I can do without a provobot. But, big daddy, if you are worried about me, zap in a trivid pak, and you can tune in on me anytime." A long silence followed, during which Cy felt the console was shuffling its feet.

"Well, have fun. Be cool. Don't do anything dumb. And take a force-field isomorph with you."

"Do I have to brush my toothies?" Cy said, playfully patting the console's credenza and walking toward the eletube. He took a silver B–1 reprod from the flitter loft, the craft lifting silently from its pod and into the air traffic pattern toward the ancient Bolling Airfield. He wanted to fly close to the shimmering film of curtain that hung over the Potomac Trench, but found that he could not override the coded flight plan. He landed the craft at about thirty MPH and walked to the pits, where the holographic rerun of the ancient sports car race was ready. He bent into the tiny cockpit of the silver Cobra and clapped Gurney on the back. The car left twin tracks of smoking rubber as it roared off down the straightaway.

"Red-lined at *ninety-five hundred?*" Cy shouted at Gurney, looking at the needle sweeping across the tach face. The car seemed to soar from a busy thick clacking to a deep scream that rattled Cy's ribcage.

"The absolute end!" Cy shouted, as the car swept through the esses. "Nirvana, Apocalypse, and Revelation!" He pushed the multilocator switch on his energy-pak, and alternated between a seat high in the stands and the tiny seat beside Gurney. He rode a lap with Surtees in a prototype Ferrari, superimposing himself over the driver's holographic form. He sat on the grass, drank a quart of ale, and lit an eight-inch pencil-thin Reina Isabel. He flicked the energy pak to trivid, dialed his billet, and monitored the strength of the signal. It was weak. "I can't hear you very well," he said softly to his consolbot.

"You're on the very edge of my monitoring range," the voice came through. "Your life-support systems are wavering at minus two point-one standard deviations. I'd advise you to move as little as five-hundred yards closer to me."

Cy glanced around quickly. One consolbot was in the pit area, and a few provobots hovered over the crowd. He looked out over the weed-filled meadow to the force-veil, about one thousand yards away. The veil hung like a waterfall of the purest mist. He had seldom been this close to it. He walked toward the veil some fifty yards, watching the strength of the home signal weaken on his pak.

"Two-twenty-seven s.d.'s on life-support," the voice said weakly. "You are nearing the perimeter of the quad, Cy. Listen to me, don't do anything foolish, you can't survive across the river trench. I can show you trivid tapes of what is over there. You wouldn't want to go. Shall I hook in to the consolbot there?"

Cy moved closer to the edge of the meadow, nearer the veil. He strained his eyes to look across the fetid sludge of the Potomac Trench. Hey, he said to himself, I can see through the veil. He looked, fascinated, and saw the Masonic Tower in Alexandria. It was mottled with lichens, and bull-bats big as condors were streaming from the high niches.

"Cyrus? Cy!" The home voice sounded urgent. "You're in danger, boy—my son, your signal is fading fast—move back into my range. Are you all right? Two-seventy-three on life support. Can you hear me? I AM DISPATCHING THE PROVOBOTS TO SAVE YOU—"

"The hell you are," Cy said, breaking contact. He stepped to the edge of the trench. With his levitator registering strong anti-grav reserves, he lifted off, eased into prone flying position, and thrust off across the dappled mud flats toward the curtain of beautiful mist. A provobot swished down the runway as Cy rammed the force-field at ground level, fought through what felt like plastifoam netting, and rolled through onto a dirty white sandbar. The provobot caught up with him easily, but did not cross the force-field. The bot hung there, like a silver chalice, flashing a red pilot-tube light on its cowl. Cy sprinted along the sandbar and into some fleshy green brush.

"Alarm! Alarm!" the provobot sang out. "You are in imminent danger—identify yourself—" Cy flicked on the pak long enough to say, "Go to hell," and began to trot down the sandbar toward a crumbling jetty. He felt a thick bubble in his throat, and stopped jogging. He was breathing hard. He reached for a handkerchief, and saw a dime-sized, grayish-green patch of mold on his hand. He blew his nose lustily; fatty gray particulates blackened the cloth. He wiped at the mold, and saw another erupt on his thumb. Quickly he palmed on his own force-field isomorph, but noticed that the energy level was already lower than expectancy. The molds faded; the air inside the iso felt clean and refrigerated. He climbed up the jetty, and began to walk toward the shoreline. Already the surface of the isomorphic body-suit was graying with particles. He walked down the center of a street. A snail as big as a sea lion was rasping the soft paint off the front of an old beauty shop. Cy drew his fusion torch and notched it to stun. A crystalline cluster began to form on his shoulder. He felt a burning sensation, brushed the growth off, but saw that it had actually permeated the iso. Oh shit, he thought, talk about hostile environments. I've got to find a down-under. No bunch of tin-box robots is going to tell me what to do. A hairy bush moved from an alleyway. Cy's heart beat wildly against his ribs as he saw that the bush had segmented legs. It was a tarantula as large as a VW, backing slowly into the street. It reared on its back legs, awesome fangs raised, and Cy saw that another tarantula was the cause of the attack-ready posture. The second tarantula approached warily, leglike palpi glistening with sperm. The reared female started a lunge, but before she could strike, the spurred forelegs of the male shot up, catching the fangs. Thus protected, the spider forced its mate upward, exposing an abdominal furrow, and depositing the sperm.

Cyrus felt faint. He used some precious levitational energy to

get atop a theater marquee. Tufts of orange pollen were budding
into ridges on his sleeve. He felt a very convincing diarrhetic
twinge. He took one of the nutritional activators, and immediately felt the expanding stomach blastula. Swallowing was difficult for him; he cleared his throat and spat out mucus and tiny
white crabs. Good Christ, he thought, what kind of a world is
this? Panic welled up inside him, he hacked, and gagged, and spat
again. He leaned against a rusted cable; it shredded in his hand,
the parterre swayed and collapsed. He wrenched the levitator just
in time to minimize the *g* forces, rising from the crumbled debris
like a rocket lifting ponderously from its pad.

He felt sick, hunkered down in the center of a parking lot, and
felt fluid seeping past his anal sphincter. I shit my pants, teacher,
he thought, remembering one hawk-faced pedagogue who had
refused to let him go to the third grade bathroom. He closed his
eyes. They felt pasted shut. His ears began to itch, something was
crawling up his back, and a small mutant lamprey had affixed its
saxophone mouth to his mastoid surface. Cy rubbed his eyes
clear of wax and tiny fibers. A fanlike crystal blipped into life,
splitting his earlobe. "I've got to get the hell out of here," he said
aloud, but he was lost. He lumbered out onto the street, looking
for the force-field. Maybe I can make it back, he thought. A
leather-winged pterodactyl dove at him and banked away,
screeching. Cy veered heavily toward the curb, crashed through
a soft wooden fence, toppled into a shallow grease pit. He moved
as if in a dream, lifting to upright position like a crane hoisting
a heavy weight. His body isomorph glistened with oily waste from
the pit, and the surface was covered with strange spores, molds,
buds, barnaclelike growths, the lamprey, and a large slug. He
lifted a few feet off the ground, feeling the weakened levitational
energy. Black fluids sluiced from his spleen and watery excre-
ment dribbled from his rectum. He settled on a mound of soft
earth, took a tentative step, and fell like a puppet with severed
strings. A wolverinelike creature crept up from a hole in the
mound, snarling. Cy flicked the fusion torch to sear and pulled
the trigger. A cone of orange fire enveloped the creature, and it

somersaulted wildly before dying in the flames. A wet, translucent tuber grew on Cy's chest, his brows and lashes bloomed with
crystal growths. He vomited and excreted in dual projectile
gushes. I'm dying, goddammit, he thought, goddammit it to hell,
goddam all you solid-state, latency-spouting consolbots, holobots, provobots—all you fucking tin spheres and boxes and cylin-
ders. You're not human. There is nothing like a true human. Fine
cartilages, bones like tree trunks, valves and kingposts and tubes
and ducts. Marble skin, golden hair, agate eyes, and holy neuro-
logic brain in its bony case. You're nothing but a bunch of machines—circuit breakers, fuses, Hong Kong transistors. Cy sali-
vated gelatin, trying to breathe past the thorns erupting in his
nostrils. He rammed the levitator to full lock, and his body dug
a shallow furrow down the rutted knoll, back to the Potomac
Trench, a scant fifty yards away. The energy supply gave out as
he moved very slowly out onto the spongy dark river bed. He saw
the softly glimmering force-field veil in the distance—so near and
yet so far away. Little things scuttled across his eyes, blurring the
picture. With his last bit of strength, he rolled supine and spread-
eagled, firing the torch at sear. He tried to aim it like a flare-
pistol, but it fell flat on his stomach, cremating him from the waist
down.

The torch burned for three days and nights before expending
its cells. A trio of service bots sent to repair the force-field
watched Cy try to make it back home. They even found themselves cheering him on.

Back at his billet, the consolbot clacked out the data cube:

"Cyrus Beta Livingston, assigned to my care these two years
past, has died in an attempt to escape from the Washington DC
continental quadrant. I had hoped sincerely that he would prove
malleable and adaptive; however, he has consistently shown a
willful strength, a resistance to programming, a stubborn endogenic egocentricity, as well as a certain subjective likeability. He
seems to have been admired in the peer-group, but is formally
classified as robopathic. The current population of the area is
three hundred twenty-three. I am ready for reassignment."

FALL OF PEBBLE-STONES

He was a good person, that cop. There weren't
any rotten people around there. (But have
you looked under your eaves lately?)

R. A. Lafferty

And heal my heart and bless my bones
With nightly fall of pebble-stones.
> Ellenbogen, *Rainy Morning Rimes.*

Bill Sorel stood at his nineteenth-floor window and shied pebbles
and stones out over space to land in the sidewalk and street. It
had rained the night before, and there were pebbles on that little
ledge under his window after every rain. It's always fun to throw
stones, even small stones, in the morning and see what they will
hit.

"Hey, that cop's going to come up and get you again, Bill
Sorel," Etta Mae Southern called from her window next door.
"Where were you last night? I called every guy I know for a date
and couldn't get anybody. You remember the other day the cop

came all the way up to your place and told you the people in the street were getting crabby about getting hit on the head with pebbles."

"I have been awarded the big red plum, Etta Mae," Sorel boasted to the early morning air and his neighbor. "I'm not a professor; I'm not a doctor: I'm just a hardworking and dirty-scheming popularizer and feature writer. But I have wrested the big red plum from the big boys in the Q. and A. scientific field."

"Well, don't throw the plum-pit down on someone's head when you're finished," Etta Mae said. "You told that cop, 'They're not very big pebbles,' and he said, 'No, I know they're not.' You told him, 'People just like to complain about things,' and he said, 'Yeah, I know they do. Now you just cut out hitting people on their heads with pebbles so they'll have one less thing to complain about.' You said, 'How did you know it was me?' and he said, 'Who else in this building would be the mad pebble-thrower?' He sure is a nice cop but I bet he won't be so nice if he has to come all the way up here after you again."

"I've been awarded the big red plum," Sorel repeated, and he continued to pick the pebbles out of that little ledge below his window and throw them down over the street. "I have been selected to compile, edit, write or whatever *The Child's Big What and Why Book*. This will pay me well. All I have to do is answer the scientific questions that children of all ages will ask, and do it in the style that the most doltish kid can understand and the smartest kid will not find patronizing. And really most of the work is already done before I start."

"You hit a man with a pebble, Bill. He's looking around to see where it came from. He's on the edge of being real mad if he finds out someone hit him on purpose."

"I didn't," Sorel said. "I discovered that I can't hit any of them on purpose, so I concentrate on hitting them by accident. I just throw them and let them find their own targets. But it wasn't a very big pebble and it didn't hurt him much. Now all I have to do is find out half an answer to one question and a full answer to another, and I'll be able to put the book together. Where do *you* think the pebbles come from, Etta Mae?"

"My idea is that the rain makes them. Pebbles are made out of silicon mostly. And silicon and nitrogen are almost exactly alike. I used to go with a smart fellow and he taught me things like that. When it lightens, the rain makes almost as much silicon water as nitrogen water, and it deposits it as pebbles. That's one way. Hey, do you know that rotten people never have pebbles around their houses? The other way is that little pieces of sand come together and the lightning-impregnated water fuses them into pebbles. It has to be one of those ways or there wouldn't always be pebbles after it rains. There's a third way that pebbles could happen, but it's a little bit doubty."

"Tell me the third way, Etta Mae. I have to consider lots of fringe things for the *Big What and Why Book.*"

"It's that somebody doesn't want you to run out of pebbles because you have so much fun throwing them. So, whoever it is, he keeps making pebbles for you every time it rains. You know Mrs. Justex on the eighteenth floor. She always used to live in a house before she came here, and she had a little ledge outside her kitchen window where her milk would be left every morning. She took the apartment here and saw that there wasn't any ledge. 'How will I get milk?' she asked herself. So she nailed up a little ledge like the one you fixed for yourself there. And every morning there would be a quart of milk for her on the ledge. This went on for a week till she happened to think, 'Who is my route man here? And how does he get up to the eighteenth floor on the outside of this building?' She heard him then—it was early in the morning—and she went to see. She opened the window suddenly and knocked him off. He fell down and was killed on the sidewalk. But he faded away, and there wasn't anything left of him when she went down to look. After that, she had to start buying her milk in the store."

"No, Etta Mae, I know Mrs. Justex. That's just one of the stories that she tells when she's wet-braining it in the Wastrels' Club."

"It did seem kind of doubty. I don't believe she drinks milk at all. What is the half an answer and the whole answer that you have to find out before you can put the book together?"

"The half one is, 'Why does a baseball curve?' I think I have that half whipped. I'm going to see a man today who is supposed to know the answer. And the whole answer I'm looking for is to the question, 'How do the pebbles get under the eaves?' "

"Oh, well, it's got to be one of the three ways I told you."

Bill Sorel stood there at the window and threw every pebble away. That is important. He didn't miss a one. Then he got a little broom and swept that ledge clear of everything.

Bill Sorel should have had an easy job of putting that book together. He already knew all the answers except for that half answer and that full answer. He had once handled a lot of the questions in a little daily feature before it was canceled out on him. He could use that material again. And most of the other answers he had already filed in his head for ready use. Besides, there were already many such books that he could draw upon, besides the real reference books, and besides the palaver of his own keenwitted friends. He had had it down to three unanswered questions when he applied for a shot at the *Big What and Why.* And now he had it down to one and one-half.

When Bill Sorel had come on the scene there had been three questions going around wearing blatantly false answers. These were: "What Makes it Thunder?" "What Makes a Baseball Curve?" "How Do the Pebbles Get Under the Eaves?" It is hard to believe the answers that had been given to these questions by scientists, some of them grown men.

Listen to this one:

"Thunder is produced when lightning heats the surrounding air and causes it to expand and send out waves. The expanding wave is heard as thunder."

Well, what can you do when you come on something like that? Possibly it was better than the answer that earlier generations gave, that the lightning burned up the air and the thunder was caused by new air rushing in to fill up the place.

Well, Bill Sorel had found out what causes thunder. It was really a wonder that somebody else hadn't stumbled onto the right answer before he had. Read it. Read the amazingly evident answer in *The Child's Big What and Why Book*.

Listen to this about a baseball. And it's been repeated again and again for more than a century.

"The curving of a baseball is caused by denser air on the bottom of the baseball than on the top. Therefore the bottom spin will be more effective than the top spin, will have more traction on the air, and will cause the ball to curve. The ball will curve to the right if the pitcher throws it with a clockwise spin, and to the left if the spin is counterclockwise. Artillery shells behave according to the same rule."

Oh, great bloated bulls! What? A three-and-a-half inch difference in elevation would cause enough pressure difference between the top and the bottom of a baseball to make the thing curve up to eighteen inches in sixty-six feet? Where is your sense of proportion? Suppose the difference in elevation-pressure should be a hundred thousand times as much, the difference between low ground and the height of thirty thousand feet or so. Would the thrown ball then curve a hundred thousand times as much? Would it curve thirty miles off course in sixty-six feet of travel? As Etta Mae would say, "It's kind of doubty."

But now Bill Sorel halfway knew what made a baseball curve. He had heard the explanation at second hand. Today he hoped to hear it at first hand.

And listen to this one about pebbles in the little rain-worn ditches under the eaves of buildings:

"It is sometimes asked why there are usually small white pebble-stones under the eaves-drops of buildings when there do not seem to be any other pebbles around anywhere. But the answer is that there are always pebbles around everywhere. They are mixed with the great bulk of the earth and are not noticed. But rain washes the finer and lighter earth particles away and leaves the pebbles behind. That is the reason that there seem to be so many pebbles under the eaves of buildings, particularly after a rain."

Aw, heel-flies! Bill Sorel didn't know the answer to that one, but he knew that such drivel wasn't the answer.

Yeah, he had a big red plum. He wasn't going to let it get away. He was going to make sure of it. He got in his Red Ranger (a type of motor car) and drove off to find the man who could complete his half answer to the second question. And as he drove, he reviewed in his mind that momentous third question.

Some pebbles are limestone, but most of them are quartz. *And there are not always pebbles around.* In much earth there are no pebbles at all. In most earth, the true pebbles will make up less than one part in fifty thousand. Ah, but you put up a building or house and move into it, and after the very first rain there is a thick accumulation of pebbles in its eaves-drops. Has fifty thousand times their amount of earth been washed away to reveal them?

Bill Sorel had made a nuisance of himself around building projects in checking out the pebble situation. In one place he had taken a cubic yard of dirt, hauled it aside, and gone over it all with a toothbrush and sieve. And he had not found any pebbles at all. The only things too big to go through the sieve were organic things, roots, hickory nut hulls, twigs, pieces of bark and pieces of worms. There were not any natural pebbles at all. He kept track of all artificial pebbles (pieces of mortar, cinder block fragments, bits of limestone gravel and of flint chat). He would always know them from genuine pebbles, and he already knew that they would not accumulate under eaves.

He continued his surveillance as the seven houses on this particular tract were raised, were finished, were first rained upon. He examined them. The rain had made little under-the-eaves ditches around all the houses, but there were no pebbles in those ditches. Something was missing from the formula. The premonition of what it might be excited Bill Sorel and almost scared him.

People moved into one of the houses, and Sorel waited impatiently for it to rain. But it didn't rain for a whole week. People moved into a second of the houses, and that night it rained. Sorel was around with a flashlight at dismal, drenching dawn (it was partly for such devoted labor as this that Sorel had won the big red plum), and he discovered that the two inhabited houses now had pebbles in their eaves-drop runnels, and that the five uninhabited houses had none.

He followed it up. As soon as people moved into another house and there was rain thereafter, so soon was there a full complement of pebbles around that house.

You do not believe this? Pick out a housing development in your own region, and make a nuisance of yourself by observing it closely. You will be convinced, unless you are of such mind-set as defies conviction.

Sorel observed other housing developments, apartment projects, commercial constructions. Wherever eaves-runnels were not precluded by roof guttering and spouting, there would be white pebbles appearing in full force as soon as the structure had been put to human use and it had rained thereafter.

Sorel tried it at his own nineteenth-floor apartment. He figured a way to divert rainfall from the roof. He made this diversion, and he made a little ledge outside his window on which the diverted rain might fall.

(A little misunderstanding was created by these activities of Sorel. Firemen and policemen and psychologists and deacons came and soft-talked him and tried to capture him with hooks and ropes and nets. They thought he was contemplating jumping off the building to his own destruction. He wasn't. There just wasn't any way to divert the rain-drop without climbing around on the outside of that building.)

Well, it rained the night after Sorel had made these arrangements. There sure had not been any pebbles there before it rained. There had been nothing there but a little ledge or trough made out of number two pine boards and fastened to the brickwork with screws and lead anchors.

It rained and rained, and Bill Sorel kept night watch on his little

ledge by the lightning flashes and the diffused night light of the
town. One moment there had not been any pebbles. And the next
moment there had been a complete complement of pebbles on
the ledge. Sorel knew that the pebbles were for him. He knew
they wouldn't have appeared on the ledge of an apartment that
nobody lived in. But how had the pebbles got to that nineteenth-
floor ledge? This was the question that still lacked even a hint of
an answer.

Bill Sorel in his Red Ranger arrived at a little acreage and came
on a tall middleaged man who was eating round onions; and with
him was a bright-faced little girl who was eating gingerbread.

"They're good for the circulation," the man said. "I bet I eat
more onions than any man in the county. I'm George 'Cow-Path'
Daylight. You sent me a postcard that you were coming to see me
today."

"Yes," Bill Sorel said. "I'm told that you really know what
makes a baseball curve. I've been looking for the answer to that
one for a long time."

"I'm Susie 'Corn-Flower' Daylight," the bright-faced little girl
said. "Mr. Cow-Path here is my grandfather."

"Yes, I really know what makes a ball curve," Cow-Path said.
"It's because I know what makes it curve that I've been striking
out batters for thirty years. You ask the batters in Owasso and
Coweta and Verdigris about me. You ask them in Chouteau and
Salina and Locust Grove. Yeah, ask them in Oolagah and Tiawah
and Bushyhead. They'll tell you who keeps the Catoosa Mud-Cats
on top of the heap year after year. I am the best small-town
pitcher in northeast Oklahoma, and I'm the best because I know
what makes a baseball curve."

"And I am the best third-grade girl pitcher in Catoosa," Susie
Corn-Flower Daylight said. "I can even whizz them by most of
those big girls in the fourth and fifth grades."

"Cow-Path, they tell me that you maintain that the direction of
the spin has nothing to do with the direction of the curve of a ball.

And you say that there isn't a gnat's leg's difference in the pressure on the top and the bottom of a ball.''

"Not a millionth of a gnat's leg's difference," Cow-Path Daylight said. "A pitcher's mustache with one more hair on one side than on the other would have more effect on the ball than any such difference in pressure. The reason that I understand the physics of the situation is that I spent two years in the sixth grade, which is why I learned that book *General Science for The Primary Student* so well. There was a paragraph in there about how a gyroscope top spins and leans and holds. I applied it to a baseball and became a great pitcher.''

"Well, if the direction of the spin doesn't have any effect on the direction of the curve, what *does* have effect?'' Sorel asked smoothly. He had heard the explanation at second hand, but he wanted to hear it from the master.

"The direction of the *axis* of the spin is what causes the curve,'' Cow-Path said, "but it doesn't matter which direction the ball spins on the axis. Look!''

Cow-Path Daylight took a pencil from Sorel's pocket and, with his strong fingers, he jabbed it clear through one of those big round onions that he liked. He had it centered perfectly. He spun the pencil with its spitted onion, and that was the axis of spin. He moved the whole thing head-on down the centerline of the hood of Sorel's Red Ranger, but with the direction of the axis about eleven degrees off to the right of the direction of movement.

"The curve will be in the direction of the angle of the *axis* of spin,'' Cow-Path said. "The ball, on the gyroscopic principle, tries to align its direction with the direction of the *axis* of spin. But the direction of the spin itself doesn't matter. See!''

Cow-Path reversed the direction of spin while keeping the same axis of spin and the same forward motion. "See, the spin is exactly reversed, and reversing it will make no change whatever. But every change of axis, whatever the direction of spin, will have an effect on the direction of the ball.''

Cow-Path showed, with the gyroscopic onion, how a ball would behave with the axis tilted to the right or the left, or up or down.

And he showed that it was all the same thing whether the spin was clockwise or counterclockwise.

"It is for this understanding that I am known as the artist of the backup ball," Cowpath said. "I can throw a fork-ball that moves like a slider, or a slider that moves like a fork-ball. And I can throw my floater and my drop with the same motion and the same direction of spin: only the tilt of the axis will be changed."

Sorel saw that all of this was true with an eternal verity. It was one of those big Copernican moments. Things could never again be as they had been before. Infinitesimally and particularly there had been made a contribution towards a new Heaven and a new Earth.

When he had his feelings a bit under control, Bill Sorel made small talk with the two Daylight people. Then, believing that their well of wisdom could not be exhausted even by such a huge cask as had been drawn from it, he asked them questions.

"Do you know what causes thunder?" he asked them.

"Do you mean thunder, or do you mean the sound of thunder?" Susie Corn-Flower Daylight asked around her gingerbread. "They're two different things."

"I suppose I mean the sound of thunder," Sorel said. "Thunder itself has no cause."

"Why, how smart you are, for a city man!" Corn-Flower admired.

"I very nearly know what causes the sound of thunder, the sound of lightning really, but I don't know exactly," Cow-Path said. "Lightning is resinous, as we know from the color of it as well as from the odor. I believe that when lightning cracks or fractures the air, it coats both parts of the air with a sort of rosin dust—not too different from the rosin that pitchers use. Then, when the two parts of the air come together again immediately, they are a little bit offset from each other. So they grind and set themselves together, and the two rosined surfaces rubbing together make the noise."

Bill Sorel was amazed. Cow-Path's explanation was gibberish, of course. But it sounded almost like the real explanation would sound if given in code, and it may have been just that. And Susie Corn-Flower's divination that the thunder and the sound of thunder were two different entities was—well, it was a thunderous sort of intuition. Sorel felt very pleased and gratified with these two persons.

So he tried them with the final question.

"How do pebbles get under the eaves of houses and buildings?" he asked.

"Oh, I suppose they come off the roof," Cow-Path said. "The rain must loosen them, and then they roll off the roof into the eaves-drop ditch."

"No, Grandpa, no," Susie Corn-Flower Daylight said. "Why would they ever be on the roof to fall off? The pebble angel puts the pebbles directly into the eaves-drop ditch. He puts them there as a sign that he is guarding that building and that everything is all right. Buildings without people living in them never have pebbles under the eaves."

"No, I know they don't, Corn-Flower," Sorel said. "But did you ever hear that rotten people don't have pebbles around their houses either?"

"I've never known any rotten people," Susie Corn-Flower said. "We've never had any rotten people in our town."

"That's right. There never have been any here," Cow-Path said.

Bill Sorel had *The Child's Big What and Why Book* finished a week later—he was a fast worker—and it was ready to send off. But he had two versions of one page, and he had not yet made his selection between them. This was the page that covered the question, "How do the pebbles get under the eaves?"

Sorel went to the Wastrels' Club to drink white rum and think about it. One version gave the old safe answer, that there are always pebbles around everywhere, and that the rain washes the dirt away from them and leaves the pebbles. This was the safe falsehood.

The other version was somewhat different. It was true, probably: or at least it was a coded statement of a truth. But could Sorel get away with a truth like that in the *What and Why Book?*

Etta Mae Southern was already in Wastrels' with a handsome, rich, and goodhumored man. She made very small horizontal circles with her finger in the air.

"That's the world's smallest record playing, 'I wish it were you instead,' " she called across the clubroom.

And Mrs. Justex was already in Wastrels'. She was drinking one of those lacteal gin-sloshes that are called Milky Ways. So Mrs. Justex *did* drink milk, sometimes, and in a way. That fact changed just about everything. It meant that the widest of improbables was still possible.

On the wall of Wastrels' was a paragraph of wisdom:

"When one has discarded all absolutely impossible explanations of a thing, then what is left, however improbable it seems, must be accepted as the explanation until a better explanation comes along."

Bill Sorel had seen that paragraph on the wall a dozen times, but it had never so hit him between the ears before.

A cop came into Wastrels' and said it had started to rain outside. He had a Salty Dog. Cops are the only people left in the world who still drink them.

"You will be in my apartment in fifteen minutes," Bill Sorel said.

"Why will I be?" the cop asked him.

"To try to make me stop hitting people on their heads with pebble-stones," Sorel said. And Sorel left Wastrels' and went to his apartment. He selected one of the two versions of the disputed page and put it with the rest of the pages. He sealed and stapled the completed *What and Why,* and went out and down in the elevator and out into the rain to mail the thing in the stand-up mailbox on the corner. And then he came back to his apartment with happy anticipation.

Then he was standing at his opened window in the early dark. It was raining and blowing and getting him pretty wet. He was scooping up handfuls, double-handfuls of pebbles from the ledge under his window and flinging them out at the lower world. He scooped out twenty, thirty, fifty handfuls of pebbles from that little ledge-trough that wouldn't hold three handfuls at one time. But now that trough stood full of pebble-stones no matter how many he scooped out of it.

Somebody was banging at Sorel's apartment door, and he let him bang. And pretty soon somebody was shaking Sorel's shoulder, and he let him shake.

"Hey, you got to quit throwing pebbles down there," the cop was saying. "You're hitting people that are trying to get taxis in the rain, and you're tearing their umbrellas. Those are bigger pebble-stones than you usually throw, aren't they?"

"These are the biggest ever," Sorel said happily. "These are prime pebbles. Say, I used the page about the pebble angel in the book. That's going to hit a lot of people crossways. I mailed the whole thing off with that in it. I'm glad I did."

"They come in just as fast as you throw them out, don't they?" the cop said. "I wonder where they come from? I never noticed that that's the way pebbles come when it rains. Can't you throw more of them faster and get ahead of them?"

Oh, it was with a wonderful clatter that the pebbles arrived!

"Man, this is as fast as I can throw them," Sorel panted. "I bet I've thrown a thousand pounds of them down already. It sure is fun. It looks like I made a breakthrough in pebbles. The pebble angel is showing that he likes the mention."

"Maybe if we both scooped them and threw them as fast as we could, we could almost keep up with them," the cop said. "Yeah, it is fun." The cop threw lefthanded, and the two fitted well together at the window.

He was a good person, that cop. There weren't any rotten people around there. (But have you looked under *your* eaves after a rain?)

The Memory Machine

I am sure they will be considered guilty until they are found not guilty. That's the American way.

—Richard Nixon

O Where Hae Ye Been, Colin Wilson My Son, Since 1930?

It was now mid-October; they were scheduled to leave for earth in the second week of November, arriving in mid-January. (At top speed, the *Hermes* covered four million miles a day.)

—*The Space Vampires,* by Colin Wilson (Random House, 1976), p. 14

The *Vega* was one of two big space cruisers that had set out for the derelict a month ago. They could achieve up to four million miles a day.

—*Ibid.,* p. 26

"You astound me, sir. An incredible coincidence."

"That's what I think. You didn't report any meteor showers, did you?"

"There weren't any, sir. Meteor showers are always associated with comets, and there wasn't a comet within forty million miles."

—*Ibid.,* p. 28

Poets' Corner

". . . It seems as yesterday that I started
In the fine new ship that stood
In the red-gold rays of the setting sun . . .
And my legs—they seemed like wood.

". . . The terrible jar
Of the ripping start
It laid me flat on my back,
And I could only stare . . .

". . . As the crowd flashed by . . .
And the earth fell away
And space loomed dim and vast . . .
And I was afraid to the core.

". . . My calculations, they have failed me . . .
The fuel is almost gone.
The oil is thin—the bearings hot,
And the cold, it chills to the bone.

". . . Oh Red Star, I can see you——
I wonder if I'll ever touch you . . .
Perhaps, who knows, I'll never reach you . . .
Perhaps, who knows, I'll die . . .

". . . I'll just go back to the stern once more,
And one last look I'll take . . .
At the tiny green ball that's floating
Far in the rocket's wake.

". . . And then I'll return to the cabin
And measure the oil and the fuel,
And wonder and wonder as I figure
How I ever expected to win this cosmic duel."

—"First Flight," by Wilson Shepherd,
in *The Phantagraph*,
July-August, 1939

Hip, hip . . .

Three rousing cheers for Donald G. Turnbull for his valiant attack on those favoring mush. When we want science fiction, we don't want swooning dames, and that goes double. You needn't worry about Miss Evans, Donald, us he-men are for you and if she tries to slap you down, you've got an able (I hope) confederate and tried auxiliary right here in the person of yours truly. Come on, men, make yourself heard in favor of less love mixed with our science!

Isaac Asimov
174 Windsor Place
Brooklyn, New York

—*Astounding Stories,* September, 1938

Try Harder

When one sees his sketches of flying machines, parachutes, submarines, tanks and guns, and realizes that he knew the distant stars to be suns and postulated the existence of other earths, it is difficult to believe that Leonardo da Vinci was not a science fiction fan.

—*The Immortal Storm,* by
Sam Moskowitz (Atlanta
Science Fiction Organization
Press, 1954)

Me Tarzan, Him Cthuthu

I have seen Yith, and Yuggoth on the Rim,
And black Carcosa in the Hyades.
And in the slimy depths of certain seas
I have beheld the tomb where lieth Him
Who was and who shall be; . . .

—"Beyond," by Lin Carter,
in *Amra,* II, 47 (1968)

TOMUS

Here is a story on a theme that has been treated
before in science fiction—in "The Story of the Late Mr.
Elvesham" by H. G. Wells, in "The Master Shall Not Die"
by R. DeWitt Miller, and in "The Indesinent Stykal" by
D. D. Sharp, among others—but never as poignantly as this.

Stephen Robinett

He is utterly humorless and determined. This morning he
learned he will die. He has said nothing since. Brooding? Possibly. He had never brooded before. The sensation is annoying. I
have my work to do. His silence is more unnerving than his usual
chatter. This morning, idly, just after breakfast, he asked about
death.

Tomus, what is death?

I answered frankly. I always try to answer frankly. We have
come, over the years, to an uneasy, communicative peace. *I don't
know.*

You must know, Tomus. You know everything.

I noticed his voice. It came through the thin barrier between
our personalities with a changed quality, retaining its usual im-
pression of wide-eyed innocence, but somehow different. The
quality escaped me.

Not everything. I don't know everything, I answered, only half paying attention, my mind occupied with my own work. My mathematical model of our galaxy, the core of my interstellar navigator, had yet to crystallize in my mind. Reconciling the converging series of equations demanded by the curvature of space with the infinite series demanded by the expanding universe, is, as one might imagine, taxing. His questions, by comparison, are merely annoying, tedious, usually simpleminded, seldom humorous, always without wit. He is uncultivated.

You must know, he insisted.

Will you please shut up!

Tomus, this, I think, is important.

Not very.

You must tell me about death.

It is one of the few things I have never experienced.

But you know about it.

It is the maximum entropy of a biochemical system.

He chewed on that awhile, allowing me to work through several equations. Ultimately my galactic model will be used to program a navigational computer, the perfect map. I was deep into a conflicting pair of equations when he finished chewing.

Tomus.

What?

Somehow your answer is unsatisfying.

It is accurate.

What is entropy? What is a biochemical system? Tomus, what is death?

Do you remember the dog? The dog, a friend of our early years together, the years after I allowed him to remain, had died, as dogs do, after fifteen years. It grew old. Entropy increased. It died. Maximum entropy, its scampering quantum of energy spreading back to the universe.

I remember the dog.

That is death.

I got a great amount of work done after that. Occasionally he began to ask something, then fell silent. About noon he broke the silence.

Will I die?

Yes.

And you, Tomus? Will you die?

It's possible.

But I will die. You are sure of that.

Yes.

He said nothing else. He says nothing else. He is brooding. I sense his determination. He wants to live. To think of himself gone, nonexistent, expired, *kaput,* upsets him. He broods. At least he is quiet.

I finish my day's work and go out to eat. The sun, a dull fat orange on the horizon, autumn fruit, has nothing in it of summer. Winter approaches. It is still beautiful. My four hundred summers and winters merge in my mind, each beautiful, each different. Only my work is the same, unchanging, new problems but the same mental processes.

I walk across the broad lawn in front of the Center. I recognize few of the strollers. It is too much trouble to keep track of who is where. If I need them, I can find them. The faces change. Only the people remain the same.

I walk out the gates and glance back at the building. It is anonymous. Since the Life Riots three hundred years ago, there has been nothing but anonymity for us. Once a sign hung over the main entrance, *Center for Anentropic Maintenance.* I was one of the first. In those days I was a black man. It helped during the riots. The mobs, thinking on a primitive, stereotyped level, could never conceive of a black Longevitor. They left me alone. I worked out the basic principles of the modular city while they rampaged, destroying the old, permanent city. Now, new modules—neighborhoods, they were called—are installed at regular intervals. The old modules are reconditioned and used elsewhere. Times change. Places change. Only the Longevitors remain the same.

Over dinner, he continues to be troubled. It disturbs my digestion.

Tomus, he says during dessert, *why do I have to die?*

It is the nature of things.

But you—
I have my work to do.
I could do your work.
I doubt it.
Test me.
If the polynomial equation F *times* X *equals zero—with rational coeffi-*
cients—has a root of A *plus the square root of* B, *where* A *and* B *are*
rational and B *is greater than zero but not a square, is* A *minus the square*
root of B *also a root of the equation* F *times* X *equals zero?* I sense
confusion.
I could learn.
I doubt that, too. The problem I gave you is simple, fundamental.
What was it again?
I tell him.
And if I do not know the answer, I will die?
There's more to it than that.
That is enough for now. I will work on it.
I finish eating and go to Madline's. She is the only Longevitor
with whom I keep contact. This time she is tall and thin and bony.
Last time she was short, dumpy and slightly repulsive. I avoided
her. When she reembodied, tall and thin, I had already been with
him forty years. He had ceased gibbering and begun to speak.
The gibbering, romping around in the unused portions of the
brain, throwing tantrums, crying out in the middle of the night
like a wild man so that I was startled awake, passed into mumbling, then speech.

His first word surprised me. I was at home alone, trying to deal
with several Naperian logarithms, a simple manipulation. Unable
to concentrate, I sat back and heard it, a sound like a sparrow's
peep. I looked around the room, thinking it originated externally.
Again I heard it, a single sound, *Me.* I should have killed him
then.

Madline, dressed in a low-cut, clinging garment—proud of her
knobby frame—meets me at the door. Externally, we are a
chronological mismatch. Father–daughter. Hers is in its twenties,

mine in its sixties. I want to finish the navigator program before reembodiment.

She puts her long arms lightly on my shoulders, interlacing her fingers behind my neck. She smiles, satisfied she is still attractive to me, letting me see how attractive she is—this time, thin and bony—and kisses me.

Stop that.

It is something he dislikes. It makes him feel selfconscious. I kiss Madline.

Stop it!

Mind your own business.

Madline leads me to the sofa, a contragravitational field she developed once (fifty? seventy-five years ago?), holding my hand. The sofa, its field decorated with a green pastel smoke, enfolds us.

"You look tired, Tomus."

"I've been working hard. I want to finish the program before the next exchange."

The comment reminds her of something. She goes to her desk, an ancient plastic rolltop she has kept through four embodiments. She holds up a letterdisk. I recognize the seal.

"Have you read this?"

"No."

"They've found two more."

"Where?"

"One in Peking. The other in Vermont. They're the first two we've found on Earth this century."

"It's too stable here. Adversity breeds intelligence." I indicate the viewer on the desk next to her. She drops in the disk and hands me the viewer. Two men, both well over the two hundred I.Q. threshold, both with substantial personal achievements, one a chemist, the other a poet. The poet interests me. I point at him.

Madline nods, understanding me. We have known each other too long for misunderstandings.

"We've never had one," she says. "They've allowed him one

probationary embodiment." Part of Madline's job is screening potential Longevitors. "He probably won't last more than one exchange anyway. Poets burn out early."

"And mathematicians?"

She smiles and returns to the sofa. "You're approved. I saw the recommendation myself. There was no trouble."

I had expected more resistance. My output, due primarily to him, has diminished. They might have interpreted it as a trend.

"We'll always need mathematicians," says Madline.

"They said that about engineers before Caster."

Caster, the inventor of flexible computer engineering, permitting computer design of anything mathematically possible, had been too old to retrain. The device he thought would guarantee his reembodiment made it unnecessary. Society no longer needed engineers. When they cease needing mathematicians, will I be in a young phase, young enough to retrain? Intelligence always finds a place in society. Only when the skills trained into that intelligence become outmoded does it become expendable. If they are physically able, most men retrain, satisfy the Center of their usefulness. Intelligence does what it must to survive.

"Madline, have you ever thought about dying?"

"Once, the first time. Before I was chosen."

"Lately?"

"No, why?"

"He brought it up. He realized today he's going to die."

Her expression takes on an air of disapproval. She frowns, grave and solemn. "Why did you let him live in the first place?"

"Is there a law against it?"

"No, but it's cruel."

"Everyone else dies. He has it better than most of them. He has no problems, no worries about making a living."

"How old is he now, mentally?"

"Eleven or twelve. I'm surprised he's developed that far."

Madline shivers. "It's so cruel. If you just overwhelm them, smother them as soon as you're in control, it's much more humane. Why did you let him live?"

I remember the embodiment, sixty years before. It is the best part of an exchange, the old carcass discarded, suddenly seeing through new eyes, feeling new muscles, weak but adequate, a feeling of vitality. I remember the laboratory table, the computer, flickering, dying, ending the program that transferred me. I looked at the overhead mirror. The transfer cap, its myriad wires blurred and out of focus, looked frothy on my new skull. I tried the arm. It jerked across the chest, unused to so strong a stimulus. I tried again, more gently. The arm moved and stopped. I sensed the presence. At that moment, when you gain control, you are supposed to kill. I hesitated. Why? I had done it before. Something, some latent ethic from my past, asserted itself. I let it live.

I look at Madline. "I don't know."

I've got it!

What?

The answer.

What answer?

To your equation.

I smile.

"What is it?" asks Madline.

"At dinner, I gave him a simple algebra problem. He thinks he has the answer."

I do! I do have it!

"Does he?" She looks worried.

What is it?

True.

That's all?

What else do you want?

A proof.

Oh. Just a minute.

"Does he?" repeats Madline.

"I framed it like a true-false question. He says the answer's true."

She relaxes, smiling. "Can he flip a coin?"

Tomus.

What?

Pay attention. He begins, haltingly, to give me a proof. The terminology is wrong. He recognizes only that *A* and *B*, *X* and *F* are symbols. He has observed roots and coefficients, watching me work. Still, I become interested in his explanation. It is good, simpleminded and unsophisticated, but good. It is also correct.

I nod. "He got it."

A expression of utter horror comes over Madline's face.

"What's wrong?" I ask.

"Don't you see?"

"No."

"We have been afraid something like this—" She shakes her head. "Tomus, please go home. I have to think. The Center will have to know."

"That he can do algebra?"

"That he is twelve and without training and can do algebra."

I see that she is right. I nod and prepare to leave. She stops me at the door, her long fingers light on my forearm.

"I'll have to tell them."

"I know."

"They'll reevaluate your application for exchange."

I nod. "Probably."

She frowns again, uncertain how to read my expression. "Does it worry you?"

"My energy goes into my work, not worrying."

Momentarily her fingers tighten on my arm. "I hope—"

"You hope what?"

She shakes her head. "Nothing. The decision isn't ours." She kisses me lightly. "Good night, Tomus."

Outside, the sun has set. The sky, awash with stars: clear, crisp points of light, seemingly eternal. I look for the nova, a bright buckle on Orion's belt. It became visible from Earth a decade ago. Even stars end, collapse and explode, their vitality reabsorbed by the whole. The stars change. Only the people remain the same.

A cold wind catches me off guard. I walk to the nearest gravity tunnel. I punch in the number of the stop nearest my apartment and take a capsule. It drops several stories, is routed, rerouted, starts upward and emerges at Newport Beach Station Three. The journey from Los Angeles has taken three minutes.

I walk toward my apartment building, remembering Madline's face when she realized the implications of his algebra. For me it is only a fact. It has no emotional significance. Somehow I knew he would develop. His progress has been geometrical. He gibbered for decades, perpetually infantile, the child locked in the closet through middle age, never developing, without the normal means of asserting itself, bound and gagged in his closet, able only to think. He mumbled only a few years. He spoke, first one word, then several. I took an interest in him. I explained the world he saw through my eyes, the sounds he heard through my ears. Once the nucleus of a vocabulary developed, he learned quickly, putting two and two together. Now he puts F and X, A and B together.

Madline is anxious for me. She thinks they will disapprove my reembodiment. It is one thing for them to allow us to smother babes in their beds. It is something else for them to allow reembodiment, knowing the old husk must be discarded still containing life. The Representative Panel—all mortal—has qualms, scruples, ethics. They see death from the wrong end of the telescope. They see a tiny grim reaper, inexorably marching toward them. They feel it is wrong to collapse the telescope and speed his arrival.

I see only entropy. As long as my energy can be channeled effectively into my work, as long as they judge my work useful, irreplaceable, I am permanent. For them, death is inevitable, tragic, a dark room to frighten children. For me death is a matter of choice.

I reach my apartment and sit down to work. He has been

suspiciously quiet. What is he up to? Escape?

Are you there?

I am here, Tomus.

What are you doing?

Thinking.

Does it hurt? I sense confusion. He is too serious to have a sense of humor.

No, he answers.

Good. What are you thinking about?

I want to live, Tomus.

You sound like you've already got one foot in the grave.

I begin work, listening to his idle chatter. It slows me down but amuses me. Is that why I let him live? For amusement? For company? I remember the dog.

I want—

You want what?

I want to be a nuclear physicist.

There are no more nuclear physicists, and where did you learn about them anyway?

In an old book you were reading.

Spying again, eh?

He is flustered. He hates being accused of anything. His ego, though strong, is unused to the abrasion of other egos. He feels, justifiably, that being unable to act should relieve him of responsibility.

Eventually he settles down.

I want—

What do you want?

I want to be a mathematician.

How about a fireman?

What's a fireman?

A man who puts out fires, but they don't exist anymore either.

Good. I do not want anything put out.

I am surprised and pleased, a metaphorical turn of phrase has, lamely, popped into his conversation.

How about an Indian chief? There are still some of those.

What's an Indian chief?

You have to be an Indian first. Are you an Indian?

No.

How do you know?

You are not an Indian, I think, so I am not.

I'm not, despite appearances, your blood brother. Whatever I am is irrelevant.

True.

I laugh out loud.

Why are you laughing?

Your wit's improving.

What wit?

Good question. Keep at it.

I want to be a mathematician.

I decide it is time to shut him up.

Okay, mathematician, try this. I give him one of the problems I am working on.

Pardon me?

That's the type of problem mathematicians do.

Tell me again.

I tell him. He ponders, befuddled.

I will work on it.

Next day I find a letterdisk on my desk. The Center is reevaluating my exchange application. New evidence, requiring reconsideration, has come to light. I disregard it. There is work to do. Only the work is important. As long as it is done, little else matters. At noon I am in a state of intense concentration. He interrupts.

Tomus.

Buzz off.

Tomus.

Later, please.

I am a mathematician.

Good for you. So am I, a mathematician with work to do.

I have done your work.
He has my attention. *Go on.*
The answer is true like last time.
And the proof?
He begins the proof. Because of his success with the algebra,
I pay close attention. Halfway through, I begin to laugh.
Tomus, what is wrong?
His proof is ludicrous, ridiculous. He has misunderstood the
problem, committed blatant errors of manipulation, ignored
what refused to fit, tried to chop the problem on a Procrustean
bed. He is hopeless. A dunce.
When I finish laughing, he is still bewildered.
Tomus, the answer is true. I am certain it is true.
Get your pointed hat out of the cupboard and sit in the corner.
Pardon me?
Your proof is hopeless. I begin to explain his errors. The sense of
wide-eyed astonishment grows. He has never seen anything so
complex. It makes the questions of death and entropy shrink to
minuscule proportions in his mind. He is awestruck. But he is still
listening.

I spend the afternoon going over the problem, step by step,
showing him, showing him again. Finally, when he understands,
he is dumbfounded by its beauty.

He remains dumbfounded throughout the evening, allowing
me, for once, a quiet dinner alone.

Weeks pass. From time to time, I show him more. He masters
things quickly. He is learning geometrically, omnivorously. I try
to impose some system on his learning. Discipline, the grammar
of thought, is his weakness. He is insatiable, a mental whale—
maw open—taking in the plankton of thought. He wakes me in
the middle of the night with questions, some foolish, some irrelevant, some probing. He is on fire with learning. I wish, instead
of a mathematician, he had chosen to be a fireman, putting out
infernos.

A year passes, two years. I give up complaining about his interruptions of my work. His unintentional interruptions are the worst, a peripheral sense of intensity, edging into my mind, a clamoring, a clanging, a one-man band.

Because of this distraction, my own work creeps. The Representative Panel, delaying judgment on my application—on my worthiness to survive, to serve them—is anxious. They want results. Madline tells me of the controversy over my application. Many of them are using my unproductiveness as an excuse to oppose another reembodiment. They prefer to avoid meeting the question directly. They prefer to avoid killing him. A canceled application kills no one. It permits a normal death, age, death, entropy.

I have thought of it. Even without the scholar in my closet, the furious engine of learning, rattling and clanking and puffing steam, even without him, my output would be small. One day, I realize why. I am bored. Bored stiff. Ho-hum. Though I still believe in my work, work that must be done, it bores me. I have experienced most things. Everything of interest, except—I remember a conversation I had with him. No, I have never experienced that.

I sit back in my chair, hands behind my head, thinking, reflecting, ruminating on too many years.

Have you ever thought— I begin.

Not now, Tomus.

I am stunned. He has never refused to talk. *Not now?*

I am busy.

Busy? What can he be doing? Digging out? Tunneling out? The rebuff angers me. *What the hell do you have to do that's so important?*

Please, Tomus, I'm concentrating.

On what, my navel?

No, your program. I have it almost finished.

I sit up in the chair. *What do you know about—*

I have been watching, learning. You made a mistake in the equations that describe the Orion nova.

Mistake? The upstart! The ingrate! *Mistake, my foot!*

It had better be yours. I have none. He laughs.

A joke, his first, an incongruity observed. A joke. I laugh. I laugh and keep laughing and laugh until tears run down my cheeks. Tension and weariness and anger drain from me.

Finally, breathing deeply, I control myself. I reach across my desk and punch up the equations for the Orion nova. I scan them quickly, indexing through several sequences, before I find the error. I stare at it a moment, then punch in the correction.

Do you want the rest of it, Tomus?

The rest of what?

The navigational program. I have it.

All right. Cough it up.

He hesitates, wondering about the phrase, then talks. I punch it into the computer as he talks. I know, as he dictates, he is correct. The simplicity and beauty of the construction alone confirm it. Still, hours later, when he finishes, I get computer confirmation. The mistake, an oversight, a moment of bored inattention, has unsettled me. The computer confirms his program.

Madline meets me at the door. He no longer objects to my kissing her. He is curious. He would like to kiss her himself. I imagine him trying it, a passionless kiss generated by intellectual curiosity, a pensive moment afterward, frowning, quizzical, analyzing the kiss into oblivion. I expect him at any moment to say, *Tomus, step aside, let me try.*

I have come to Madline's to get word on the exchange application. We sit on the sofa, now smoked a rust red. I wait. Her information is supposed to be secret until official promulgation. Hear ye! Hear ye! The following named minds please step forward! You have been chosen to serve mankind, eternally!

She knows why I have come. I have seen her seldom since the reexamination of my application began. She knows by my infrequent visits and by the way I kissed her. Finally, to break the uncomfortable silence, I ask, "Have they decided?"

She nods.

"And?"

"They evaluated your program. It was superlative. The best work you've done, Tomus." She smiles. "It startled them with its brilliance."

"And?"

"They also examined the potential projects that would justify reembodiment. There were several."

"But—"

Unable to appear solemn any longer, she grins, throwing her arms around my neck. "Even the dissenters gave up. A mind like yours, Tomus, it will live forever."

She kisses me, slowly, seductively. Even this weary carcass begins to respond.   .

Tomus.

Go away.

Tomus, they have approved the program?

The doctor is busy. Call back later.

Tomus, will I die now?

The next few weeks, those before reembodiment, I spend with him. The navigational program is finished. Technically, officially, I am retired until next time. I take him places and teach him things. Mathematics has beauty but it is not the whole of life. He must be exposed to as much of it as he can before we are separated. Separated, a euphemism. Before total entropy, before death. I owe him that.

He drinks in the world with the same intensity he drank in my world. It is a marvel to him. He wonders why we have never done this before. I tell him the truth. The work had to be done. It came first. I try to impress that on him. It is all that matters, the work. The rest is froth and foam, big bubbles on a short beer. To survive, I had to work. He understands the need to survive. The other things I have taught him are the tools of survival. But that one fact, the need to survive, is the reason. Without it the tools are useless.

Madline, good friend, tall and bony friend, is there on the day of the exchange. She smiles and kisses me.

"The last for fifteen years," she says. Some residual sense of propriety would never let her start earlier.

"You like younger men, I take it."

"I like you, Tomus."

"Madline, I want you to do something for me."

"Name it."

I take out the letterdisks, one addressed to her, an explanation, the other addressed to the technician in charge of exchange, a Longevitor, another old friend. His contribution, his reason for being inserted continually into the ranks of the able-bodied, is his integrity. If a mortal ran the equipment, his bitterness toward Longevitors—the same bitterness that keeps selection of Longevitors in the hands of mortals, who must be shown compelling reasons to grant another person perpetual life—would corrupt him or drive him insane. I hand Madline the disk addressed to her. "Read it after the exchange."

She accompanies me into the exchange room. I pass the second disk to the technician, asking him to read it now. He completes the setup first. The table is hard beneath me. I feel the familiar cap fitted to my head. How many times before? Madline takes my hand.

"Are you comfortable?"

"Not very. They haven't changed that."

She smiles. "No. They haven't. Perhaps next time we can do something about it."

"Perhaps."

Tomus.

What?

I am afraid.

Don't be silly. There's no sensation. It just happens.

I am still afraid.

The technician comes back, asks Madline to leave, and nods

curtly to me, acknowledging the letter. Has he had such requests before?

"*Ciao,* Tomus."

"Good-bye."

I wait. There will be no sensation. I know that. Still, I am anxious. And, I notice, interested.

I feel strange. Something is in front of my eyes. An arm. It is pudgy, short, floppy. I try to move the arm. Unexpectedly, frighteningly, it flings away from me. I remember what Tomus said, carefully, slowly.

I will try it later, when I am calm. Now I am giddy. The sights, the sounds heap in upon me. Yet there is something I must do. Tomus has told me. I sense the presence. It is like me. It is fearful. Tomus, you told me what to do but it is so helpless. I cannot do it. Tomus, I cannot.

I am frightened. Tomus, I am frightened without you. Where are you, Tomus?

I remember. Now I know where you are. You are gone, dead, Tomus. You are like the dog. There is only me and it. I cannot do it. I will not do it. I will let it live as you let me live. I will call it after you. I will call it Tomus. I will name it after you, Father.

UNDER JUPITER

Before the starry threshold of Jove's court
My mansion is.

Michael W. McClintock

To reach Ganymede from Earth the purposeful traveler must first secure passage to Trojan Port, from which all interplanetary traffic departs. The other space station, Gateway, at the rim of whose great Wheel an Earthman may stand erect and coffee may be drunk from cups, looks chiefly inward, as befits an instrument of the Conservancy. Few of the station's eyes are turned toward space; from Earth come all its visitors, and to Earth they all return. But at Trojan Port the longrunner *Vega* was hanging out, so to Trojan Port the purposeful traveler went. Slugged with benotex to ward him against claustrophobia during the fifty-hour transfer, he rode out in a passenger capsule lashed in a cargo module among cartons of microfilm and bales of paper. The capsule had been borrowed from Canaveral, because Zanzibar hadn't boosted live payload for fifteen years. It had been that long, too, since Trojan Port had had to deal with an upbound

115

Earthman, but the technician at the portal got the capsule open
and started the little adrenalin pump without mishap. The traveler yawned, shivered, and looked at the two lanky orbiters hovering beside him.

"I'm falling," he said, "so I must be up."

"Do you feel nauseated, man Kalkas?"

"Thank you for your concern. I don't feel nauseated; I do feel
hungry."

"Hey, that's a good symptom, and we can treat it, too. Oh, I'm
Neal Abramowitz, Communications Officer." With the unfailing
egalitarianism of the Spaceborn, he also introduced the technician.

Kalkas held out his hand, first to the technician, then to the
diplomat. "Your comrade, man Abramowitz. What's the local
treatment for hunger?"

"Best food in the System. I hope you like it."

The provender of Trojan Port was not uniformly depressing;
several fruits and vegetables flourished in weightless hydroponics. But protein appeared as either little cubes of vat beef or eggs
from the automatic chicken, and the only condiment was salt.
Among his twenty kilograms of luggage Kalkas had brought
fifteen grams of oregano, forty of paprika, and seventy-five of
powdered garlic. During his first months on Mars as Agent Delegate in Libya Dome, Kalkas had attempted to introduce a few
mild spices into the bland cuisine of his official entertainments;
the subsequent complaints of gastritis among those of his guests
who swallowed more than a bite or two had puzzled him until he
learned that he was contending not only against tastes, which
could be educated, but also against biochemistry, which couldn't.
Kalkas told Neal Abramowitz that eating a good lunch would be
a pleasure.

When the adrenalin pump stopped, the technician disconnected Kalkas from the capsule and Abramowitz led him to the
personnel hatch. The Spaceman spidered easily along the net
that lined much of the wall, while Kalkas moved painstakingly lest

he cast himself adrift. His muscles had to work continuously against themselves, as if he were moving a heavy weight or a stiff lever just a millimeter or so; resistance must be overcome, but it must not be overcome too vigorously. At the hatch Kalkas needed to catch his breath. He had an uncertain sense of having passed this way before: perhaps he had been brought, for his last drop to Earth, to the same portal through which he had just returned to space. But all the portals are similar to each other, and on the day of going down he had been stupid with the drugs that would buttress him as he resumed the burden of his home planet's gravity. Amid the fuss and melancholy of the Retirement he had too long extended his tour of duty on Mars; then he had paid for his added weeks there with an invalid year. At the end of this journey he would, he hoped, not need the lyserganol or the walking armor. To the pacemaker, the kidney drain, and the calcium seep, Woomera Clinic had added two stabilants and a broad-spectrum trace implant. If he kept up his exercises and his potassium intake he should be able to go home without danger.

Beyond the hatch, cables of various colors hissed along the wall, towing orbiters at a quickstep pace. Open-frame buggies, propelled by electric fans, whirred more rapidly through a screened central passage. Fashion in dress had apparently altered more in space than it had on Earth; the deep green leotard worn by Neal Abramowitz was conservative among the florid bikinis, cutaways, mesh vests, jockstraps, shorts, longs, and odd wrappings aswarm in the tube. For Kalkas the invariable seventeen degrees of the spaceworlds had always been sweater weather; he had many years ago become inured to the second glances or the stares of the acclimated.

"Do we go now to the hostel?" he asked Abramowitz.

"We can if you want to, but we're only a hundred fifty meters from the best cafeteria on the Port. Are you nervous about riding the cables?"

"There's some slight technique involved, I believe? Perhaps you'll refresh my memory."

"It helps to give yourself a little push and match speeds with the cable. And you have to remember to go overhand past the pulleys. Or I can get a buggy if you'd rather go that way."

"I'll do well enough on the cable, I believe. I have ridden them before. By the way, how is my luggage being handled?"

The Communications Officer was puzzled for a moment. "Hey, I don't know, exactly. The freight rack, I guess, or a buggy, if that's handier."

"It will, in any case, be placed in my room at the hostel?"

"Room. Oh—right, right."

Kalkas found once more that riding the cables was a simpler though more conscious skill than cycling; he was at leisure to look about as he rode. Trojan Port appeared not to have changed substantially since he had last been in its tubes and volumes. Its characteristic colors were still the off-whites and greys of various plastics, its characteristic sound was still the hum of fans, and its characteristic odor was still the vaguely fecal scent from the food-machines. Its people, however they dressed, were mostly long and pink. Kalkas was accustomed to the compromises struck between the needs people carried with them and the requirements of the places they came to; those compromises marked all of the Spaceborn's homes, built where there was no air that men could breathe, where no grain grew. But the new homes were not identical each to each. Outside the wall of Libya Dome on Mars were hills and plains and craters, land and dust, a kind of air and a kind of life. Beyond the hulls of Trojan Port was the void. In a sense, the orbital station was the furthest from the old world of all the new worlds, even though it was the old world that the station orbited, and not many more generations could pass before Trojan Port was as alien to the other spaceworlds as they all now were to Earth.

The best cafeteria on the Port was a smallish volume nicely paneled in imitation redbrick and genuine moondust tile. Dining cotes, their frames covered with brown velvet, were anchored along a web of stationary cables sheathed in leathery scarlet plastic. The lighting was the dimmest Kalkas had ever seen, except in radar rooms, anywhere off Earth. He remarked to Abramowitz that the Spaceborn were beginning to develop sophisticated tastes.

"We've got a little time and energy to spare these days, so we can afford some fancy touches. Nothing wrong with a little nostalgia, either. The woman who designed this volume worked from holos of some of the big . . . cafés? Do you call them that?"

"Restaurants. Or clubs."

"Right, right—clubs. Clubs in Miami and Honolulu. Does it remind you of them?"

"Yes. It certainly does." Kalkas omitted to add that like the designer, he had seen such clubs only in holos.

"Hey, you'll feel right at ease. That's good."

Putting the traveler at ease was the prelude to discovering the purpose of his trip, an enterprise that Neal Abramowitz undertook with vigor. Kalkas had decided months ago that only a convincing imitation of forthrightness could carry him through such interviews as this one. Few Spaceborn understood statements that depended for their significance upon implication or allusion; none that Kalkas had ever met were receptive to innuendo. If Kalkas tried to talk with Abramowitz as he would under comparable circumstances with, say, the Clerk Plenipotentiary of North America, the orbiter would almost surely be puzzled, even vexed, and might feel insulted. Since Kalkas had not only to reach Ganymede but also to gain a prize there and return with it to Earth, he must take care both to keep his way clear ahead and to leave no suspicions or dislikes behind. Fortunately, the Blushing Tunnels themselves provided a serviceable public motive for his journey.

"So the Conservancy has heavy hopes for the N'yerere process?" Abramowitz asked.

"We hope eventually to reforest all the Northern Rockies, perhaps re-establish grasses on the Great Plains. Terrestrial stocks of europium will be quite inadequate for the task."

"If the Conservancy were negotiating through us, we'd save you the flight."

Kalkas smiled at what passed for subtlety among the Space-born, knowing that Abramowitz would understand the smile to be an acknowledgment of Trojan Port's commercial acumen. He specifically reinforced that understanding by saying, "I'm sure you'll devise means of collecting your share, and probably more, of the transfer costs. And the transaction will be sufficiently expensive for us without our paying you ten per cent for making arrangements."

"Even so, we're a little surprised that the Conservancy would break its own rules for a few tons of rock. And our charges are always reasonable."

"What would you have asked this time? A couple of Calder stabiles, perhaps, and a Pollock or two?"

The ploy succeeded; for the next twenty minutes they talked not of why Kalkas was traveling to Ganymede but of abstract expressionism. Trojan Port's Culture Committee had offered a million megawatt-hours for *Broadway Boogie Woogie;* the Ministers of Conservancy were debating whether or not the sale would be an unwarranted expenditure of an unrenewable resource. Abramowitz had a holograph of the work in his private volume. It was one of his favorite paintings, in part because he thought that Mondrian had worked from traffic-flow statistics. Kalkas said that, for all he knew to the contrary, the artist might have done so.

"I really hope you make the trade. Holos are neat, but they don't have the feel of the real."

"No, of course not. But you mustn't be greedy; Trojan Port already has the best gallery above Earth."

"Right, right. Hey, would you like to see it?"

"Yes, I would, but only for a short while, please. My adrenalin seems to be close to normal, so I expect I'll begin to tire soon."

Trojan Port had begun its Art Space just after the turn of the century but had acquired the most important works in the collec-

tion during the past two decades, as the Port Commanders and
the Exchange Committee grew ever more knowing not only
about trade but about art. When Kalkas had last seen it the Space
had been a slender tube near the hydroponics volume, featuring
many holos, a few Klees, and a single Chagall. Now the first thing
he saw as they entered an enormous sphere was *Guernica,* upside
down. Like the cotes in the Port's best cafeteria, two hundred or
so paintings, sculptures, stabiles, and mobiles were suspended in
a scarlet web that filled the volume. A few score orbiters drifted
along the strands or hung still before various works, turning
occasionally to alter the perspective, sometimes pivoting very
slowly on the long axes of their bodies. As Abramowitz towed
him along the radii and chords of the display, Kalkas might have
been one of his own Attic forebears being given a conducted tour
of the Elgin Marbles in the British Museum. Kalkas had little
discernment in art and little affection for the works of the Consumption Age, but now he began for the first time to appreciate
emotionally how much the Conservancy was paying for the mega-
watts, the metals, the rare earths, and the machinery to keep its
folk alive while the lands grew green again. It is earthborn, he
thought; someday it must come back to us.

Abramowitz had not utterly forgotten his diplomatic intelligence assignment, and before they had completed half a circle he
asked whether Kalkas might be followed by other travelers coming up. Kalkas found it easy to say that, with luck, there could be
several more; hovering before Kelly's *Colors For a Large Wall* he
thought of adding that some, once up, might stay, but he knew
that that would be too suggestive of the truth. He must not
provoke the Spaceborn to any thorough and coordinated investigation, for the vital connection could be discovered from a few
questions asked in Libya Dome. The risk was already so high that
Ferenc Troyant might realize that the inane suspicions he had
harbored nearly two decades before had been well founded, that
Auckland's procomps had refused to venture a prediction beyond Kalkas's transfer to orbit. The only thing that made the

gambit practical was the coincidence that the N'yerere process, which would, indeed, require large quantities of europium, was succeeding in the Bitterroot tests.

Soon Kalkas was honestly able to plead weariness. He and Abramowitz rode in a buggy to the hostel. The Communications Officer spoke casually of new facilities or extensions of the port; Kalkas seldom replied with more than a nod or a murmur. At the hostel—a short hexagonal tube boasting a bathcloset in each of its twenty-four private volumes—Kalkas pressed his thumb to a record card, thanked Abramowitz, and went to what he persistently thought of as his room to check the integrity of his luggage. He assumed it had been scanned, and it could have been opened, but nothing was missing or noticeably rearranged. Clearly no one had been ingenious enough to discover that the stainless steel liquor canteen was a cryogenic flask. Neither had anyone cracked the seal on the full cologne bottle to discover that the liquid inside was nothing like cologne. Kalkas broke a different seal, fitted a self-closing straw to the nozzle, and, in defiance of Woomera Clinic, drew a sip of Djokjakarta's finest scotch.

The Conservancy's purposes, he thought, might have been better served by a different agent; he had said as much to the Minister of Futurity. But a form of the seduction that had first drawn him up thirty-five years before drew him again: Once more he would be going far and going into strangeness, where the light of the sun is not the light that falls on Earth; once more, too, he would be putting behind him, for a space, all that he most desired to have when he returned. Thus he had agreed to travel some billions of kilometers and fetch, if he could, a gram or two of Cris Troyant's skin.

He would also arrange for the shipping of several tons of europium oxide, with which N'yerere's crews would try to turn North America's sad grey mountains once more black with conifers, but the only prize would be the chromosome sample for the New Breed project. If Cris carried the sort of genes that her heredity suggested, and if those genes were unmixed with catastrophic recessives, and if the requisite clonic crossbreeds could be fixed, then the Conservancy might be able, within a few decades, to send its own colonists into space. Perhaps it would be no easier for these theoretical spacegoing Earthborn to return to their birthworld than it was for the Spaceborn to visit it. The Conservancy's biochemists, however, would insure that they remained of Earth, and the psychologists would insure that they never forgot it. Most important, they could continue to crossbreed with ordinary Earthborn. The genetic disaster of cross-infertility would not recur. Thus the success of the project would insure for the Conservancy a supply of energy and raw materials not to be endangered by any vagaries of Spaceborn taste or evolution.

"You want a species of inverted Janissaries," Kalkas had told the Minister of Futurity, and then had had to explain the allusion.

The Minister had agreed. "Yes. Because we cannot depend upon ourselves, and we dare not depend upon the Spaceborn. The procomps forecast a four per cent probability that the woman's genes are precisely what we require. Even if they are not, the procomps forecast almost eighteen per cent that they can be clonically crossbred to the optimum."

"Forecast?"

"The procomps don't think they know enough about the mother's genetic endowment for a prediction. When the conservation of every earthborn species may be at issue, I think we must pursue even these odds."

Snug now in the padded, anchored sleeping pouch, Kalkas drew a last sip of scotch and recalled one of his infrequent visits to the Troyant compartment. Cris had been walking sturdily, so it could not have been many months before the Retirement. The little girl had nothing of Ferenc in her, save perhaps a lack of laughter, but she had her mother's green eyes and shaggy red hair. Kalkas was pleased with that resemblance, which appeared in neither of the child's brothers. Nothing about her as an embryo or as a puling infant had pleased him, but she had begun to charm him now. He was showing her parents the near-mint copy of the Bonestell Centennial Portfolio that a historical survey group had found in the abandoned Maryknoll Dome when she bounced over to look too. Both Macky and Ferenc were amused by the primitive, though sometimes surprisingly prescient, visualizations of planetary surfaces, but Cris, to whose point of view the reproductions were upside down, gazed at them soberly, occasionally tracing a line or two with one finger. When they came to the painting of the Milky Way as seen from an extragalactic rogue planet, Cris said "Oooo" and for many minutes would not let the page be turned. Macky said something about the child's liking mandalas.

Kalkas wondered what patterns stood or spun in the body and the mind of the young woman who had been that child.

Neither the Logistics Board nor the Transportation Subcommittee ordinarily levies a fare for passage, but both are scrupulous in the allocation of volume. Of the nineteen primary craft that the Conservancy traded to Luna and Mars at the time of the Retirement, only the five emigrant carriers are properly fitted for passengers, and of those the four oldest, all first launched before the beginning of Trojan Port, are no longer quite safe. Travelers, therefore, must either suit their plans to the schedule of *Altair* or attempt to wangle part of the supercargo volume of a freight craft. To avoid any formal involvement of Ferenc Troyant, the Conservancy had negotiated Kalkas' passage with Luna, consigning him thereby to a voyage longer by a week than one undertaken in a Subcommittee craft. Kalkas did not begrudge the time spent in transfer, but he was sorry that celestial mechanics and the acceleration tolerances of Moonmen would require him either to return tediously by way of Mercury or to wait seven months on Ganymede for *Betelgeuse*. The Director of Information Resources had argued for the layover, but Kalkas had persuaded the Minister of Futurity that two weeks was adequate. Negotiations with the Board grew complex, but finally Kalkas had the option of returning with *Vega* or waiting for *Betelgeuse,* and Luna was guaranteed the freighting of europium oxide from Ganymede for five years. Luna also had a choice between *Blue Poles* and *White Light.*

A day after his arrival at Trojan Port, Kalkas rode in a vacuum boat the five hundred kilometers out to *Vega.* Despite Woomera Clinic and Djokjakarta's finest scotch, or perhaps because of their interaction, he had slept badly, dreaming in fits and snatches of his life on Mars, his many journeys, the horrid year in the walking armor. At last, unable to sleep at all, he had gone to breakfast, then wasted a gram of garlic and half that much paprika attempting to make palatable the fare served by the hostel. His dyspepsia was intensified by Neal Abramowitz's honest cheerfulness when the Communications Officer came to see him to the boat portal. Kalkas was certain that the orbiter would have come out of mere friendliness even if he had had no official business.

"We've been hoping that the Conservancy would find a way to launch out the gamete trade again."

"You may as well hope for immigrants, which, I assure you, the Minister of Demographics wishes he could send. But Auckland has no reason to think that the results would differ from those of the last experiments."

"Stein Bayly has a good argument for the mechanistic interpretation. Hey, maybe you saw his paper? We tried to make sure it was broadcast kinda widely."

Five years earlier the Officer's predecessor had been less circumspect: "If we have to, we'll saturate every RTV frequency on Earth."

"I read it," Kalkas said. "I read Li Hong's refutation, as well, and like the Ministers I found the geneticist more persuasive than the biophysicist. But as I understand the situation, Bayly's thesis did suggest certain interesting new lines."

He did not add that the lines, when they did not reach dead ends, only reinforced the Conservancy's determination not to reopen the gamete trade but to pursue New Breed instead. That intention had not disturbed Kalkas until he learned that the pursuit required his services. A third- or fourth-hand rumor of the project had reached him some five years ago, by way of an anthropologist on a working visit. Kalkas had had little interest, then, for anything but his diplomatic history; he was trying to bring the orderliness of hindsight to a concluded age, and he preferred not to speculate whether that age might open anew. But soon the project directors, pressed by nearly all the Ministers to produce results quickly, had set aside their attempts to construct the appropriate chromosomes from purely terrestrial bases and had begun examining the records of Earthmen in space through the fifty years preceding the Retirement. Within a few weeks it had occurred to someone to interview the Earthman who had been longest in space and who had been among the very last to come down.

Thus Kalkas was the first Earthman to come out of Retirement. As he handwalked gingerly through the short tube joining the vacuum boat to the longrunner he felt again, more strongly now, the sense of repetition that had touched him yesterday as he left the portal. This time, however, the sense had a clear association: he recalled, not his first transfer out nor his last one in, but his return to Mars after his rotation leave of 2140. Then he had felt that whatever direction he took he would return to something earlier left behind, as if he could not go away from but only toward. The perception had gratified him, but its notional recurrence, eighteen years later, was subtly disturbing. He intended to have no home on Ganymede.

A long young woman, dressed in the snug, many-pocketed coveralls common to longrunner staffs, awaited Kalkas in the lock at the end of the tunnel. She introduced herself as Nadya Strode, Head of the Astrogation Unit, and Kalkas recognized a diplomatic pattern. The Spaceborn, not wanting to offend the man who might signal the Conservancy's re-entry into space but also not wanting to appear overanxious, were delegating first officers to escort the traveler. Twenty years ago Kalkas would have been met in Trojan Port by the Logistics Officer, if by anyone; the Associate Quartermaster would have welcomed him aboard *Vega.* But he suspected that now the Commander's first impulse and the Captain's had been to greet the Earthman himself, that impulse diverted by the reflection that the Conservancy occasionally misled by being entirely straightforward. Kalkas guessed that the Blushing Tunnels had already been advised to have the Executive Engineer at the landing zone.

Nadya Strode's own concerns were obvious: She wanted to store the supercargo for which she had been made responsible and hurry back to the control bay where she belonged. Although she betrayed no curiosity about the only Earthman she could have seen since she was ten or twelve, she did try to put Kalkas at ease in an environment she seemed to assume was thoroughly strange to him.

"Things will seem more normal when we start blasting," she said. "That'll give us up and down again."

Like any flight attendant demonstrating the safety bubble, she showed Kalkas how to use the netting strips and handholds, then led him along the gallery. The interior of *Vega* differed from the interior of Trojan Port chiefly in scale and the frequency of straight lines. There were no buggy cages, of course, but the elevators had a similar function. Kalkas remarked that the long-runners had apparently not been altered in fifteen years.

"It's a good design," said Nadya Strode. "When we build our own they won't be a tad different."

In a more amiable mood or of a less businesslike person Kalkas would not have permitted himself to ask, "Do you expect ever to serve on a Moonbuilt longrunner?"

"No, we'll probably ask Trojan Port to build them. I've heard we're beginning to stockpile capital materiel in Grimaldi."

Kalkas would have been less discomfited had there been any hint of sardonicism in Strode's manner.

The design of supercargo volume in a longrunner intended primarily to transfer goods owes much to George Pullman. Dur-

ing the years since the Retirement Kalkas had forgotten what thin
partitions divide one acceleration couch from another and what
modest arrangements are made for privacy. His own bungalow
in Canea was small, of course, but he could never feel cramped
while the Mediterranean was soughing forty feet from his window. Now he had neither window nor door but only the grey
screen of a tape deck and an accordion-pleated panel. After un-
folding the panel and checking the bins to make sure his bags had
been stowed, he strapped himself to the couch and, on a whim,
asked the library if it had Hugo. He wanted to read "Driving
Montana" again, because he had remembered, in this most
purely manmade place, that "you are lost / in miles of land
without people, without / one fear of being found, in the dash /
of rabbits, soar of antelope, swirl / merge and clatter of streams."
The library responded with a sette of *Odes et Ballades,* leaving
Kalkas with nothing to do but doze until the blast started, wondering hazily what sort of bird an antelope had been.

A klaxon announced five minutes until blast, and at one minute
a taped voice began counting down. The return of weight, unlike
that provided briefly by the vacuum boat, was instantaneous and
continued, a jerk that never tapered off, so that Kalkas could not
for a moment repress the emotional certainty that the longrunner
was plunging out of control. In a magnetic bottle a hundred and
fifty meters astern the fusion bomb had been detonated that
would explode throughout most of the next three weeks. The
traveler, committed now to his farthest travel, felt at once blank-
minded and exuberant, caught up utterly in the wonderful fact of
departure.

For twenty minutes or so, while the possibility was greatest that
the blast might have to be canceled and rezapped, Kalkas remained on his couch, given up to wandering thoughts of where
he had been and where he was going. Once he had been to the
Eagle's Pylon in Tranquilitatis; he guessed, as he read the names
and dates etched into the anodized metal, that none of those men
had expected to die without seeing a second series of exploratory

footprints scuffed in the ancient dust. Once he had been to Pasadena; there the administrative engineer, speaking in the tones of a man who likes his job and wants to continue doing it for a long time, told him that there were enough sulfates in the local ecosystem to keep the cracking plant pouring out water and free oxygen for fifty or sixty years, provided the power were not cut off. Never once had Kalkas been to Boilerplate, the first colony settled exclusively by Spaceborn, but now he was on his way to the Blushing Tunnels, the first colony in whose establishment the Conservancy had taken no part. The range of his travels was implausible. As a young person newly certified by the Canea Institute, he might have joined one of the terrestrial Ministries with fair prospects of becoming sometime a Clerk, a Minister, an appointed Delegate. He had never explained to himself nor had anyone, even Macky, ever asked him why, after a week's hiking on the fringe of the Rhone Barrens, he had applied for a posting to Space Affairs. Perhaps in another time he would have become an agnostic monk.

After the same voice that had counted down announced the security of the blast, Kalkas released himself from his couch and looked for the stalls; the embarrassingly ingenious apparatus built into the couch, since it had to be emptied by hand, was to be used only when one was strapped down for hours or while weightless. The stalls, meant to be used only under acceleration, were little different from those in any earthbound aircraft. They were both occupied when Kalkas found them.

Within a few minutes a man emerged from one. He looked at Kalkas' clothes and said, "You must be the Earthborn." They chatted briefly, and Kalkas, learning that the other traveler came from Mars, agreed to join him for coffee in the common room.

Apparently everyone aboard but the duty crew had foregathered in the semicircular volume a short way around the deck from the supercargo. Twenty people were sitting or standing about, most sipping from mugs or from tall glasses filled with the garish waters that passed for soft drinks. Kalkas presumed that the longrunners still maintained the custom of limiting alcohol to dinner-time.

The Marsman, having gotten coffee for Kalkas and himself, had taken a table near the serving station at the middle of the inner curve. The chatter of conversation did not stop as Kalkas moved to join him, but it did stammer and change pitch for a moment, as it would were a white person to enter a chewing room in Cape Town. Kalkas nodded, pleasantly and casually, to those who turned to look at him, receiving "hi's" and "harya's" in turn.

"You show up like flygrass in Noachis," said the Marsman. "I'm Ed Smith, man Kalkas."

"Your comrade, man Smith. I find the attention mostly agreeable; it's difficult, you know, for an individual to be noticed on Earth."

"The teeming millions, huh? Be rum if we could trade you space for population."

"It must be one of Finagle's Laws that the most attractive barters are the ones that cannot be made. You may recall the negotiations about the longrunners just before the Retirement? Everyone involved knew that Trojan Port was the logical choice to hold most, if not all of them, but for one factor: they couldn't possibly staff them with their own people."

"Real hard. I don't know much about it; I was still in studies then."

"Your field?"

"Exobiology. I'm going to Blushing to do a project on the squirms with Rosenbaum's team. See if we can find out how they eat X-rays."

"I'm fascinated. Tell me more." Kalkas was disappointed. Neither a physicist nor an administrator, Smith probably did not even know Ferenc Troyant, save by name, much less work with him, and so could scarcely provide Kalkas with pertinent information. Kalkas began to give more attention to the other passengers. Marsfolk, no less than Earthfolk, must move more selfconsciously under Lunar acceleration than do those who were born to it. But his observations were made superfluous when Nadya Strode came to the table. She carried a glass full of mauve liquid that Kalkas guessed was meant to imitate grape juice, and a crescent of it stained her upper lip. Seating herself, she asked whether they had realized that they were the only non-Moonfolk aboard.

Kalkas smiled. "Of course: You see how we gravitated toward each other."

Smith only looked blank, but, surprising Kalkas, Strode grinned and replied, "Light-footed, light-witted."

"Light-hearted, too, then," Kalkas added, but that turned out to be an idiom no longer current among the Spaceborn. He had to explain that it named an attitude, not a physiological condition. Ed Smith said that it sounded to him like a way of giving irresponsibility a biophysical excuse.

"Man Kalkas," asked Nadya Strode, "would it be fair to say that the Earthborn know more about irresponsibility than anyone else?"

"It would be fair—if you added that we have also learned more about responsibility than anyone else."

"I don't want you to read this personal," said Smith, "but you had to learn. You didn't have an option."

Having resigned hope of learning much about Martian conditions in general or the Troyants in particular, Kalkas had begun to wonder if he would have no better way to occupy his time in transfer than reading or playing bridge. Now he was certain that he had found a more engaging diversion. Besides the twelve other men among the little crowd in the common room, he could assume two more among the duty crew. Allowing for instances of indifference or distaste and assuming that Strode would, indeed, be in the game, he could expect that she would chum at least six or seven during the transfer, some repeatedly. Kalkas, unlike many Earthborn, had never been fond of competitive venery, but Smith was so model a Marsman that outplaying him at anything would be like old times in Libya Dome.

" 'Option' may be the wrong word," he told Smith, "if we identify the growth of the Conservancy with our learning process. Some of the institutions that now seem to serve us best, grew up almost accidentally. And no one can certainly predict that the choices we have made and must continually make will prove correct. We may fail in the end."

"But no one would *choose* failure," Smith objected. "Success is the survival factor. You had to try what you could."

Kalkas practiced a wry smile. "Man Smith, I believe you wish to deny us credit for whatever tentative success we have enjoyed."

Nadya Strode interrupted: "Man Kalkas, are all Earthfolk . . . I can't think of the word." She scowled, not, as Kalkas would have, with embarrassment but with simple uncertainty.

Smith suggested "pessimistic."

"No, that's not on. Not 'sad,' either. 'Melancholy.' That's the one. Are you all melancholy?"

"Not at all. For example, I'm a quite cheerful person, but I don't demonstrate that I am in such ways as you might. We have different vocabularies of emotion."

"So we'd need a translator."

"I doubt that there is one. We'll have to devise our own mutual glossary."

"Who wants more coffee?" Smith asked.

Kalkas never learned the exact ratio of his success to Smith's in the contest that Smith never realized had been joined, but he was confident that Strode came more often to him than she went to the Marsman. He was glad she was active; he would have found it tedious to hunt.

Kalkas became acquainted with the other passengers and staff; he found a bridge game, and during the rest of the transfer he spoke to Smith no more than half a dozen times. The Marsman's couch was too far around the curve of the supercargo gallery from the Earthman's to allow Kalkas to mount even an informal watch. Thus he had to infer from irregular observation and tangential conversations with Strode the state of affairs between Marsman and Moonwoman. The triangle bore some resemblance to the one he had made with the Troyants. Kalkas was Kalkas, Ed Smith was not unlike Ferenc Troyant, but Nadya Strode had little in common with Macky. Even had Macky ever traveled, she would have been no player; her loyalty to Ferenc, bound up as it was with her dedication to Mars, had never broken, no matter how the stress of her passions distorted it. Occasionally Kalkas had wondered if her desire for him was anything but some oddly mutated element of her diplomacy; certainly his own involvement had proceeded as much from his exasperation with Ferenc as from his taste for Macky.

Often enough he had regretted that the involvement had ever grown past that early duplicity, for he had learned that he could purchase joy only with detachment. The execution of no other duty had hurt him so much as retiring from Mars, yet even as he departed from his last hour with Macky he felt relief at the completion of the affair. The news, eight years later, of her death had struck him as hardly more than a fact.

When Kalkas saw his daughter for the first time in fifteen years, she was seated at a programming console making patterns flash in a readout globe; he scarcely glanced at her. Neither did she look up from her work as the Executive Engineer explained how the tunneling machines and, indeed, all the robots were directed by the procomps arrayed here. The Instruction Center was the third stop on the tour Kalkas was being given, following a quick hike along the primary tunnel and a glance into the main extension in progress, preceding a more leisurely inspection of the slag dumps, the labs, and, as a climax, the surface dome. Kalkas had no need to pretend interest; the factitiousness of the Blushing Tunnels absorbed and disquieted him. Alone of the permanent settlements, Blushing began and continues with neither a political nor an economic purpose. The four older colonies expend energy and capital materiel, Libya Dome and Boilerplate contributing some of their people, for an enterprise from which none can expect any goods in return. Blushing is the most permanent research station ever established. The United States at their grandest never ventured such a pure extravagance.

"I hesitate to open an unpleasant subject," Kalkas said, "but do you have contingency plans in case the inner space-worlds discontinue their support?"

The Executive Engineer seemed to be surprised by the notion. "There'd be no reason for 'em to do that. Jupiter's got to be the biggest thing this side of the sun." Then he shrugged and made the qualification *pro forma:* "Well—star flight."

"Whether or not it ever needs to be, could Blushing become self-sustaining?"

"I doubt it. There's probably no recoverable iron in the whole ball. I random we'd move to Io."

"You wouldn't petition Luna for immigration?"

"What damn for? Our rationale's Jupiter studies."

By the time they reached the conveyors that rose to the dumps, Kalkas was certain that he wanted to secure his passage home on *Vega;* the tedium of a three-month transfer could not be worse than a seven-month confinement among these appalling epistemophiles. But first he must devise a meeting with his daughter. He wished he knew what she looked like.

The Executive Engineer had hinted, very broadly, that the vision of Jupiter from the surface dome would be entrancing; he was prepared, he implied, to allow Kalkas an hour or so of contemplation before dragging him down again. In the event, it was Kalkas who suggested after fifteen minutes that they go below and who had twice to repeat the suggestion. The colors, the banded clouds, the rather foreshortened Red Spot, the visible moils of the deepest, most agitated planetary atmosphere in the System, all combined into a handsome display, but Jupiter was no more imposing than any other planet seen from a close orbit. The violet blush along the horizon was more interesting but no more seductive, since it reminded Kalkas of the energies and ingenuity required to insulate this place.

As they descended in the elevator Kalkas tried to lighten the Executive Engineer's disappointment by asking questions about the progress of the Jovian researches. The Ganyman turned out to be a competent popularizer; Kalkas learned about gas-giant tectonics, quasi-phoenix reactions, and ammonia organics. It was not information that Kalkas cared to retain beyond the moment, but the Executive Engineer's enthusiasm for it suggested a minor cultural puzzle.

"I should have thought," Kalkas said, "that Jupiter would allure you more as studied through procomp readouts than by unaided vision."

The Executive Engineer was silent a few seconds. "I never thought about it," he said. "Maybe we respond to it directly because we know what it means."

Having wearied of science reportage, Kalkas did not ask what it meant. Although he wondered if such mysticism could have drawn Cris Troyant to Ganymede, her motives scarcely concerned him. Yet he needed, for the sake of his errand, to know more about her, so, over coffee in the canteen, he turned the conversation to the staffing of the Tunnels. The Executive Engineer would rather have talked of squirms or grazers or scaphes, perhaps, but he accommodated himself to his guest's wishes.

"More from Libya Dome than Boilerplate, pos, more to give. But that makes no problems. Most Mercuryfolk're only a generation, two, away from Mars. I random there'll never be real difference. Possibly a little in the musculature."

"You're a Mercuryman, aren't you?"

"Pos, how'd you random? But I'm a Ganyman now."

When the Executive Engineer's great-grandchildren thus named themselves, Kalkas thought, they would be no less than morphogenetically precise.

"Do you, perhaps, know a young Ganywoman, who used to be a Marswoman, named Troyant?"

The Ganyman did, identifying her as one of the best procomp handlers in Blushing, and Kalkas explained that she was the daughter of a Martian acquaintance. Since the Executive Engi-

neer was not curious about the connection, Kalkas did not bother
to lie about it; he turned his attention, instead, to persuading the
Engineer that the notion of asking Cris to join them for dinner
was the Engineer's own. They spent the rest of the afternoon in
preliminary discussion of trade ratios: so many tons of unproc-
essed europium oxide for so much cloth, so much paper, so much
liqueur, and so forth. Kalkas had been prepared to invent minor
difficulties in the interest of plausibility, but the lack of any standard medium of exchange or any precedent for this transaction
made that unnecessary. The Ganyfolk—two others had joined
the Executive Engineer—were hard bargainers, and so Kalkas
had two motives for agreeing that business talk should be forbid-
den during dinner.

The characteristic fare of Blushing depressed Kalkas less than
the food of Trojan Port or *Vega;* the Ganyfolk, dependent upon
a supply line and more interested in Jupiter than in colonization,
had no automatic chicken, no nowcow, no vat for beef, no ac-
celerated rice. Fruits and vegetables they had in plenty, of course,
but most of their protein was, more or less unabashedly, sea-
weed, yeast, and algae. With the aid of his spices Kalkas found
it easier to swallow the honestly insipid pastes of the canteen than
the artificially flavored foods of the cafeteria or the common
room. Unfortunately, Blushing did boast a turkeypot which was
harvested for special occasions. The first Earthman to visit Ganymede was a special occasion, and at dinner turkey was regularly
set before him. He drew heavily upon his diminishing reserves of
spice without being able to generate the illusion that the texture-
less white discs were anything but edible plastic.

Cris Troyant was slightly offended by the spices, not, it
seemed, because their use implied a comment about Blushing's
premier food but because they were an Earthborn taste that no
Spaceborn had ever acquired. Her nose was sensitive; she wrin-
kled it immediately when Kalkas opened his little box of paprika,
and asked him if that was one of the flavorings he had used in the
famous Agency dinners.

"Ferenc told you about those? I experimented with paprika once, very lightly, on cabbage. It wasn't such a disaster as garlic, but it convinced me not to go on to cayenne."

"These things change the flavor of the food."

It wasn't a question, but Kalkas replied as if it were. "In a sense they do. They have their own flavors, and they can also be used to emphasize the flavors of the foods to which they're added. They help us pay attention to what we eat."

Looking blank, Cris turned back to her plastic turkey. By the time the meal ended, Kalkas had begun uneasily to wonder if there were any possible approach to the girl. She seemed to be unresponsive, not because she was shy or preoccupied, but because she had no interest that Kalkas could touch. Her eyes, opaque rather than dull, received but did not send, and her lips were compressed. He imagined her exercising to relax, preferring water to coffee, and studying thoughtful books in her spare time. He understood why he had not recognized her when he saw her earlier, in the Instruction Center. Her hair had lost its flame; she was nearly chubby. She dressed in the stylized utilitarianism of Mars, but her clothes lacked the usual clashing bright colors; her pullover was light grey, her shorts were pale blue, and her only accessory was a narrow peltex belt that held a brooch in place over her navel. The brooch was a disc of polished olympi-stone, orange rather than crimson, lightly carved with a Greek cross. Kalkas thought she might talk about it, but she said only that it had been a gift. She didn't stop for coffee, and Kalkas was left with no choice but to prospect among the other Ganyfolk.

"She doesn't seem much like her parents."

"Never met 'em," said the Executive Engineer. "Mother died. Cris doesn't communi much. Ever beep bids with Ferenc?"

"Often, but more often with Macky. Ferenc didn't sit on the Communications Subcommittee until shortly before the Retirement. He was never voluble, but he was never so locktaped as his daughter seems to be."

"Voluble?" The Executive Engineer didn't know the word.

The Head Beep Programmer said, "Long-interval polytalker," and went on to tell Kalkas that Cris connected better through readouts than through speech. "She's a booster on the pro-comps. I've been gramming for thirty years, and I'm not many diblets quicker than she is now."

Two days later Kalkas found an excuse to adjourn the session early and relaxed from the negotiations by strolling through the Tunnels. Using the creddy his hosts had provided him for such casual occasions, he sampled the flavored alcohol served by a tiny step-in, rented a few music settes for the player in his room, and bought a charming little crystal pendant that held within it a complex three-dimensional pattern traced with europium oxide. Presently his wanderings brought Kalkas to the procomp section. No one objected to the Earthborn guest looking in on some of the daily labors of the colony, so he stayed for a while and grew interested in Cris Troyant's work. When, once, she paused and leaned back from her console, he asked her a question, which she answered shortly but clearly, and then he asked if she would spend a few minutes over coffee telling him about her work.

She would, although she hadn't much time to waste and she didn't—as she said when they reached the canteen—like coffee, preferring instead a bubbly concoction called Greenwhistle.

"What do you want me to tell you?"

Kalkas wanted to know what his genes could possibly have contributed to her, but he began talking with her about the extent to which Blushing relied on the procomps. His own quite informal acquaintance with the devices had come chiefly in Libya Dome, where every office, every kitchen, every lab had a terminal, and most drudgery was performed by slaved specialty robots. Afforded such sybarism, Kalkas had promptly shed the housekeeping habits in which Earthborn children are trained, but he had never grown easy with the quasi-cyborgs that made his domestic laziness possible. Both the energy-extensive policies of the Conservancy and the naturistic element of the global village culture inhibited the use of procomps on Earth; even the Clerks and Ministers who relied most heavily on them felt some distaste for the things. But the Ganyfolk used them even when metallic circuitry or human labor might be more efficient: some of the research teams, Cris said, were composed solely of procomps whose handlers only checked program obedience and methodology patterns.

"I handle quasi-phoenix study a lot," she said by way of illustration.

"And you don't know precisely what your procomps are doing, but you know they're doing it?"

"Pos."

The certainty of her knowledge perplexed Kalkas just as the mode and content of it disturbed him. He was familiar with readout globes as auxiliaries to screens and printers; to the procomp handlers of Blushing, screens were useless and printers only supplemented holographs recorded directly from the globes. Cris read the shifting patterns as easily as Kalkas read Kuoyü. The analogy was imprecise, of course, because the procomps employed a language that could not be spoken, whose tagmemes were points, lines, colors, and motions. It was not a tongue, it was a face, and Kalkas doubted that any Earthborn had ever made it.

For a short time Kalkas supposed that facility with the procomps was to Cris what talent was to some painters and sculptors and composers, either cause or symptom of a radical inarticulateness. But as he tried to improve his acquaintance with his daughter, he realized that she was simply impatient with the linearities and cadences of ordinary language. She preferred the meaning mandalas; she disdained what she thought a poor substitute. Kalkas was at the worst disadvantage of his career.

Weeks later, as *Vega* decelerated past the orbit of Earth in vector to Mercury, Kalkas concluded that it had been, after all, the inhuman symbography of the procomps that had led finally to his success. His reflection was prompted by the image of Earth displayed on the big screen of the common room; the planet happened to be only a few million kilometers from the longrun-

ner's course, and the astrogating scope had been fixed on it for
several hours. Examining his responses to the display, Kalkas
found among them, as he had expected, no hint of any feeling
that the image was making a statement to him, that the planet as
shown meant anything—anything, at least, but itself. Yet Cris,
certainly, would endue it with some recondite signification; her
inability to make clear what she meant when she spoke of the
physicality and the *inevitability* and the *connectingness* of the signs in
the globes had been what provoked her to lead Kalkas up to the
surface dome.

"Jupiter'll show you," she said.

She would not have been trying to explain or even to state what
she meant, perhaps would not have bothered to mean at all, had
she not been made loquacious by scotch. To give himself appar-
ent leisure for his real work, Kalkas had concluded negotiations
for the europium oxide in four days, at a cost that would strip
three rooms of the Retrospect Gallery and commit to Blushing
half of Sulawesi's coffee crop for the next five years. Then he
concentrated upon his secret diplomacy. He was prepared to be
egregious, if he must: break into the cubicle Cris shared, waylay
her in a deserted corridor, the sort of antics in which the Garbage
Authority occasionally indulged. But he preferred other tactics,
so he happened to meet his daughter at breakfast or lunch or
supper or odd moments, two or three times he visited the procomp section, and once the Head Beep Programmer had an
impromptu yayho to which Cris came for a short time. Cris liked
the crystal pendant, offhandedly given, casually accepted, and
opened, in her fashion, to the interest in procomps that Kalkas
painstakingly simulated.

Yet for all his efforts Kalkas had made little progress toward the
isolated fifteen minutes or so that he needed, and was nearly
settled upon a Garbage method, until the shalom party given him
two nights before *Vega* was to blast. Before leaving his own cubicle Kalkas filled his little cryogenic flask with the last of his scotch.
As he anticipated, both flask and scotch became talk things at the

party. The flask, not inspected too closely, was admired as quirky craftsmanship, and the scotch, once sniffed, led to discussions of taste and chromosomes. Cris, sipping Greenwhistle, became interested when Kalkas, with a straight face, asserted that the Spaceborn were handicapped.

"We can all smoke or drift or dazzle," he said, "but to drink, you—not I—must camouflage the alcohol with dextrose or sucrose or plastic flavors. Even then your tolerance is low."

"What do we dump?" asked Cris.

From among his disreputable reading a quotation occurred to Kalkas. " 'The troubles of our proudly angry dust / Come from eternity and will not fail. / Bear them we can, and since we can, we must. / Shoulder the sky, my boy, and drink your ale.' " He was glad he remembered it in English; in Persian, of course, it did not rhyme. Neither did it appear to say much to Cris, even after he explained "dust" and "ale" to her, and he abandoned the notion, never very promising, of getting her intoxicated. But when he poured a second forty millies for himself, she asked if she might have a taste. She sipped delicately, did not gasp or choke, and finished the few millies Kalkas had given her, and asked for more. Kalkas, his hopes rising, poured a long squirt.

Although she thus began her fall by attempting to show that Spaceborn could drink just as neatly as Earthborn, when she grew talkative her subject was the procomps. For her they were not the essence but perhaps the *sine qua non*—although she didn't know the phrase—of the Spaceborn achievement; through them and by them and in them the Spaceborn not only knew the universe but spoke with it. She did not, however, mean "spoke," so she had to try to explain the language: "It's not like words, because the connections are inevitable. In any system you can use." "See, we can assume reality, because it doesn't count if it's not real, and every quiddy is real as it is." "If there's a vector, it's physically *there*." "You don't memorize compsy, you see it. Like you see stars." "Jupiter'll show you."

Standing again in the surface dome, Kalkas would have given

his attention, as he had before, mostly to the auroras at the horizon, where the charged particles bound in Jupiter's magnetosphere were turned away from the dwellings of men. But Cris wanted him to attend to Jupiter, fifty degrees up the curve of the sky, flaunting its racing bands, its sodium cyclones, its presence. She described, not very clearly, some findings of the quasi-phoenix studies.

"See," she said, pointing to the gibbous disc but looking continually at her father and now touching his arm, "all meaning and beautiful."

For many seconds Kalkas stared at the gas giant; he had been touched suddenly by sympathy for Cris in her frustration, as she tried to make a language she despised serve her. Speaking carefully he said, "Yes. The sight of Jupiter is powerfully emblematic to you because the planet is the reason you're here, the focus of all your labors. Furthermore, it's an enormous and complex thing, yet from here you see it singly and at once, so the perception is intense, extremely intense. Is this analogous to the functioning of the readout globe patterns for you?"

Cris had begun to look disappointed before he finished. In the space between them or between worlds, a link had been broken or had never been forged. After a few mute seconds, Cris looked away from Kalkas to Jupiter, then away from both. Tired, vexed, still wondering how he might complete his errand, the purposeful traveler began to follow his daughter down the circular stairs that led into the safety lock and so to the elevator. As she went, Cris lifted one shoulder in what seemed to be a kind of shrug.

"I random Earthborn never will reckon," she said. "We'll run without you."

Hoping she'd break her neck, Kalkas pushed her, and she clanged down the spiral in a flurry of arms and legs.

The fall was not lethal, but it was stunning; Kalkas had the opportunity he wanted. In the dome's tiny washroom he rinsed the flask of the remaining scotch. With his penknife he sliced several grams of skin from Cris's left forearm. He scraped the wound roughly, as the edge of a step might have done, and sealed his prize in the flask; the suspensor fluid would have to be added when he returned to his cubicle. He had what he had come to get.

Many years later he would have to count what he had given for it.

A Little Lexicon for Martians

Alexei Panforearm	filet of palm	nasole	pigeon-fingered
B. F. Bonesner	Fleger in the Sky	noseball	potafingers
Chesley Skintell	four-in-foot	Oheart Twist	private nose
coathead	George Alec Eftoe	Oralog	sweetliver
eargay	glass nose	Oreille Perce	tailmaster
Edmond Shoulderilton	Hugo Gernsbelly	otoceros	trompe-le-nez
elbow breeches	Jack Legstrong	oversmell	underfooted
eyewax	manual pushers	palmcism	Ursula Ar Muin

TO THE DARK TOWER CAME

EDGAR: Child Rowland to the dark tower came,
    His word was still,—Fie, foh, and fum,
    I smell the blood of a British man.

Gene Wolfe

"He's senile," Gloucester said.

Kent, who would die that day, shook his head and shrugged. He was standing at the room's nearest window looking out, his broad shoulders wrapped in an old goatskin cloak.

"Senile," Gloucester repeated. Hoping to lighten Kent's mood he added, "I like to think that the first syllable derives from the Anglo-Saxon *sendan,* meaning 'to transmit.' The second from the Latin *Nilus,* the name of a mythical, northward-flowing river in Africa. This river was supposed to be lined with antique structures; so that transmission to the Nilotic region indicated that a thing was of ancient age."

Kent said nothing.

"Can you see anything through that ivy? What are you looking at out there?"

"Fog," Kent said.

Gloucester walked over to the window. The bronze tip of the

144

scabbard hanging from his belt, weighted by the broad blade of the sword within, scraped the stone flags. He peered out. The window was no wider than the length of a man's forearm, cut in a gray stone wall several times as thick. "Fog my bung, sir," he said. "Those are clouds. But never mind, we'll get down, clouds or no."

"They might be clouds," Kent answered mildly. "You never can tell."

"They blasted well *are* clouds. Throw your dagger out of there, and it would spit an eagle before it struck the ground. There's no telling how high up we are."

"I prefer to believe that it is fog," Kent said. He turned to face Gloucester and seated himself on the clammy windowsill. "I could leave this place at any time, simply by climbing out this window and jumping to the ground. Conversely, if I leave the window unguarded, it is possible that a bear or jaguar or other wild thing might enter."

"Poor creature," Gloucester muttered. And then: "So you say it's fog. All right, sir, climb out. So soon as your feet are on good, solid ground, call to me, and I'll come too."

"I prefer not to," Kent said. His sad, handsome face creased, though only for a second, in a smile. "I believe in intellectual democracy; I know that I am right, but I concede the possibility that you're right too."

Gloucester cleared his throat. "Let's stop amusing ourselves with fancies and look at this logically." He thrust his hands behind him, under his own tattered cloak, and began to pace up and down. "The king's senile. I won't argue definitions with you. You know what I mean, and I know you agree with me, whatever you may say. Now, let's list the options available to us."

"We've done this before," Kent said.

"Granted. But let's do it again. I pride myself, sir, on being a sound sullen scholar; and when there is nothing more to be done, we triple 'S' men recast the data—integrate, integrate, integrate, and three pump handles."

He took a deep breath. "Now then, what is the desired result?

What is it we wish? To be away—isn't that so? To courtier no more? That will do for a beginning. I'd like to leave aside those highflown plans of yours for the time being, and get to something practical."

"One of my ancestors was supposed to be able to fly," Kent said. He was craning his neck to look out the window again. "My mother showed me his picture once. The climate must have been warmer then, because his cloak was silk. Red silk. He flew through the air, and it streamed out behind him."

"A symbolic figure," Gloucester told him. "He represented the strong man who, ridding himself of the superstitions of the past, devoted himself to improving his own powers and achieving mastery of others. Actually there have been a number of people who've tried it, but someone always shoots them."

"Bullets ricocheted from his chest," Kent said dreamily.

There was a beating of vast wings outside the window.

"Listen!"

"Don't go out there," Gloucester warned, but Kent had already turned around, and was scrambling on hands and knees through the aperture in the wall until he could thrust his head and shoulders through the curtain of leaves into the faint, free air.

Above his head, and below it, the tower extended until sight failed in white mist. Though Kent knew it to be round, to either side the wall seemed flat—so great was the radius of that mighty curve. (Some, indeed, said that it was infinite.) Vines overgrew the wall; Kent set his foot upon a stout stem, and took another in his right hand; then, drawing his dagger with his left, stepped out, so that he hung suspended in a dark green jungle of foliage over the yawning void.

The wing-wind tugged at his hair and fluttered the fur of the collar at his throat. A vampire flapped systematically up and down the wall, beating the ivy with pinions that were to Kent's cloak as the cloak to an Ivy leaf. There were climbers in the ivy, pale figures Kent knew to be men and women. When the vampire's wings dislodged them they fell; and the flying horror dove after them until it had them in its claws, then rose again. What it did with them then, Kent could not see—it folded itself in the black membrane of its pinions as though shamed by its own malignancy, hanging in the air, head bowed, like a scud of sooty smoke. When the wings opened again, its victims were gone.

"What was it?" Gloucester asked when Kent stood on the floor of the room once more.

Kent shrugged, and sheathed his dagger.

"Are we high up?"

"Very high. How can it be that there is air here?"

"My theory is that the tower draws air with it," Gloucester said. "Its mass is so great that it attracts its own atmosphere."

Kent spat, and watched his spittle fall. It struck the flagstones in a pattern that suggested the skull-face of the vampire; but he ignored this, and said, "If what you say is true, then the direction we call 'down' would necessarily be toward the center of the tower."

Gloucester shook his shaggy head. "No, down would be the resultant of the tower's attraction, the earth's, and the moon's. The construction of the floors may take that into account."

"The moon's? Do you think the tower rises high enough for that?"

"The moon's gravitation has an effect even on the earth's surface," Gloucester told him, "drawing the tides. And yes, I know that the tower rises very high indeed. One of its commonest names is Spire Sans Summit."

"Poetical exaggeration," Kent said. Although he did not like turning his back to the open window, he had wandered over to the stairs—down which they had come, and down which, as he knew, they would eventually go again.

"Suppose that it is not. Suppose that the king himself is the originator of that phrase, and that it reflects sober truth. How can it be true?"

"If work is still in progress," Kent said slowly, "the tower could be called summitless, because the summit is not yet in place."

"A mere quibble. But suppose another foundation exists—on another sphere. Imagine this tower stretched between the two, like a cobweb of stone."

"Then in going downward," Kent said, "we may be progressing toward either end. Is that it? When we reach the lowest floor, we may step out onto the surface of the moon?"

The other man nodded. "There are footprints on the surface of the moon, you know. Even though the king would have us believe all this is happening long before that time."

"Then let us go, even if it is to the moon, or a farther place; when we reach it we will be able to see the earth, and we will know where we are." He began to descend the stair.

"You're going down again? I'll come with you."

The room below might have filled all the tower, from wall to wall, with a domed ceiling higher in the center than the room was wide; so that it seemed like a world unto itself. The stone stair they trod might have been a bit of gossamer in that immensity.

"It's an orrery, by God," Gloucester said. "At least it's not another throne room."

"It may still be another throne room," Kent cautioned him.

In the center the sun burned with thermonuclear fire. Far away, at the dim borders of the room to which the two descended, cold Pluto circled. The walls were wainscoted, the wooden panels painted with the symbols of the zodiac; a rearing bison, shot to the heart, snorted gore near where they stood when they attained the floor at last.

Here the stair ended. "We must find another way down," Gloucester said.

Kent nodded and added, "Or up, if we are going up."

The rearing bison seemed to speak: "Long have I ruled—a hundred years and more." (But it was the king's voice.)

"Yes, monarch of the plain," Kent answered, "long did you rule."

"Hush," Gloucester whispered, "he'll hear you."

"Long have I ruled," the king's voice continued. "I have starved my enemies; built my tower."

"You are old," Gloucester ventured. There was a stirring behind the painted panel, but Kent knew that the king was not there.

"In the dream of serving others, they have served me. Pisces the whale I penned in a tank of glass, sheltering her from the waters I poisoned. Does not that show the love I bore her? The poison was needed for the making: scientist and sorcerer am I."

From a hole gnawed between the rearing bison's feet, a rat's head peeped forth. It was as large as a bucket; seeing it, Kent drew his sword.

"It is as I feared," Gloucester said when his own blade was in his hand. "The lower parts of the tower are worse than the higher. Or the higher are worse than the lower, as may be."

The rat was through the hole now, edging along the wall, while a second rat glared out with shining eyes.

"To the center of the room!" Kent urged.

But Gloucester cautioned: "No. Let us stay here, where we can guard one another's backs, or put our own to the wall."

The king's voice had continued all the while, though neither had heard it. Now it said: "Some insinuate that I grow old. Do they think that I, who know so much, cannot renew myself? And do they not know that if I should die, the tower will fall upon them? The rats are at the foundation even now."

The rat sprang for Kent's throat. He hewed it with his sword, and plunged his dagger into its chest as it flew toward him; but as he struck, the septic fangs of the second rat opened his left leg from thigh to ankle. Grizzled Gloucester, awkward but bull-strong, clove its spine with a single stroke; still, it was too late.

"I will carry you wherever you wish to go," he told Kent when a tourniquet had eased the bleeding. "Back to earth or to the moon. Wherever you think there may be help."

The bison had fallen silent, but the claws of the dying rats still scrabbled on the floor. "I'll carry you wherever you want to go,"

Gloucester repeated, thinking Kent had not heard him.

But Kent only said: "Be quiet. Someone is coming."

Gloucester thought him delirious. "I see no one."

"That is because the sun is at his back," Kent said. "You cannot see him against the glare."

After a moment Gloucester muttered: "A boy. I see him now."

The boy wore a crown. He was about thirteen, but his eyes were the cold, mad eyes of the king. Maidens followed him; these had no eyes at all—only little flames, like candles burning, in the empty sockets. "Who are you men?" the boy asked.

Gloucester bowed as well as he could, still holding Kent, and said: "We are your courtiers, sire. Kent and Gloucester."

The boy king shook his head. "I do not remember those names."

"In the beginning you called us Youth and Learning, sire; you promised us a great deal."

"I don't remember that either," the boy king said. "But if you will behave yourselves and amuse me, I will give you whatever it was I promised you before."

Gloucester asked, "Will you heal my friend?" but the king had already turned away.

Later Kent whispered, "Gloucester . . ."

"Are you in much pain?"

"Gloucester, I have been thinking."

Gloucester said, "That is always painful, I know," but the younger man did not smile.

"You said that if this tower reaches to the moon, it has no top. . . ."

"Yes."

"But isn't it equally valid to say both ends are the top? From the moon, the foundation on earth is the summit. Isn't that correct?"

"If you say so. But perhaps you should try to rest now." The wound in Kent's leg was bleeding freely again; Gloucester thrust the fingers of one hand through the tourniquet and twisted the cloth to tighten it.

He was still fussing with it when Kent murmured: "Call back the king, Gloucester, and carry me to the window. With one single bound I will leap this tall building; and that is something a boy should see."

VAMP

Perhaps not all art corrupts; but
absolute art corrupts absolutely.

Michael Conner

Sunlight reflected dully from the polarized cap of the Stockton
Condo Dome that rose out of the winter-morning Tule fog. Inside, a young man peered through the gloom toward the central
plaza. To him, the fog presented a paradox of arrested movement, an ethereal ocean that embraced the entire circumference
of the complex. Dieter, nervously gripping his portfolio, thought
how dark it was for mid-morning; it was not dark enough, however, to shroud Dwalae Workshop.

There it was, almost at the center of the low curved layerings
of Condo units that radiated outward from the plaza all the way
to the shimmering margin of the Dome field. It stood apart,
different, tawny styroflo exterior a little more massive, sculptured
just enough to set it off markedly from any other building within
the Dome.

Dieter crossed the plaza, scuffing his feet cautiously on the terrazzo surface, as if the fog could somehow have made the tile slick. It wasn't, and the sharp echoes across that empty space made him a little embarrassed, made him walk a little faster to the Dwalae's front entrance. There he halted to stare at the stylized lettering on the door:

K. KINCHON'S DWALAE WORKSHOP
Fine Transfers

Galleries: Tahoe, Marin, Mendocino, Santa Cruz
DEALERS ONLY

Kinchon: Dieter read the name again. The man whose elegant scrawl had graced Dieter's letter of acceptance was one of the best—no, *the* best—transferist in all of North America. From Canada to Mexico, Kinchon's work was in demand; now he, J. Dieter, was going to work for him. "Join my little stable," the fuzzy voice had told him over the phone. And he would. It was hard for him to push through the swinging panel without a complete surrender to panic. But he did it, and opened his eyes to the cool white of a waiting room.

Dieter stared. It seemed a joke, a mocking understatement. Certainly, it was not what he had expected: Ivory wool (yes, wool!) carpet, simple fluorescent panels spaced at odd intervals along the concave surface of the walls. Indeed, the only color in the whole space was the red of two painfully artificial poinsettias which stood on a rough wood dais not quite in the center of the room.

The effect was unsettling, and Dieter wandered around the pedestal attempting to locate a place to sit. Abruptly a young man leaned, penstyle in mouth, from a receptionist's window.

"May I help you?"

"What? Oh." Dieter glanced quickly at his portfolio. "Yes. I'm contracted to work here."

The man stared.

"M. Kinchon requested that I see him first thing today."

"Hm. Oh, yes. M. J. Dieter, is it not? This way, please."

He opened a door for Dieter, then indicated another, stenciled with Kinchon's familiar signature. Dieter hesitated.

"Go on in," the man said. "K's been waiting."

Dieter opened the door to a room decorated in the same manner as the lounge, except that light was provided by a staggered array of skylight bubbles. In a far corner, he noticed two large viewing consoles; on either side of these stood easels and a worktable. Directly in front of Dieter was a large freemold desk where Kinchon sat gazing at some papers. For a moment, Dieter feared that he wouldn't be noticed, but suddenly Kinchon stood up.

All the pictures Dieter had seen of the man did nothing to prepare him for his presence. He was shorter than Dieter had imagined, but powerful, with a bull's chest deeply tanned where his open-fronted cream velcro jumpsuit revealed a thick mat of bleached golden hair. A platinum cross with a soldered Redeemer twisting across its face hung from a heavy chain around his neck. Kinchon smiled; it was a wide smile, hung between shiny protruding cheekbones and below a drooping dark-brown moustache.

"M. Dieter, welcome!" he said, quickly glancing up the length of Dieter's thin body.

"Thank you, M. Kinchon." (Oh, the feel of that warm steel hand!) "I'm a little late, I'm afraid."

"Nonsense, forget it. We're not peasants, eh?" He gently placed his hand on the small of Dieter's back, guided him to a silk brocade styrobag in front of the shining desk. "Sit down." Kinchon returned to his own chair, then pointed to Dieter's portfolio.

"May I see that, please?" Kinchon opened the portfolio and began leafing through the work. One by one, he glanced at the sketches and holo reproductions Dieter had selected as his best. Occasionally he grunted, and Dieter had to fight the temptation to lean closer. Finally Kinchon put the work down.

"You like to sketch, I see."

Dieter responded a trifle too eagerly. "Yes, M. Kinchon, that's what I concentrated on at Sorbonne Complex."

"Mm-hm. That's good, Dieter. Allow me to say that there are not many here so proficient as you." He smiled, eye-corners crinkling in a flattering way. "*In* this area. I see you have some transfer reproductions here also. Forgive me, I know my representatives have been over this all with you before. Ah, how much console experience have you had?"

"Three months, M. Kinchon, intensive exercise in console operation and technique. However, as I told your interviewer, these transfers were made from imagined console projections, not actual beaded images. I felt—"

Kinchon held up a hand. "No need to explain—that is simply all the more impressive." He stood up and walked over to one of the consoles. "But please, I wish to show you something." As Dieter stood up next to him, Kinchon activated the screen. "The particular advantages of beaded images."

Even before Kinchon switched to holoproject, Dieter realized that he could make no sense of the image he was looking at. It *seemed* to be a corniced blackness, scuffed with gray dust, with a stark angular shadow thrusting out of the bead field. But the angles and the depth were all wrong—or all right—or simply incomprehensible. Dieter finally looked helplessly at Kinchon, who grinned, twisting his thick silver wristband.

"You see, this is something you could not imagine, because you can't even identify it. I'll tell you. I sent someone to San Francisco last week to bead the shoe of an aged alcoholic in the old Halladie Plaza on Market Street. The unfortunate man was subsequently arrested, and this is the view from just under the back seat of the police vehicle. With a boosted light level, of course."

Dieter whistled, amazed that the man would attempt a transfer from an image containing so little real information.

"Good, good, you see it. My point is that here at the Dwalae we deal with a certain effect, different from anything the other plastic arts can produce. Of course, this effect is determined by the technology, but the selection of materials and the craft of the transferist do play their part. At any rate, it is the final product that matters, and the transfer, removed by bead and console from its subject, allows appreciation by many more people than do the older forms."

"Much less subjective," Dieter offered.

"Ah, yes." Kinchon strode back to the desk and pressed a button.

"*Yes, K?*"

"Call everyone in for a moment." He sat down again. "Dieter. I want you to meet my other artists. They are good people, though given at times to excess, eh?" He laughed. The door opened, and five people walked in.

"Persons! This is M. J. Dieter of Sorbonne Complex. He is joining us, our good fortune, as his talents are most considerable."

Kinchon gestured toward a short man with steel-gray hair who nodded curtly but did not extend his hand. "Maximus."

"Dwight." Neither the clipped smile nor the gold brocade tunic impressed Dieter.

A gaunt creature shook his hand limply, leaving a scent of fermenting orchids. "Mm. Silva."

"Bryon you've met already." The receptionist grinned, sagging slightly with a bend of his knee.

"Finally, M. C."

"Excuse me?" Dieter felt distinctly uncomfortable.

"C," C said. "I prefer it to Carruthers, wouldn't you?" He was sullenly British.

"Back to your projects now, children," Kinchon said, waving them away. Dieter thought he heard someone—was it C?—mumble "Good luck," but he did not count upon the sincerity of this wish. Already the names were fading away, and Dieter was not sure it was worth the effort to keep them in mind.

Kinchon smiled. "They are quite a group, are they not?" He put a heavy hand on Dieter's shoulder, kneaded his neck muscles, a massage that was at once immensely relaxing and a new source of tension. "We want you here, Dieter. Go back to Bryon and he'll show you to your console. Just tell him what materials you'll need—he's quite efficient. Make good use of them and you'll succeed, eh?"

"Yes. Yes, I will. Thank you very much, M. Kinchon."

"Please." The massage ended. "My artists call me K." Dieter nodded, mumbling thanks, then left Kinchon's room.

Just as Kinchon had promised, Bryon directed him (much more cordially) back to a small cubicle that was to be his work area. It was spartan, but complete. In a corner were his console, an older and smaller unit than Kinchon's, and his chair. Beside them stood his plotting easel, and across from that a large worktable equipped with storage bins. After Bryon left, Dieter tilted several of them open and was pleased to find the bins filled with fresh materials. Finally, satisfied with his working environment, Dieter sat in the contour chair and activated the image.

Since his first assignment was more a test than a real project, a subject had been beaded for him. A single fact sheet informed him that the subject lived in the maintenance compound outside the Condo Dome, and that a fabric-textured bead had been placed on the right sleeve of a work jumpsuit, just above the front part of the hem. The uniform was short-sleeved, so that the bead hung just below the subject's biceps, a position almost impossible to detect, given the quality of beads used by the Workshop. This particular model was a transparent disk that had even been successfully textured to blend with bare human skin.

At any rate, the bead provided an image of exceptional clarity. Dieter sat back and watched. According to the fact sheet, the subject was a waste cycler working a four-hour afternoon shift, so his mornings would usually be spent in his room in the compound. That room, in fact, was on screen now. By making a few exploratory sketches and comparing them to the screen display,

Dieter was able to determine that the subject was sitting on a mattress in the corner of the room with his back against the wall, facing a brown wooden door. The subject read a book propped against his thighs, and he periodically brought a cigarette to his mouth by a slow bending of his long forearm.

It was interesting enough, but there was not much material for a transfer. Dieter thought about the theory of art he had often expounded to friends at Sorbonne Complex: that the purpose of art was to make the unnoticed noticeable in such a way as to reveal to the viewer the defects in his own perceptions. As he tried to make *something* out of the flat screen image, Dieter wondered whether his own perceptions were defective. But the fact that he was sitting in a console chair as an employee of the Dwalae Workshop made it an easy thought to dismiss.

Shortly before noon (and an hour after he had become bored, despite his desire to perform well) the image on the screen tilted crazily and grew larger as the subject rose to open the door. Then the image resumed its former angle while a visitor, a young red-haired woman, pulled a chair away from the wall. Hoping for additional information, Dieter activated audio. The woman sat down, petted the cat she had carried in (how perfect, Dieter thought, hands through fur), and asked the subject how long his beard had been growing. She called him Coe.

The conversation was not very interesting, although Dieter was amused by Coe's blunt efforts to resist what was plainly an attempt to initiate a sexual liaison. Eventually, she gave up; then Coe put on a jacket, blacking the image out for nearly forty-five minutes. It resumed inside the metal-gray confines of the cycling plant. That was a subject Dieter had no wish to deal with, so he spent the remainder of the afternoon experimenting with the console, making occasional prints whenever a partial view of Coe's face appeared.

Next morning, Dieter decided to concentrate on details and was ready to search for them when he activated the screen. Search was unnecessary, however. When the image popped into focus it revealed a wealth of the very particulars Dieter had hoped for. He could see a worn, fuzzy carpet scattered with cigarette butts, sections of old newspapers, balled socks, along with a few books and food wrappers. Never in his life had Dieter seen such an accumulation of refuse! Fascinated, he made several prints of the scene, and was even tempted to begin a transfer. Yet he waited, hoping for more.

Several hours later Coe stood up and walked to the closet. When he turned, Dieter saw a large window just above and to the right of the mattress, centered between it and a cheap lampstand that served as a base for a hotplate and various other pieces of cooking equipment. Despite a thick coating of grease, noon light blazed strongly through the glass, resulting in an amazing visual quality Dieter recognized at once. He wondered if Coe liked the room because of that window. He printed it a few times, but again he waited for the exact image he wanted. Soon it blanked again, however, as Coe went to work. Dieter, feeling there was nothing to gain by spending the afternoon behind the console, decided to go home early to attempt a few full-face sketches of his subject. After all, as Kinchon himself had said, he was not a peasant.

Since Dieter was a new resident of the complex, his three-room unit was at the very edge of the developed area. Still, it was an easy half-kilometer walk, most relaxing to Dieter, who enjoyed exercise. When he arrived he went immediately to the largest and farthest back of the three rooms, one designed as a living area but which Dieter had converted to a workshop. Here the white walls were unadorned, save for a few prints—Van Gogh, Rand—and some of his own landscapes sketched inside French domes. An easel stood next to a tall narrow window that revealed, when the drapes were open, wavering light that passed through the Dome field, and beyond that, the city of Stockton itself. Somehow, the view of the dusty Central Valley depressed him; consequently, he was only able to work with the drapes drawn.

Dieter tossed his portfolio onto an old stuffed chair, then prepared an early dinner. When he was finished, he sat down and began studying the prints he had made of Coe. He was pleased with the contrast between Coe's place and his own spotlessly sterile unit.

Idly he went through the prints again, pulling out several of the window views and arranging them on the floor next to his sketch of Coe's face. Imagine what that man felt when he looked through that filthy glass! The window frame was bright red enamel against the leeched pink of peeling wallpaper, and Dieter stared at the colors until his eyes grew tired and he dozed off.

After a night in the chair, Dieter was not at his best the next morning at the Dwalae. Nevertheless, he was alert enough to seize his opportunity when it arose. He was watching Coe warm some soup on the hotplate, leaning over it slightly to peer out the window. At that moment Dieter lunged at the console panel, slamming the HOLD stud with his fist. He leaned back slowly, almost afraid to see if he had succeeded, but it was there: hotplate, from above, chipped enamel with milk-red soup just boiling up around the edges; Coe's left arm, shadowed, leaning palm-down on the sill. And the window in oblique view, grease split by sun and shadow. Dieter fiddled with the gain until his cubicle was flooded with this light, then sat down, suddenly intent upon an idea.

Reaching over and pulling his easel closer, he punched out print after print of the held image in a variety of projected views. He taped these prints to the top of the easel, then swiveled around to the worktable to get a large rectangular piece of neutral backing plastic. This he placed on the easel below the prints. Carefully then he began scoring the image onto the plastic with an etching stylus. As always, he took all possible care in the crafting of proportion and relationship of objects. And only when he was completely satisfied did he bring out the rolls of shiny acrylic from another bin, along with the appropriate knives, sealing irons and adhesives.

The work went quickly. He stayed late each night for the remainder of the week, making templates and cutting acrylic of various shades of red, gray and black. When he finished, he glued the cut sheets together to create a terracing of color with the window as focal point, built up high enough to throw an actual shadow inside itself. Dieter fancifully embellished it with a tiny red trash canister embossed upon the alley below the window amidst a riotous littering of garbage.

Dieter further altered the original image by eliminating Coe's arm from the scene. Human forms appeared too stiff in acrylic layering, and anyway, he felt that the bubbling soup (he had had great stinking fun blistering the plastic) provided enough of a human element. He thought it was good; when he had squared all the edges precisely and sprayed the piece with acrylic finisher, he *knew* it was. He decided to ask Kinchon to view the finished piece.

Kinchon answered his intercom summons quickly, bounding into the cubicle with an amazing burst of energy, then halting abruptly to stare at the easel. Dieter watched tensely as Kinchon picked it up, tilting it slightly at arm's length. Inwardly, he was quite proud at the way light reflected off the fine topographic variations.

Finally Kinchon spoke. "What are you calling it?"

"Ah—" Dieter chuckled nervously. " 'Soupçon,' I think."

Scowling, Kinchon turned to face him. "No, please, don't ever fool with titles." He fingered his cross. "Hm. How about 'Red in Filtered Red'?"

The wit of his own title faded against the glow of a Kinchon suggestion. Dieter nodded. "Yes, K, that's amazing. Thanks." Still, Dieter found it impossible to look Kinchon in the eye when the artist put the transfer back on the easel.

"This is not bad, Dieter, much better in fact than I expected. It breaks down in places, here." He pointed to the silver-gray forks and spoons near the base of the hotplate and laughed. "Yes, you do see. These are very gross." Dieter did not see, exactly, but laughed anyway.

"However, I do not think anyone can really criticize you for it, *if* they notice." He placed a hand over his mouth, then snapped his fingers. "Do you know Rudi Gersch?"

Dieter shook his head.

"No matter, you will. He is a close friend with a gallery of his own in Tahoe. This is not quite up to Dwalae standards, Dieter, but . . . let's see. There will be a large showing and party there in two weeks. I'll have him show this, and some of your things from the Sorbonne, and we can go, and you will certainly make a sale and meet some important people." His grin spread as he reached out to pat the back of Dieter's head with a cupped hand. "How does that sound?"

Dieter found it difficult to say anything.

"Do not be modest! Your success is deserved. But do not become self-satisfied, begin work on something else right away! Another medium, perhaps, with the same bead. You can set up holoprojections!"

"Yes. Sine-curve aspects of the conversion were—"

"Well, whatever you decide, work hard so that Gersch can follow up on you." Then, as quickly as he had entered, Kinchon started off. ☻

"And don't worry," he called over the partition, "I get my commission." The workroom door shut on his laughter.

Despite Kinchon's admonitions, it was several days before a renewal of interest in Coe prompted an eager Thursday-morning reactivation of the console. On the screen was the old held image, which Dieter smugly took as an affirmation of his success. Feeling guilty about the layoff, however, he did not stare at the screen long. He punched RESUME and settled into his chair.

The new field was most puzzling. Not only were its angles very odd, but it moved too, rhythmically sweeping the walls of an unfamiliar room. The periodic appearance of Coe's right hand provided no clues and at last Dieter became exasperated enough to activate audio.

Coe was playing a guitar, and playing rather well, too, despite the inadequacy of the audio transmission system built into the bead. The music had an intriguing rhythm to it, matching the sweep of the bead field. Dieter was disappointed when it stopped.

Then the image stabilized. For the first time, Dieter was able to tell that Coe was surrounded by a group of young people dressed in various Maintenance uniforms. Their conversation seemed to concern embarrassing objects found in Condo units during cleanup. Some of the stories were amusing; nevertheless, the sarcastic attitude of the storytellers made Dieter faintly uncomfortable.

A resonant voice, distorted beyond comprehension until Dieter lowered the gain, came over the console. Dieter recognized it as Coe's.

"Yeah, old Charlie, he told me he was cleaning up after a big party in a fiver near the plaza. Got down on the floor to pick up some kind of mess and he found an open box with damn near a gross of cylanite ampules. 'Damn Condopigs,' he says, 'easy to implode when you don't have to work!' "

Some of the people in the room had a rather nasty way of laughing, Dieter decided.

"Then he looked at the nice white atrium." Coe timed his pause effectively. "Which wasn't white—stains of every color, and in the corner, one dead terrysuiter, stained the same way."

Coe laughed. "Well, you know Charley wasn't going to touch a mess like that. Fortunately, the suiter was dead, so Condo Security had to handle it." He played a few chords on the guitar. "Hm. Charlie might have killed the terry anyway, just to stay away from work."

This postscript delighted Coe's companions, but it had a strange effect on Dieter. It wasn't the drugs, or the dead man, or even the flippant attitude toward them. It was everything taken together, disturbing the spherical equilibrium Dieter had always supposed existed under the perfect, nonmaterial Domes. Off-center: like the flowers in the Workshop waiting room?

Suddenly Dieter winced as a flash of afternoon sunlight came through the windows directly opposite Coe. Dieter moved to flip some filtering into line, then froze.

Someone sitting across from his subject was pointing directly bead center.

"Coe. Hey, Coe, what's that shiny thing on your sleeve?"

"What?"

Dieter saw the top of Coe's forehead as he peered at the bead. He had to fight a physical impulse to leave the cubicle. A hand came into view, grabbing Coe's arm and twisting it until Coe's face was directly centered on the console screen for the first time. Dieter printed the image.

Coe had sandy hair cut short and a thick beard which covered his square face.

His nostrils flared slightly. "I'll be damned!"

Dieter was startled back into his chair.

"You know what this is, Morry?" Coe's hand descended, thumb and forefinger looming large, separated, ready to pinch the bead. Abruptly, the image blacked out, but audio continued. "Shit. An image bead."

"Hey, someone's been watching you?" The image resumed, first of Coe at arm's length, then over to window light.

"It's not government, is it?"

"Naw. This here's for Condopig scribblers." Coe's voice was nasal enough to rattle a loose screw somewhere inside the console chassis. Fascinated, unable to deactivate the unit, Dieter simply stared.

"With this I play rat-sack man for some vamp with money enough to buy me."

Not me, not me.

"What you gonna do with it?"

"First . . ." Dieter saw Coe's face instantly enlarge so that the screen contained only his mouth and teeth, which reflected the window light in long sculptured rectangles. PRINT, Dieter punched compulsively, PRINT, PRINT while Coe yelled.

"Hey, artist—" *God, can Kinchon hear?* "You eat shit, all your people eat shit!" The image shifted wildly, stabilizing finally as Dieter realized that the bead lay on the floor with Coe and Morry standing above it, their legs thick and tapering, their predatory heads bent.

"You think he can hear this?" Morry said.

"Don't matter. He'll *see* this." Coe brought his foot down on the bead as Dieter wildly punched HOLD, just before the audio terminated in a storm of static.

Even though Dieter knew it was ridiculous, he could not rid himself of the notion that the image of the gigantic heel, with Coe's face tiny along one edge, had been aimed at him. Try as he might, Dieter could not deal with the image and the emotions it stirred in him.

By Friday afternoon, even Kinchon had noticed Dieter's lassitude. "How are you approaching it?" he asked, reaching over Dieter's lap to change console settings. The heel popping in and out of holo right in front of his face annoyed Dieter, but he was too depressed to express what he felt. Instead he complained vaguely about the light level.

Kinchon sighed, ran a hand through his straight black hair, then brought a chair over and sat.

"Ah, I understand the problem. Do you know how many times my own beads have been found in this way?"

Dieter shook his head.

"Well, there were times when the ending was not so quick and easy. I have had the misfortune to bead persons with access to courts of law."

That, Dieter thought, would have been easier to take: a formal exchange of grievances—

"It happens, Dieter, and if you desire material you must take the risk. And after all, it is only a display of beamed electrons, no?"

He smiled thoughtfully and leaned closer.

"All right, Dieter, I must be plain. The first thing you must understand is that the man there"—he jabbed toward the screen with his finger—"counts for nothing. Nothing! We are concerned with one thing only—the image. The situation which produced that image is none of our concern." Kinchon emphasized his last remark by squeezing Dieter's thigh.

"K. Would it be all right for me to rebead this man?"

Kinchon's eyebrows rose.

All right, in your terms then. "I wish to prove I can deal with this subject in an objective manner. Let me get some new material and I think I can get over this block."

Kinchon rubbed his chest hair as he considered. Then, curtly, he consented. "But it is a shame you don't work on this one," he said, leaving. "It has so many possibilities."

Dieter chose to ignore this advice. Coe's violent act had disturbed the quiet relationship Dieter had enjoyed with his subject, and that relationship had to be reestablished before Dieter could hope to deal with the material. Plainly, Dieter felt like a cheap voyeur, and he *knew* he was anything but that. Only Coe could free him.

He went quickly to Materials, obtained several beads, then went back to Bryon's office to find Coe's address. Bryon was reluctant—he insisted on confirming Kinchon's permission—but still Dieter was able to get what he wanted and was out of the workshop, headed for the Maintenance compound before three. To get there he had to pass through a busy service checkpoint. This was a wide portal in the Dome field crowded with Maintenance personnel and their vehicles. Condo Security examined his membership certification and held it, issuing him a chit. Then Dieter walked past, feeling a faint tingle on his face as he emerged from the field.

Dieter had spent most of his life inside domes, and the experience of standing in the open air always unnerved him a little. Now, with the apprehension he felt toward the task at hand, he felt nauseated. The sky was large—too large—and its clarity seemed like some amorphous weight pressing on him. But Dieter managed, with several deep breaths, to control his stomach; when the dizziness passed, he studied the map Bryon had drawn for him.

Coe lived on Av D, Number 135, easy enough to locate since the compound was laid out on a grid. As Dieter passed Av A, he was most impressed by the design and arrangement of the old buildings. It was said that the compound had been an undomed complex late in the last century, and he believed it; the wood-framed structures were covered with a patchwork of weathered pine shakes and yellowing styroflo, the result of the activities of wood scavengers during the Twenty-Year Depression. Dieter was glad of the vandalism, because the juxtaposition of natural and artificial building materials made for an interesting texture. These were narrow buildings, starkly angular, with many windows. In Dieter's opinion they had more character than any of their successors inside the Dome field.

He reached Av D and walked slowly down to 135. There, a dirty glass door led to a staircase. Hesitantly Dieter touched the buzzer. But there was no response; then Dieter remembered that Coe would probably still be on his shift. Somewhat relieved, he sat down, pulled out his sketchpad and furtively observed the activities of the Maintenance people who passed.

For almost an hour he sketched the unit facing him across the Av, inventing different proportions and elevations. When street traffic increased, he stopped to check his watch. Four-twenty: the shift had ended and people in Maintenance uniforms were entering the buildings all around him.

Coe would be coming! The thought frightened him enough to make him think of returning to the complex. But what would he say to Kinchon, who had shown trust, however reluctantly, in his judgment? Firmly, he slid the pad back into the portfolio, feeling the tiny bulge the beads made in the inside zippered pouch.

Then he heard a voice, *the* voice, there was no mistaking it. Dieter forced himself to be calm. He turned in the direction of the sound and saw him, shocking in his solid, vital presence. Strangely, all of it—the beard, the blue eyes, everything Dieter had so casually sketched—was less emotionally intense than on those frightening prints. But there was more, Dieter realized, a way of moving, an odd combination of the fluid and the mechanical, a pulling stride that was directed by a bent head rocking a broad yoke of shoulders. He stepped in his heavy workshoes so close to Dieter that for a terrible instant he loomed just as he had in the heel image. Dieter drew his knees up.

Coe checked his mailbox, took a key from his jumpsuit pocket. But before he could put the key in the lock, Dieter was there behind him.

Coe turned, just as Dieter was about to tap his shoulder. "Ah, ha, excuse me. Your name is Coe, isn't it?"

"Yeah," Coe said quizzically, one hand on the doorknob. "You know me. Who're you?"

"Dieter. I'd like to talk with you"—Dieter stared at the ground between them— "about that bead you found this week."

Alarm hardened Coe's impassive features. "Hey, look, if you're Security, I know right where it gives the rules about remote surveillance—"

"No! No, I'm not Security. The farthest thing from it, in fact, I work at the Dwalae, and I was at the console when you, uh, terminated the broadcast."

Coe relaxed, looked at him, laughed softly. He stared at Dieter again and laughed very loudly while Dieter gripped his portfolio tightly.

Then the laughter ended. "I ought to waste you, pig."

"You won't even find out why I want to see you?"

Impassive once again, Coe simply shrugged and turned. "Come on," he said, starting up the narrow stairway. At the second-floor landing Dieter was startled as Coe stepped around a naked woman who was talking into a pay phone. She smiled and waved at Coe, who merely grunted, continuing to the third floor. Halfway down a dark corridor, Coe unlocked a door and suddenly they were in the room.

His room! There it was—the mattress, the closet, the littered floor. And the window, different in the evening light, of course. The door closed. Coe paced in front of it.

"All right, Condo boy, tell me why you're here."

"I want to explain."

Coe nodded, continuing to pace. *Where could I bead to catch that motion?* Dieter realized that it was the wall that should have been beaded in the first place.

"You want to explain. Since when does a screen vamp have a conscience?"

"Since me. No, please, I'd just like you to look at what I was doing." Dieter reached into his portfolio, pulled out the holo reproduction of "Red in Filtered Red," and gave it to Coe. The tall man halted to peer at it.

"I watched you for a week. I got involved, and what you did was a shock. I'm still involved. That's why I came."

"Hm. My window."

"Yes, your window. I did it hoping that people would see something there that would make a difference the next time they walked into their white bedrooms."

Anxiously he watched Coe, who tilted the transfer the way Kinchon had. Suddenly he was grateful for Coe's openmindedness; the man apparently appreciated the complexity of the situation. And Dieter smiled a little too—for the first time his theory of art had practical application, and here, in a built place, it sounded solid. More solid, in fact, than all the echoing bulk of the styroflo Condo units.

"You like the window, huh? What's your name again?"

Dieter told him. Coe's deep laughter came, genuine, its phrasing matching the rhythm of his walk. "Yeah, it's a nice view. Saw Stockton all summer long. You been to Stockton?"

"No."

"You wouldn't like it." Almost shyly, he handed the holograph back. "Let's see something else."

Dieter gave him some of the partial face sketches, and, sensing a warmth between them, took the opportunity to apologize for the beading.

"I didn't do it. You see, you were my very first subject for the Dwalae, and the staff did it for me before I even came here. It's not something I really approve of, but as I sort of said before, there's always the possibility of working change in any artform." He retrieved the sketchpad while Coe settled onto the mattress to look at the rest of the drawings.

"I really prefer to sketch, you understand, and there's absolutely nothing worth drawing at the Complex." He hesitated. "You wouldn't mind if I sketched you—?"

"That depends." Coe slid the sketches across the carpet toward Dieter. "On the deal. Young man, are you still vamping me?" The blue eyes didn't waver.

"Coe, this transfer will help change this rotten system—I live in there, you live here—"

"Don't forget Stockton," Coe said drily.

"We should all be living in the same place! Look, Coe, I think my stuff is different enough to matter. Art is a way of showing people how wrong they can be, if it's done in the right way."

"Okay, okay. I've seen beadwork before. Used to work in a component shop. Maybe you can give it to those grumbies you live with. So shit, yeah, sketch, but not now. Come back later and let me see what's happening." He stretched and stood up. "I gotta take a leak. Be right back."

Without hesitation Dieter reached for a bead. He looked at the wall for a good spot, and when he was satisfied he peeled the backing off the tiny disk. He slapped it onto the stained wallpaper, then resumed his position, as if negating what he had just done.

When Coe returned, hand on zipper, Dieter obtained a vague promise to meet sometime in the future. Then he left to reenter the windless security of the force dome.

On Monday, Kinchon surprised Dieter by visiting the cubicle to remind him of the party. When he saw the new bead field on the screen, however, he scowled.

"Why place the bead in such a position? There's not much more that you can do with such a view, is there?"

Dieter was suddenly annoyed with Kinchon. "There wasn't time for me to find another place. He was gone for only a moment. Besides, I've got another idea for a different approach to the window. I want to make it part of a series."

Kinchon sighed. "Fine. So long as it succeeds." Dieter was sure the transferist thought he was wasting time, and he was prepared to argue; but Kinchon abruptly changed the subject.

"We will, by the way, fly to Tahoe in my hopper."

"Thanks, K."

Kinchon nodded, looked once more at the screen image, then left the cubicle.

The centered window threw a marvelous pattern of changing light and shadow onto Coe's furnishings, and sometimes Coe himself would come, somber, to muse by the window with arms folded. Each time it happened Dieter printed the image and taped it to the easel; soon the easel was entirely covered with Coe, frozen in various postures. After Coe had gone to work, Dieter spent his time assembling power components for a linear series of holoprojection strips in ascending tones, soft yellow to murderous red. With everything fabricated in advance, he might be able to assemble another transfer in time for the weekend showing. All he needed was a suitable image.

Next morning he watched Coe dress. Slowly, with Dieter following every move, Coe sauntered to the window. "Over a little, Coe, come on," Dieter muttered, and Coe seemed to respond. Suddenly he was dead center in the field, pausing in the window light, face absolutely void. One knee was bent slightly toward the bead. Dieter jammed his finger against HOLD: He had his image.

The crafting of this transfer took only about three hours. Once again he used acrylic sheets, this time as multicolored puzzle pieces in a planar rendition of the window, with Coe a gray silhouette inside it. Then, using this figure as core, Dieter mounted a succession of the holo strips to form a concentric layering of Coes, partly transparent, all surrounding the window. The shape of the finished piece *was* Coe, reduced in size and dimension but startling all the same.

Friday afternoon Dieter took the new transfer directly to Kinchon in hopes of having it presented with the other piece. At Kinchon's door he was nearly knocked down by two grinning dealers. They left the door open; inside, Kinchon was shouting violently into his phone. When he noticed Dieter standing in the doorway, he wiped his forehead with a damp silk handkerchief, then motioned him toward the styrobag. Dieter sat patiently until Kinchon was through with his tirade.

Wearily Kinchon blanked his screen and walked around the desk. "Ah, my apologies, Dieter. A dealer has attempted to take advantage of us. So! You've finished another one. Hold it up for me, please."

Dieter held it high between his own face and Kinchon's.

"All right."

Dieter looked at him.

"Please, enough." The transfer went back to Dieter's lap. Kinchon leaned against his desk, moved his hands back and forth along its edge.

"You have fine technique in this, Dieter." His voice rose. "But again you are fascinated with the man." He shook his head. "No, this will not sell, Dieter, do you know why?"

Though he resented this blunt rejection, Dieter tried to seem unconcerned and open to criticism. "I really didn't think about that. I just did the transfer."

"Not thinking of selling! A serious fault in a commercial artist, Dieter. But beyond that, this is not a transfer. It is a sentimental fantasy, which would not be so bad, except for the fact that it is entirely subjective. Can anyone who does not know you or the subject guess the reason for this type of presentation?"

"I would think so."

"Then you are wrong. For instance, what about this man is so gray, so small? His soul, his body, who can tell? And why this magnificent expansion? Because he had the heroism sufficient to destroy a small piece of solid-state equipment? Pure projection, fancied with Dwalae facilities." He walked behind the desk, pulled open a drawer and withdrew an enameled box, from which he took a tiny red pill. "Really, Dieter, there is no excuse for this." He swallowed the pill, sighed deeply.

"You must excuse my curtness today, there have been some business unpleasantries. My point, without attacking you personally, is that this is not commercially saleable because it ignores the boundaries of the medium. *You* see what is here, but no viewer ever will. I warned you—I felt you should have moved on to other subjects. But I was inclined to trust you. If my trust was rewarded with your mistake, well—" The phone buzzed. "That is my mistake. Yes, David, how goes it!"

Dieter turned to leave.

". . . a moment, David. Dieter, it is an exercise, so do not become discouraged. Next week we start again, eh? Oh, and meet me here tomorrow at nine?"

Numbed, Dieter nodded and returned to his cubicle. The console screen was still activated, but since Coe had left for work the room was empty, a held image without the tension generated by his presence.

Searching for that presence, for that part of Coe that appealed so powerfully to him, Dieter closed his eyes and with an act of will placed Coe in the screen image. There he was, clothed, nude, clothed again; on the floor, legs apart, leaning against the table, cigarette burning dangerously close to that dry lower lip. Finally the fantasy stabilized, oh so beautifully. There was his man, near the window, his naked body edged in a beige glow that dissolved like sugar to shadow-suggestions of limb and torso. It was vivid enough for Dieter to hit the HOLD stud; vivid enough for Dieter to be desperately confused when he confronted that empty, static image. He didn't bother punching RESUME. He cut the power and went home, taking the new transfer with him.

Dieter woke groggy from the effects of a half-liter of anisette. A hot shower clarified his mind. He was going to Tahoe, work in hand! Tahoe, the most affluent complex on the entire western coast of North America, a center of art and culture. Everyone he had ever wanted to meet, everyone who mattered—patrons, promoters, all with money enough to indulge a taste for fine art— lived there at one time of the year or another. People he wanted to change—but to change them he had to meet them and be taken into their confidence.

He spent the day gathering energy; when evening came, he put on the royal blue jumpsuit he had bought in the duty-free shop at Orly Transmat. He felt quite decorative, felt even more so outside the Dwalae when he saw Kinchon's chrome hopper resting on its three rollers, its opened bubble reflecting the low crescent moon in curved slashes. Gingerly, Dieter bent over to admire the crystal panel display, the monogrammed joystick, the upholstery of the contour seats. It was beautiful. Not something to be owned, necessarily, but something to be seen in, definitely.

Kinchon called from the doorway and urged him to get in. He did so, staring as Kinchon approached. The transferist wore a golden jumpsuit, open to the navel and bound at the waist by a sash formed of tiny linked rings of white metal shiny as the hopper. The platinum cross was gone, replaced by a choker of the same metal as the sash.

Nodding to Dieter, Kinchon dropped a briefcase behind the pilot's seat, then stepped in and turned on the panel lights. Even in their soft glow Dieter could tell that Kinchon's tan had been chemically renewed. For the first time since Dieter had known him, Kinchon looked like the old idealistic concept of K Kinchon, Master Transferist. He was beautiful, all jeweled flash and white-toothed glint. Still, Dieter wondered whether there was any substance to the man to compare with the solidity of Coe's far different life. He found the comparison unpleasant.

"Ah, now we have a *complete* cockpit, eh?" Kinchon said as they taxied through the hopper portal. They lifted off with barely a whisper from the air induction tubes. Kinchon said nothing until they reached cruising altitude. Then he leaned back from the controls.

"You look good tonight, Dieter. You will fit in well." Dieter was flattered, but relieved when Kinchon excused himself to examine some papers from the briefcase. It was enough simply to be able to watch the Sierra foothills pass below as mottled pools of black/gray in the transparent moonlight. The newsfax forecast had been correct—it was a clear night in the mountains, and the sight of the Sierras, jagged and dusted with the season's first snowfall, obliterated any trace of the strange thoughts that had disturbed him all day.

As they traveled into the mountain range, Dieter peered ahead until he was sure of the bulbous glow he saw well up the side of a large peak. It was Tahoe Complex, just as he had seen it in holo reproductions. Four kilometers of dome blistering the side of Silver Peak, the Complex dominated the entire Tahoe Basin. The mountainside had been carefully stripped and reworked so that a terracing of subcomplexes ascended to the peak, all protected by the obliquely bulging dome. Now, in the basin, Condo light competed with moonlight, a harmonious duel which cast a pale yellow on the snow. Kinchon continued studying his papers as if they were doing nothing more than driving over a dirt road. *He's used to it—he lives here.* Still, Dieter was convinced that Coe's reaction would have been at least appreciative.

"Here already?" Kinchon crammed his papers back into the briefcase, then pressed a stud on the panel. They descended slowly.

"Do you see, Dieter, there is our party." Kinchon pointed out what appeared to be a flaw in the dome high above the rest of the subcomplexes. In it, Dieter could almost make out tiny figures, but the hopper landed before he could be sure. A valet attended to the hopper; they got out, entered a small pneumatic tube that whisked them up the mountain? through it? to the party area.

The tube ended at a round platform perhaps a hundred meters

in diameter, illumined by wedge-shaped floor panels. Along the perimeter was the exhibition—various works of art interspersed with large potted plants and pieces of furniture which stood unused, possibly because they provided no good view of either art or people. Most of the guests were crowded about the bar and buffet in the middle of the platform, where the gray noise of conversation drowned out the electronic efforts of the music generators.

Such scenery! Of course, the pale mountains surrounded everything here, but they were pale indeed in comparison to the people—hundreds of them, arrayed in a dazzle of color. There were several faces Dieter recognized immediately, but when he turned to Kinchon to ask about them, he discovered that his companion had been led away by an eager group.

Left to himself, he scanned the display area for his own work, and spotted it on the opposite side of the platform. He circled toward it, avoiding the knots of guests in the center.

There it was. Not near the best mountain scenery, of course, but nicely mounted on a slab covered with black velvet. His pleasure faded, however, when he discovered that his name had been misspelled "Deiter" on the small white card below the transfer. Glumly he stood back a little to watch the guests as they drifted by.

"*Tsk.* My god, Jorma, look at this! How absolutely depressing!"

"Oh, I don't know, Edith, it's—"

"It's not something I should have to look at. This Deiter person ought to have known better. Or at least Rudi should have, I'm going to talk to him. To even *think* of living this way!" She pulled her escort away.

"Condopigs," he muttered. People like her knew nothing, could learn nothing. In his frustration he walked blindly into a crowd that had collected in front of the piece to the right of his. He pushed his way through until he could see the object of their interest.

He stared, horrified. Here was a mixed-medium oil-and-holo competently executed, but of a completely degenerate character. Two stallions were fighting in a field; the mouths of both animals were open, hideously grinning, teeth smeared with holo-projected blood.

Turning away in anger, he found himself facing Kinchon. Something was wrong with the man. His mouth was like a gaping wound; his eyes were glazed, he blinked continually. "Dieter," he said, almost in a whisper, caressing the back of Dieter's neck. "Here." His other hand came around under Dieter's nose, popped a tiny ampule, releasing a puff of lime-green dust.

Instantly Dieter's eyes filmed over. He tried to blink the tears away, but could not. It was as if his visual field had expanded horizontally, narrowed vertically, while thoughts sped through his brain like a plaza faxstrip display. All of it was helplessly observed by a tiny bubble—for that was how it seemed—of fascinated objectivity. The discrepancy between the two thought-forms was immediately, sickeningly funny. Dieter giggled, awash in the moist warmth of Kinchon's hand.

"You do like cylanite, yes?"

"Oh, yes. Never, thank you, K, never had it be—"

"Good, good." Then the touching stopped and Dieter, coasting on the dwindling sensation, realized that Kinchon was gone again. He turned, vaguely searching, until he lost his balance and fell upon a providential couch to watch the distorted movement of color and form around him. He longed, achingly, for Kinchon. But the small part of Dieter untouched by the drug picked out only one face—was it Carruthers'?—from the muddle before it.

Then, gradually, the ocean cleared, the bar and the music generators rolled silently away from the platform center, leaving a space adorned only by the inlaid shield of the complex, an ambiguous heraldry of crystal and rosewood placed (deviously placed, the bubble insisted) just off center, a nagging, incorrectable deviation from the perfect. Dieter licked his lips.

"Entertainment!" someone called; from the tube exit spilled a running stream of black-clad attendants bearing armfuls of small objects which they piled in the middle of the platform. Dizzily Dieter got up and circled the ring of spectators, his wide-band perception noting that the objects were stuffed animals of some sort, the bubble determining that they were either lemurs or tarsiers. A smaller group of attendants clad in scarlet moved to the pile, each one holding an instrument resembling a large gilded garlic press. Dieter blinked; the yellow sparkle from the animals' eyes was almost too much.

Back to back, the attendants put their animals into the presses, then gently closed the handles until only the soft furry-brown heads were visible.

How orderly. A jarring screech startled him. Whizzing lemur eyes separated from exploded heads, saucering high overhead; screaming guests retreated from a heavy spray of red liquid which rolled, like mercury, on the floor. The bubble protested weakly, while the rest of Dieter watched the last few eyes caroming off the dome. He was jostled in the scramble for lemur souvenirs, and he wanted very badly to see Kinchon again.

A servant with a squeegee touched his arm impatiently, then, when Dieter failed to respond, pushed him aside to continue moving the remaining drops of fluid to a small glistening pool near the bar. Light from the floor panels began to fade. Suddenly Carruthers was there, frowning.

"C! Oh, ha! You've got some of that stuff on you." Dieter tried, clumsily, to brush the glistening droplets off his sleeves.

"Leave it, Dieter. God, K's done it again."

"K. Yes, K, I must see him. C, all in gold—"

"Shh." Around them, the party noise dwindled. Carruthers whispered: "You'll see him soon enough." Then he was gone. Unsteadily, Dieter leaned forward to see that only the shield remained illuminated, silhouetting the ruins of the exploded toys. No one spoke.

Suddenly someone ran past Dieter, a lithe androgynous figure dressed in a pale body stocking. As it flashed into the open space,

Dieter saw, blearily, that a softly pointed cap of the same material covered its head and shoulders. A young Amanita mushroom, the bubble noted.

"M. Kinchon to do the honors!"

And there he was, Kinchon, jumpsuit shimmering in the interrupted light, a long knife held in both hands above his head. Dieter reached out in the darkness toward the devastating radiance.

Slowly Kinchon walked an eccentric route about the figure, which held its position, trembling. The knife was put to use; Kinchon cut the costume around the circumference of the cap. Then, winking, he reached up and grasped its point.

"Now—"

The lights came on full as he pulled the cap away.

Galvanized, Dieter stared at a face obliterated by glossy flesh putty that concealed eyes, nose and ears. Only a slick and vivid red mouth remained to open and close slowly below the word "head" stenciled on the forehead. Spasmodically the figure arched its back to applause that began softly, then rose to a laughter-filled crescendo.

"Circumcision!" Kinchon screamed, both hands high again. The figure (a dancer, the bubble told Dieter) settled into graceful repose at Kinchon's feet.

Kinchon! The drug ravaged Dieter's stomach, but oh, how he wanted Kinchon. Even so, the bubble still had a voice of its own: Coe, Dieter seemed to hear, Coe, Coe, but it wasn't right. Kinchon was there and he wanted to leave with him now.

He drifted into the circle, where Kinchon was talking to the dancer and two women. Touching K's shoulder, he waited for him to turn and then stared with everything he felt into quizzical, then decidedly satisfied eyes.

Dieter began perspiring. "K, please. Could we go now?"

Kinchon laughed a little nervously in the direction of the women, who regarded Dieter suspiciously. "You do not like this? Dieter, you haven't yet met Rudi—"

"Another time. Now, please." He closed his eyes until the new drug-waves passed.

Kinchon shrugged. "Camella, excuse me please. The young man has had his first sniff of cylanite, so-o-o . . . Perhaps I will be back."

"I doubt it." The dancer laughed as her two companions helped her move off into the crowd.

They returned to the hopper pad in silence, Dieter unable to express his confused thoughts and emotions. Finally, when they were well away from the complex, he put his hand on Kinchon's shoulder.

"I'm sorry, K," he said blurrily. "The entertainment—I just couldn't—"

"No need, no need, it's just as well, Dieter. The party was a bore. This is just fine." He opened a compartment between their seats. There was a rattling—like the rattling of beads, said the bubble—then Kinchon busied himself with his sash for a moment. "More cylanite, Dieter?"

No. He shook his head. There was enough drug in him, more than enough desire for contact, the flowing contact toward which he knew he was moving. The pale blister of the Stockton Dome was below suddenly, and as they landed and taxied toward Dieter's unit, he knew that something of this great artist would come to him. Shyly, Dieter leaned his head against Kinchon's powerful shoulder. He was rewarded with a smile; then Kinchon pushed him gently away.

"Dieter, up now. Yes, move slowly, that's it." Dieter managed to get his other leg out of the cockpit. "Now. Let's see where you live."

"My doorway's too wide, K." He giggled helplessly as Kinchon pushed him toward it. Somehow Dieter managed to get the door open and his hall lights switched on.

And there K. Kinchon stood, fingering his choker in a way that excited Dieter intensely. Apparently Kinchon had been feeling the effects of the drug too; shiny rivulets of sweat ran down the open V of his jumpsuit. Trembling, Dieter approached, hand extended, his intention to run a single finger slowly down that slick brown chest. But Kinchon grabbed his wrist suddenly, twisting it enough to hurt as his smile flowed smoothly. His eyes shone.

"What do we say, my young friend?"

"Wha—" Very softly: "Please?"

"Ah-ha. I could not hear you."

"Please," Dieter said, pulling his wrist away, melting.

"Much better. You learn quickly. Here"— he pulled Dieter onto the bed beside him—"we must sit together."

They faced each other, Dieter's thought bubble noting with resigned amusement the extent to which sweat stains had spread under both golden arms of Kinchon's jumpsuit.

Love, for this man? Attempting to express it, Dieter's lips only met Kinchon's salt palm. The man laughed and stood up, staring thoughtfully at his hand.

"Truly an eloquent invitation, J." Wide-eyed, Dieter looked up; Kinchon had never used his diminutive before. "However, reality intrudes upon the vapors of love. I have not been near a rest room all evening. Please, Dieter, may I use yours?"

"Uh, through here." Dieter switched on the light to the workroom and pointed to the bathroom door. As he brushed the hair on Kinchon's forearm, the man suddenly stiffened.

Kinchon was staring at a wall covered with the sketches Dieter had made at Coe's room. His brown face went livid.

"What is *this!* You bring me here to mock me! Perhaps you love me, eh, just as you love that man there!"

Coe? Not now, oh god— Dieter's voice broke. "Please, K."

The smile hardened, as if encased in lucite. "Please," Kinchon mimicked. His hand fumbled with his sash for a moment, then cupped Dieter's neck gently.

"Is this what you like, eh?" The grip tightened cruelly; suddenly Dieter was pushed back onto the bed. "Yes, moan, you idiot. You take me for a fool! Making overtures to me when you are so obviously fascinated with that lowlife who never should have been beaded in the first place." Again he mimicked: " 'I wish to deal with this subject in an objective manner.' Faugh!"

The door slammed and Dieter was alone.

In bed, alone between cold sheets, he realized what was wrong. He had wanted contact, yes. But he had gone to the wrong person.

Dieter's mind was clear and determined when he awoke. For the first time in weeks, his situation was plain. The job at the Dwalae had ended, he knew. But that was good; console spying would have destroyed him eventually, made him into another Kinchon, insulated, callous. All his life he too had been insulated, but only because he had known nothing else. Now he would leave the condos to travel with Coe, perhaps to the city, to gather material no other transferist could ever hope to capture. Together, they could change everything.

Outside the Dome it was cool and clear, strangely silent, with little traffic between complex and compound. At 135 Av D Dieter found the stairway door unlocked. He ran eagerly up to the third floor. There was no response to his rap on Coe's door. He knocked again. "Yeah, come in," came low and muffled from behind the door. Dieter opened it.

Coe stood by the window, silhouetted by the indirect early morning light. Dieter greeted him; Coe said nothing.

Dieter put down his rucksack. "I've got to tell you about what happened last night."

"Enjoyed it, huh?"

"Enjoyed it? Whoa, I found out everything you said was right!"

"Not what I hear, terrysuiter."

"What?"

"Your fellow snotsucker came by last night, pig. Showed me where this was." Coe held out the bead on an extended fingertip. "You like to sketch. You want to change things. You, an artist. Ha!" Coe reached into his jumpsuit pocket, took out a knife.

"Coe, I, I—listen!"

"No, you don't like working on no console, no sir. You want to break up the whole act through your own little cylanite haze!" He flipped the blade out, holding it point upward in his fist.

"I—hey, I'm not afraid of your fucking knife, Coe—I didn't use the console, but I had to be sure. Kinchon was—"

Coe came forward. "You are dead on the world, fool, I'm no stunt man for the likes of you."

Seized with a desperate thought, Dieter didn't move. "Don't you see? Don't you really see? I love you. I *love* you, I won't resist, I care." His voice was hoarse.

The blue eyes softened, but only for an instant. "You eat shit. Vamp! Finger puppet!" Then the knife hand arced upward, the blade touched Dieter's waist, he pulled back violently, screaming his love.

With a calm born of years of experience, Kinchon lightly touched HOLD. He was tired, having sat up all night, but the wait had been worth it. Quite right to bead the neck, even if the image was slightly off-center. That could be corrected, for the essence was there, on the screen: the intensity of the bearded face, the flailing arm of that young fool, the first glint of blood, red as the window behind them. Dieter had been quite right about that window.

He was planning it in flat black and red mylar cilia. He already had his title: "For My Vamp in Party Red."

BEINGS OF GAME P-U

Ouspensky told us, with his dying breath, "Think
in other categories." Here are two such categories,
combined synergistically for the first time—the world
of E. E. "Lensman" Smith, and the transcendental
discipline of L. Ron Hubbard's Scientology.

Phillip Teich

An undistinguished planet in an equally undistinguished solar
system in Galaxy Thirteen: uninteresting, that is, unless a complete analysis revealed the planet's statistical improbability: it had
no valuable minerals and was inimical to any possible life form.
Well then, academically interesting.

Beneath its crust, though, a spheroidal structure ten kilometers
deep environing *Homo saps*—or reasonable facsimiles thereof.

This was Flag Base of the Space Organization, the governmen-
tal and defensive stratum of Soul Technology, which, as everyone
now knows, is the universe's only purveyor of mental and
spiritual freedom.

Inside the planet, then, in a handsome stateroom, Rod Garrett
was lying on the bed, immersed in the forms and flows of his
personal universe. His wife, Regen, was immersed in a book.
When she put it down, she asked, "Preparing for the game?"

184

"Uh-huh. Anything dissonant affects the communication drastically."

"But doesn't *playing* the game help resolve dissonance?"

"I know; I invented the game. Want to play a round?"

"Sure."

She sat facing him on the bed. They looked into each other. Presently there appeared between them, in midair, a model of the galaxy. Flag Base was there, flowing a dark blue energy to significant points.

Rod looked at his wife's creation, and then again into her. The model changed; Flag Base became twice as large as any star. After a moment Rod extended his space until he was fully occupying the space of the being who was his wife. Then the model between the two bodies disappeared, and was replaced by another model.

Regen exclaimed in awe.

This model, too, was of the galaxy; but it was done in ethereal, aura-like colors. Stars and planets shimmered in translucent blue-violet, orange, and gold. Pouring from their depths was sound, creating a harmony of a billion chords. It was a deep, entrancing music that lifted, enraptured, and impelled.

"I think you imbue your mockups with esthetics just for persuasion." She smiled and unmocked the model, then turned and fell back onto his lap. "You're power-mad."

He grinned at her. "But you got the communication."

"Right. Agreements. A very senior subject."

"You were right as far as you went, of course. Flag does control the galaxy. But only by agreement—which is the senior datum."

He smiled, and she put her arms around him. "That's a great game!" She flowed admiration at him. "I process people all week; they get rid of what's troubling them, regain abilities, become rational—and this is almost as good. Well done, Rod Garrett."

"Thank you. Want to go for a ride to the park?"

"Fun. You drive, I'll ride."

Outside their stateroom, Rod mocked up a narrow platform with a rail. He beamed the floor at an angle and they glided off on air. They flew like this down the wide corridors of Flag Base to a large underground botanical park.

As they were sailing across a bright meadow, a thought beam lightly touched them.

"Excuse me for interrupting you two. Rod, can you come by my office?"

"Yes, sir. I'll be right there."

The beam disappeared.

"Wow! That's only the second time I've heard him in my mind. And the first was in a group." She looked sadly at him. "There goes the rest of your twenty-four-hour liberty."

"I don't know. We'll see."

He kissed her lightly, then unmocked his body and disappeared.

The office of the Commander in Chief was a huge half-sphere, one half of which was sheer glass, overlooking a large, clear lake. The other half was steel, to which clung scores of papers.

"Sorry for pulling you off your liberty, Rod. But here's the situation." The Commander in Chief spoke softly, laying sheets of paper side by side across his long desk. "Stats dropping slightly below normal variation throughout the galaxy. Every Soul Tech org, including Space Org bases. *Except* the Games Organization—their stats are soaring.

"No one here has noticed it yet. We've all gotten complacent, I guess.

"And, much as I hate to send you, I expect nobody else could handle it as well at this early stage. That okay with you?"

Fleet Admiral Roderick Garrett looked at his Commander in Chief, at the being himself, not at the white-haired and ruddy body. He marveled at the perfect integration of the Old Man's energy pattern, a pattern certainly unique in kind: along each wave followed intractable awareness.

Both beings willingly occupied the same space; each was larger than the room itself. The Fleet Admiral richly appreciated this intimacy with the greatest being in the universe, the founder of Soul Technology and Commander in Chief of the Space Organization.

"Of course, sir," Garrett replied immediately. "A change in randomity would be interesting anyway." He lied; the randomity of Flag was the fastest, and therefore the best, in the universe. He had to admit, though, this mission would have a nice responsibility level.

He left and consigned his duties to the Flag Admiral. He kissed his wife good-bye.

He strode to a nearby unmock station while considering a plan of investigation of the GO. It wasn't going to be fun, but it would be fast.

Garrett himself had founded the Games Organization as a division of the Space Organization; its purpose was to create and establish sane and challenging games for Level Tens and above. He wondered what they were up to that would cause trouble this big.

He stepped into the station and unmocked his body. He could have unmocked anywhere, of course, but it was generally considered poor etiquette to disturb other people by suddenly appearing and disappearing.

Next, infinitely more difficult than unmocking a body, he stopped creation of his personal energy pattern. This was an experience of sheer loss; his personal universe remained only conceptually.

Bodiless, then, and creating so little energy as to be undetectable, Fleet Admiral Roderick Garrett vibrated ten locations per second through the mountainous hundred-square-kilometer complex of the universal headquarters of the Games Organization. First he found and examined executives; he sought and found mental pictures of incompetence for any mental masses being directly energized; he sought and found succumb intentions for any individual picture being energized.

Then, with minute quantities of highest harmonic frequency—

esthetic energy—he delicately needled every mental mass within each executive's personal universe which contained recordings of events within the Games Organization, directly energized or not, until each mass separated slightly, like a blooming flower, into its constituent pictures.* He viewed the pictures and nailed significant incidents for time, place, form, and event.

At no time during or after an examination did any executive have even an unformed awareness that he had been examined. The quantities of energy utilized were too infinitesimal, besides being of a type abundant in a mind; and the investigator was consummately skillful.

Garrett had chosen the latest, fastest, and most cautiously used investigatory procedure: direct examination of stimulus/response minds. The s/r mind, different in kind from the analytical mind, is particularly accommodating in searching for contrasurvival situations: it enmasses only unconfronted scenes; and only unconfronted scenes can cause trouble.

Thus Garrett was justified in expecting to locate the source of the trouble quickly. Anything unconfronted enough to cause stats to drop everywhere should be as obvious as a sinking ship.

He was disappointed.

There was the usual incompetence, but no gross incompetents; there were the usual rare succumb intentions, but no outright suppressors. Even the GO's products, its games, were apparently survival—with two exceptions, possibly three.

One of the space-war games was as aberrated as hell itself, and

---

*Esthetic energy is the "glue" by which mental pictures having mass, or *enmassed* pictures, cohere into aggregates, or mental masses, and the agency by which enmassed pictures are selected into masses according to significance, termed *esthetic classification*, analogous to DNA in a meat body. Conversely, only esthetic energy can explode a mass. A mental mass, as everyone now knows, occludes its pictures, and when it is automatically energized by the stimulus/response mind, basically because of harmful actions by the being in a significantly similar area, the significance of the mass is enforced upon the being, creating all his irrationality.

                                                                              P.T.

one creation game was simply incomplete. Garrett would rectify these, but they were not what he was looking for. There was also one picture in one mind of a graph of the stats for a Game P-U. That was odd—but, no, not important, just one picture. He would have to examine the rest of the crew.

If Garrett had known then that the solution to his vital mission lay in that one picture, he could have saved over ten billion beings. For that picture indicated a game that made probable a hitherto impossible, even inconceivable occurrence: the death of spiritual beings.

Before examining the rest of the crew, Garrett decided to act on the data he had. It was midevening at GO headquarters. He intended himself just outside the limits of the org, mocked up his energy pattern, and extended his space out to the quartermaster.

A kilometer above the GO, a solitary being felt another presence, and then perceived an immensely powerful, high-waveband being.

"Yes, sir. Identity, please," the thought connected.

"Fleet Admiral Garrett, quartermaster, here to confer with Admiral Howard."

"Yes, sir!" The being disappeared and a millisecond later reappeared. "I'll inform him that you're here, sir," he stated, and disappeared again. It was not every day that the Fleet Admiral visited GO headquarters.

Three seconds later, the Admiral appeared. He had met with Garrett frequently at Flag, and recognized his energy pattern.

"You caught us by surprise, sir," Howard greeted his superior. "It's been over five hundred years. But you can have the Chief's office, which is ready as always."

"Thanks, John, but I won't be that long; just want to take up a few things with you. Can we meet in your office?"

"Yes, sir. Right now."

The two beings located themselves in the Admiral's executive suite. Howard's body was already there. It was a rugged thirty-year-old *Homo novus,* which is *Homo sapiens* in every detail except for the energized mechanism, the trap, which pins a being inside a *Homo sap* body.

Garret could tell that Howard had not been in his mahogany-paneled office when the quartermaster had announced him: the body had that spinny expression of having been just mocked up. It was recovering somewhat by soaking up the sunlight that radiated from the ceiling.

Even though this was a Level Ten org, bodies, desks, papers, and so on were still used—as they were on Flag Base. The policy was to use as much objective universe material as was necessary to establish identification, location, and, in general, order. Besides, bodies were fun now.

After checking to make sure that no other beings contained or were contained within their space, Garrett explained his visit.

"Formally I'm on a mission, John, the reasons for which are irrelevant at this moment. I'm in the first stage, investigation; however, I do have three orders which I suspect won't affect much but nevertheless are needed." Three sheets of paper appeared on the Admiral's desk with orders neatly typed, signed, and sealed.

"I also need some data," Garrett continued thoughtfully. "Everything you have and can collect on Game P-U in five days. I'll be back then to get the data and give you the particulars on this mission. That's all."

"All right, sir," Howard acknowledged. His body stood and saluted.

Garrett took his leave then, checking out with the quartermaster. He stopped his continual personal creation of energy and proceeded to examine the stimulus/response minds of the game creators for the same factors as the executives. And, finally, but most tediously, he examined the energized pictures and masses of the remaining one million crew members.

It should be understood that this exhaustive investigation of so large a group was no mere pleasant afternoon task. Mental pictures, especially when packed into their dark gray masses, are Augean stables to confront and control. After all, it had been mental pictures alone that had once degraded every being in the universe into the enslaved squalid hell of *being* bodies. S/r minds were tough stuff; only a being who had fully attained the high state of Level Ten could really competently handle the s/r minds of others.

But even more perverse was operating without creating and having energy of one's own, without one's unique and identifying energy pattern—an uncomfortable state for even so eminently able a being as the Fleet Admiral.

For most beings, such a state would be intolerable, a starkly incomprehensible void that would incapacitate them to the extent of extinguishing identity itself. But Garrett, along with some one thousand others of the Space Organization, handpicked for toughness and competence by the Commander in Chief himself, had been allowed to enter the still experimental Level Fifteen: freedom from the need for energy. Of those hand-picked thousand, however, only a dozen could still, without their own energy, handle the murderously tough mental masses of others effectively enough to escape detection. Another's mental masses were horrendous to manipulate even openly and having energy; without these, the difficulty multiplied a thousandfold.

Only by authorization of the Commander in Chief, an authorization rarely given or ordered, could one undertake undetectable direct mental examinations of others. And only one being— Roderick Garrett—was now authorized, by reason of competence and ethics, to conduct such examinations at will whenever the circumstances warranted it.

When Garrett finished his mental examinations of the entire crew of the GO, he had little more to act on than when he had started. There was incompetence, certainly, and a few deliberately destructive actions. But every org had those aberrations without creating trouble of this magnitude. The superstructure of the organization was sound; he had checked that. And the basic structure was modeled on an organization that had survived eighty million years—and what had caused their downfall had been corrected here!

Every problem in the org led to a dead end; every grouping of problems by whatever variable or group of variables led to an anarchy of dead ends. He had expected when he finished the executives that more data would isolate one thing, one individual, one game as source. Not only had that not materialized, but nothing had materialized.

Garrett flitted to Flag then. The experience was like a sudden shift of scene inside a spherical slide show, complete with all fifty-six senses. Beings, of course, perceive circumambiently; they are senior to, they contain the objective universe and thus can change locations at will. Garrett learned what he wanted to know: after a week the stats were still dropping, visibly now. And the stats of the GO had crashed. He went back to GO headquarters.

After checking in with the quartermaster, he located himself in the body mockup station, a small open rotunda near the executive division building, and mocked up his *Homo novus.*

His body was apparently a facsimile of his last born body, fifteen hundred years before, in its twenty-sixth year. Actually, however, it was three times more efficient—which is saying something, since he had been a Level Nine then, a veritable superman. Now its communication channels were even cleaner, and he had established lines for direct electrical stimulation of the musculature, bypassing the nervous system. This permitted an instantaneousness of action impossible within the physical structure alone. Thus he controlled the body like a puppet, but it was a puppet with the consummate control and grace of a danseur.

Garrett's body was lean and smooth, and to anyone esthetically sensitive, flawlessly beautiful. Esthetics had been his medium for thousands of years—it was no secret that he had been two of the greatest artists in history before Soul Technology—and a body always has expressed the being. Now Garrett's energy pattern interfused with his body's: surrounding the flawless physical beauty radiated and flowed an aura of blended white and gold.

Such was the quality of the Fleet Admiral who appeared at GO headquarters that day. Those who saw him and had done Level Eleven were awed; those who had not were stunned.

Howard ushered Garrett to the office that had been prepared for him. The room would have been a replica of Garrett's oval office on Flag if it had not avoided certain details, such as certificates, personal mementos, and unique patterns in the paneling and furniture, which might have disturbed his equilibrium.

"Thank you, sir, for canceling War Game 113," Howard began as soon as they were seated. "A lot of us kind of knew it was aberrated, but none of us took the initiative to really check it out. Same for C-U 46; we've got that straight now.

"If you don't mind my asking, though, sir, I'm in the dark as to how you found out about them. But even more, I'd like to know"—he hesitated, checking the indicators of his superior, and, finding them still good—"how you happened to start investigating here *before* our stats crashed. I know Flag is good, but . . ."

Garrett laughed. "No, we haven't perfected the ability of prophecy. That was done by stats. But first, the method of finding those games is still classified; but I can tell you it's part of Fifteen.

"As for the mission, though, here's the situation—but I'd like you to keep it sealed for a while. A week ago the Old Man noticed a galaxy-wide stat drop, just below normal variation. Nobody else did; it was too slight. Anyway, he isolated the cause—here."

"But our stats were soaring then," Howard blurted; then he understood. "Oh, the inversion precept."

"Right. The little-used 'bank robber in the family' rule; one unit brings the group up and then crashes ignominiously. The Old Man is great; he deduced our stat analysis system, remember, from the laws of the universe, and he's the best at using it."

"Agreed." Howard frowned. "Then what's out here, sir?"

"Don't know, John. It has to be something suppressive as hell. You know of anything?"

Howard thought for a minute. "No, sir." Then added: "You suspect Game P-U?"

"Just as an outside possibility. Have you got the data on it?"

"Here, sir. I have also located two people who have been in Game P-U and might have further information."

Then, alone, Garrett studied for several hours the records and promotional literature. His detailed analysis revealed that Game P-U was not intrinsically suppressive of beings. It could, however, be extrinsically suppressive: players acting crazy could make a sane game crazy.

He leaned back in his chair and, slowly at first, expanded his space to include the entire base. This was a serene state of knowing and affinity, of responsibility and creation. Truly one's existence depends not upon identity, but upon created space. From this commanding position, he considered the situation anew.

What could be wrong, *that* wrong, and not yet locatable? Procedure was correct. Funny the way Game P-U showed up, but nothing big was there. Besides, its stats were good, even fantas— Its stats! His space exploded as he cognized.

The inversion precept! *Of course!* He had been scouring the org for something spectacularly wrong when he should also have been looking for something spectacularly right.

"Howard!" Garrett yelled mentally, connecting with the Admiral.

"Yes, sir?" The Admiral, in conference, put his total attention on the incoming communication.

"What's the source of your largest stats?"

"Why, Game P-U, sir. I thought you already knew."

"I didn't, but forget it. How long has it been big—and by how much larger than the next largest?"

"It really took off about six weeks ago, sir; now it varies between three and four times the next largest. Except for the last two days. Its crash was virtually our total crash."

"Okay. Thanks, John. I'd like to have all the stats for the last two months; and I'd like to talk to those two who were in Game P-U. Can do?"

"Right away, sir."

The records arrived in a few minutes. No other game had anything like that storytelling pattern. Game P-U was undeniably, incontrovertibly, it.

While he was waiting for the two people, he spent some time in his personal universe. He reflected with pleasure that he had no stimulus/response mind anymore. If he had, it would be kicking him all over the universe now with caustic, suppressive invalidation for not applying the inversion precept earlier. Now, however, he knew what he was: a being, the only thing that was precisely and completely nothing—the true zero, containing no wavelengths, having no dimension or motion or mass or location. How could a nothing get kicked around the universe, and with what?

The two people arrived, bodiless. They had been married thirteen hundred years, they said. They had been in Game P-U only one day.

"We didn't like the space or the mood of the game or something," one said. "It seemed antagonistic, a fighting game."

"But it was a covert fighting," interjected the other, "like the game was supposed to be peaceful. But there was a constant undertone of force, police-type force. Very hypocritical."

"And suppressive to that degree," the first added.

"Anything else suppressive?" Garrett asked.

Neither could think of anything else. They left.

Garrett ordered the cancelation of Game P-U, by reason of suppression. In thirty minutes no GO in the galaxy would give the location of Game P-U to anyone; to do so would be treason.

Garrett left for Flag then, confident that his job was done. He would have been startled indeed to learn that he had not yet even begun.

Flag Base. Three days had passed since Fleet Admiral Roderick Garrett had been debriefed on his mission and had returned to the normal business of managing a galaxy.

He had not expected the stats to recover the first or second day after he had canceled Game P-U, but neither had he expected them to continue diving at the same rate. When the drop continued on the third day, he went to see the Commander in Chief.

"Hello, Rod. I was expecting you."

Garrett sat down.

"I'm puzzled, sir."

"You and me both. However, I studied your debriefing and I'm convinced you were right about Game P-U."

"Huh? Then how come the stats are still dropping?"

"Well, we'll have to go and find out, won't we?"

The Commander in Chief and his Fleet Admiral located themselves outside a rift in Galaxy Two, near where the GO data placed Game P-U. Then they approached another quality of space, which bespoke to all comers that here was another game. By definition, that meant a different operating basis.

Garrett observed his senior floating through the clear interstellar darkness towards Game P-U, his pure golden energy radiating across the starlight. He wondered at the responsibility level of this being who so casually entered uncharted areas and spaces, without thought for dangers or awe for mysteries. He had heard him talk about it once: he had said that he had taken upon himself the responsibility for everything and every being in the universe. Garrett now observed his intractable awareness and effortless strength, and understood whence they were derived.

Inside Game P-U, they shot their perception toward what they thought must be its opposite boundary. A few galaxies, then—

"Rod! Observe the space itself!" commanded the senior suddenly.

Garrett focused on intergalactic space and tuned up his perception. Smaller and smaller became the area of his attention, down to the evenly-spread atoms. Something weird about this matter, he thought; extraordinarily dense and strong. Down between the atoms. It couldn't be!

"Space is linear here, sir," he said to his senior.

"And it should be highly curved, since we're near the boundary of the universe. Check out the tone of the space, I'll check the matter."

Both went to work. They created various energy manifestations —flows, dispersals, ridges, and subtypes—to interact with the matter and space. They plotted thereby the affinity of the medium for beings, measuring its survival value, its tone.

"What'd you come up with, Rod?" the Commander in Chief asked quietly.

The Fleet Admiral, as tough as he was, was shaken. "Off the scale, sir. Definitely below. Ridges, even the weakest, persist for a long time; the space is of a demanding, possibly punishing tone. And matter, sir?"

"Similar. Below scale, lower harmonic of grief by its persistence of dispersals. You noticed the density of particles in intergalactic space? That's why. I'd call it craving, appetence. This game is inherently suppressive, matter some multiple of four points below space."

"That's why cancelation didn't work, sir," Garrett said. "Loss is the bottom of our scale, equaling death of a body. Game P-U is below loss; it's below being a game. We'd have to disconnect —at minimum."

"At minimum is right. That might not even do it. We sent one trillion beings in here; that's a contrasurvival act of considerable magnitude. We may have to unmock it—if we can.

"I'll say one thing for this Game P-U, though, Rod," the Commander in Chief continued, vibrating in a chuckle. "It's solved the eternal problem of games."

"Sir?"

"That a being loses a game when he wins as well as when he loses—because when he wins he no longer has a game."

"What a solution, sir," the Fleet Admiral replied. "Getting so far below loss you can't even know the feeling."

"True, son, true," the Commander in Chief said, more soberly. "We still need more data—and there's a ship over there. You take the top half. Energyless."

It was a teardrop-shaped vessel. Both entered and observed.

The ship was a naked hull, driven and shielded by the energy and perception of a specialized crew. It was a war vessel returning with booty from a raid: one hundred beautiful female bodies.

Garrett checked the beings operating the female bodies. Unlike the crew, they had no awareness of their true nature—they were being their bodies. But the crew, too, lacked some native abilities; they obviously could not mock up bodies as complex as the ones they were stealing.

Garrett found a common source for their incapabilities: stimulus/response minds!

On a lower deck, the Commander in Chief noticed an implant station. One girl was strapped naked and spread-eagled on a steel platform. She had been drugged and hypnotized into a stupor. A dangerously high amperage played through her body; a movie scene appeared above her of a room with electronic controls. A man opened a door to the room, saw her lying helpless, and madly rushed to pull some levers, after which the current stopped and was replaced by a slowly building, throbbing sexual sensation, and the movie faded to sexual scenes. The cycle repeated, with a different man each time.

They met outside the range of the ship's detector.

"S/r minds, Rod; did you notice? Incredible! Same function, different structure. It isn't possible; they couldn't have done it unknowingly, yet it appears to be so. . . ."

"They aren't our people, sir. The beings I examined have a time track in this game earlier than we supposedly established it."

It took a second for the Commander in Chief to assimilate this data. "Then it's not our game!" he exploded. "Or it's another universe entirely. You sure it wasn't an implanted track? They have implants here, you know; that ship's product is sex slaves."

"Absolutely, sir. I could tell the difference. Incidentally, the beings in the female bodies were all old implanters themselves. Karmic law operative—"

"Yeah, I noticed." The Commander in Chief mused, then said: "That makes it more probable this is another universe. Our game creator could have been wandering around down here and been inspired by the space. Do we always shield our games, Rod?"

"We never do, sir. It's policy."

"I didn't think you noticed—during the transition you were intent upon the change in tone. There is a shield. But it's barely perceptible. And porous."

"Porous? But why? What function—"

"For finite dimension and possibly, probably, for expansion."

"Expansion!" Garrett was horrified. "You mean it could take over *our* universe—wouldn't a higher-toned game be senior?"

"Other things being equal, yes. Since universes exist, however, only by the agreed creation of the beings within them, this universe—if it truly is one—could rank over ours by the force of agreement of a significantly greater number of beings. Or, as I suspect is the case, its very suppression, its brutal invalidation by appetence and demand, enforces a viewpoint that it is the only universe—to the exclusion of all others, even a being's personal universe. You noticed that the beings on that ship lacked bright, real personal universes?"

"Yes, sir; but wasn't that the result of their s/r minds?"

"In our universe it is; but here the s/r mind is constructed only to complement the universe, to record and enforce its data. Thus it suppresses a personal universe because a basic assumption of this universe is that it is the only universe.

"The s/r mind here is twice as vicious as the one we had. It records everything the being resists—either approaching or leaving. Thus everything unwanted, as well as everything unconfronted, persists.

"As a mind, it enforces identity and action by penalty of pain. Its rare observations are of uncertainties; it does not perceive, it evaluates. Thus a being here who is using only his s/r mind does not see things or beings, he only evaluates them.

"And, of course, a being can't get out of this game with his s/r mind energized—which it constantly must be, by the nature of the game."

They were silent for a minute.

"Rod, let's try unmocking some of this matter. Over there."

Instantly they were inside the rift of a nearby galaxy. They positioned themselves on opposite sides of a small barren planet. They nullified the esthetic frequency in the area, meanwhile interlocking energy shields impenetrable to all frequencies around the planet. They stopped creation of the shields. The planet was still there.

The Fleet Admiral chuckled. "Want to try something smaller, sir?" In the next instant he discovered that a replica of the planet was occupying his space. He relocated himself outside it. "Wise guy," he thought at his senior.

He watched as the two planets discharged energy against one another. The replica faded, strengthened; the original faded; the replica wavered and disappeared. The original remained.

The Commander in Chief had scrutinized the fading of the original. He cognized.

The Fleet Admiral now saw the planet disappear. "How, sir?" he asked, flowing admiration.

"Its persistence was dependent upon a lie, Rod, which became visible when it discharged against its duplicate. Its creator mocked it up, then claimed he didn't; so I just recreated it as it actually was created in its original time and space. And it unmocked. Apparently matter here can't survive in truth.

"It would follow that mental pictures here, since they also have mass, must be altered in some way in order to persist. Unmocking the s/r mind, then, would require viewing its scenes as they actually existed."

The Fleet Admiral mocked up the same planet. It persisted as long as he continued to create it, but disappeared when he stopped. Then he mocked it up and told himself he had created it another way. It remained.

"Because alteration of creation is basic to persistence here," the Commander in Chief said, "no one is able to take even partial responsibility for this universe. Then the matter disperses, even to atomic size. Chaos. Some job, tracing every creation to un-mock the whole thing. It is an entirely separate universe."

"I concur, sir. Incidentally, the GO names a lot of their games universes. I—*sir, look at that!*"

The Commander in Chief looked and was shocked speechless.

In trillions of trillions of years of experience neither had seen or even imagined the spectacle that was now floating near them. It was a mass, simply an encrusted solid rock one meter in diameter, surrounded, however, by a faint gray aura of discordant energy.

That rock was a being.

They did nothing for a moment, silent in their innermost depths, stunned. Then, together, they shot their perception into the mass. Garrett's personal universe reeled away from contact with this area of solid dissonance and wavered on the point of total invalidation; it held, though, and in the second of holding found its relationship—senior to the mass. The Commander in Chief barely flinched.

They withdrew then, cautiously, kilometers distant, as though their presence and communication might disturb some unknown and horrible balance. Separated now, they thought. Grim, inescapable conclusions followed grim, inescapable correlations of data. Finally:

"Could he really be considered *dead,* sir?"

"Functionally, yes," the Commander in Chief replied slowly. "It is true that the mass is his s/r mind totally solidified, and he's continually creating the energy that keeps it solid—but in that creation he is dead: he can't perceive or communicate. He certainly has no awareness of himself."

The Commander in Chief paused. "Well, that's undoubtedly the bottom of the scale. The ultimate of affinity—becoming the universe, the game. We'll have to get our people out of here if we can, then go home and disconnect. We'll worry about this universe after we handle our own.

"It's amazing how beings, in order to have games, compromise, even fight, doing the only things they can do: surviving, knowing, being fixed in position, and most horrible of all, being simple. And so they enslave themselves to their own creations.

"Game P-U, this universe, is a trap. What's that P mean? Ah, yes—physical. The Physical Universe. Some game!"

NIGHT SHIFT

It was simple and logical: why not
use the punishment to *prevent* the crime?

Kevin O'Donnell, Jr.

The grey street is quiet now. I'm grateful for the chance to meditate, yet I'm also impatient. I want something to happen. I enjoy my own company, and I don't need to be constantly diverted, but I've inspected my weapon, counted my points, and listened to the news on six different stations. There's not much more I can do.

Ah. A shadow bulged eighty yards south of me. Shadows aren't supposed to waver, not here. In this part of the city, the shadows are as rigid as the buildings. They lie across the sidewalks like lines dropped from a straightedge; they grow or shrink at the pace of the moon. I could have said sun, but I have the night shift.

After a long pause, the shadow has slithered through another shadow. Time for the infrareds. Uh-huh. A man-shape. Or a stocky, short-haired woman-shape. Sex doesn't matter to me. I'm only concerned about actions. I swing my gun around and line up the crosshairs. Not that I'm about to pull the trigger, but it's good to be prepared. When you've got your probable target all picked out, a sudden burst of excitement is less likely to spoil your aim.

What the hell's he doing? My first assumption is that he is not bound for a specific destination. He's moving too slowly, and sticking too deep in the shadows, for that. By the same token, he isn't out for a stroll, and the infrareds don't show any dog. I don't think he's looking for something he's lost, either, because in that case—even if it is a bad joke—he'd be searching in the pools of brilliance beneath the street lights. Or he'd carry a flashlight.

My second assumption is that he's up to no good, and will need close observation until he's out of my area. As always when something seems to be happening, the tinny, top forty radio station has melted into the background. In my time up here, I've learned how to do two things at once. It's become so natural that when things are slow, as they have been for the last few hours, I can hardly bear to concentrate on only one. Just a few minutes ago the radio was driving me crazy with its inane chatter and childish music. Now that something else has moved into the foreground, the simple tunes have become enjoyable.

He's right below me now. Were he to look up, he might see, in the reflecting glass bottom of my container, an inverted image of himself, made tiny by the hundred feet between us. If he knew I was watching him, he wouldn't lean so nonchalantly on the pillar that supports me. Another idea occurs to me: I focus the parabolic mike on him, to check for irregular breathing or muffled groans. I only get five points for providing medical assistance to a distressed citizen, but . . .

No. Nothing seems to be wrong with him. I could have HQ ask him, I suppose—there's a speaker set into the concrete post not two feet above his head—but if my suspicions are well-founded, that would only drive him into someone else's area, and give someone else the points. I'll wait; he can make the first move.

Dammit! He's going for the hubcaps of the Lincoln Continental parked ten yards north of me. As a precautionary measure, I ask the BMV computer for the name and description of the car's owner. It comes back in eighteen seconds: "Mrs. Esmeralda Washington, age sixty-eight, height . . ." but I stop listening. I wait till he comes around the front of the car, and then I squeeze the trigger. The hubcaps clatter on the concrete. One of them rolls fifteen feet on its edge, and I mark it mentally so that it can be retrieved later. Then I put in the call to HQ, requesting a cruiser.

It arrives in less than two minutes. One cop sprints to the inert form on the sidewalk while the other throws me a mock salute. I blink my searchlight at him. It's not much, but it's the best I can do in the way of repartee. He approaches the pillar, selects a key from the jingling ring on his belt, and unlocks the metal door. Inside is the video-tape cassette that the D.A. will use as evidence in court.

As the cruiser glides away, my point board flickers briefly, then settles down to display a new reading: GRANTED—4789. PENDING —2753. My instant curse is a ritual reply. It was a ten-point bust, added to the pending column because I don't get official credit until after conviction and all appeals. My guess is that this one won't take long—few people contest petty larceny charges.

Five thousand two hundred eleven points to go. Or eight years. The sentence was ten thousand points, or ten years, whichever came first. I've been up here for just about two years.

All things considered, it's not such a bad life. The container is a little cramped, but I don't need much space, and I can't move freely, anyway. I'm connected to dozens of tubes—for feeding, waste removal, and oxygen supply—and an assortment of wires links me to the equipment that makes me semi-superhuman. Like the auto-focusing binoculars, with their infrared attachments and their various filters. My mike can monitor the heartbeat of a mouse fifty yards away, with a filter to block out the traffic noise. And the gun will bring down anything smaller than a Tyrannosaurus Rex. About the only thing I don't have is a sense of smell, for which I'm grateful. I doubt if this place smells very good.

They tell me that if I serve the entire ten years, I'll cost the city a few cents more than a hundred thousand dollars. In one sense, I may have already paid for myself: people aren't afraid to be out at night anymore. The street was bustling till long after midnight. The Merchants' Association even awarded me a plaque for having contributed to their economic renaissance. That's something.

I suppose that if cops did my job, they'd have to stash me in a prison, and that'd cost. Plus cops wouldn't do the job as well: they can be convinced to look the other way. Money'll do it for some, threats for others. Nothing will do it for me.

Then, of course, there's the incentive for positive law enforcement. If some poor bastard in a uniform stumbles into a tight spot while he's walking his beat, he's got everything to lose and precious little to gain by going for his gun. It's in his best interests to stick up his hands and let the bad guys go on with what they were doing—that is, if he wants to see his family and friends again. But me . . . my container is bullet- and bomb-proof; the life-support system is armor-plated; and every bust brings me that much closer to freedom. I'm hungrier than any flatfoot ever has been.

Finally, from the city's point of view, my presence high above the street is an A-1 deterrent. I'm invisible to the people on the ground, who can't tell where I'm looking. All they know is that I'm up here, ready for any kind of action, from a purse-snatch to a street riot, and equipped with video-tape cameras that will document whatever charges I make. That makes them a little nervous; it tends to keep them on the right side of the law.

So I can't understand why some of them go ahead and commit crimes anyway. It's possible that they haven't read the newspaper articles about my kind, but damn near every radio or TV news broadcast includes the familiar report: "Watchtower Number —, on —— Street, this afternoon captured . . ."

My only theory is that would-be street criminals are stupid. I, for one, wasn't too bright. I figured that since mine was an indoor job, the tower wouldn't see it, and that once I got onto the street, I could melt into the crowd. Didn't work that way. I thought it did, up until I turned a corner and got blasted with the damn stun. The towers had just been keeping me in view, waiting for my victim to make a positive ID. After a couple minutes, they got it, and then I got it.

A perfect example is the guy who's in the lobby of the apartment building across the street. He's betting that since I can't see him, I don't know he's there. He's forgotten about my infrareds and my parabolic mike. I noticed his body heat an hour ago, so I've been listening carefully. Like an idiot, he talks to himself. He's waiting for somebody to come late, and may be a little drunk. He'll rob whoever it is, and then try to saunter down the street as though he belonged here. Doesn't he realize that I know all the residents of my area?

The rest of the street is dead. At this time of night, nothing moves but rats, cockroaches, and windblown papers. It's a good time to fit in some therapy. Not that I want to, but if I don't do it before the end of my shift, they'll dock me ten points. Since that's all I've earned so far tonight, I'm not about to risk losing it.

With a resigned sigh, I press the button. The shadow-dappled street scene fades from my vision and is replaced by a snug, warmly-lit living room. I blink, and lay down my book. My name is now Michael Takser; I'm a fifty-three-year-old shoe salesman who's just married off his last daughter. My eyes wander around the familiar room, picking out the frayed furniture, the shabby carpet, the cracked plaster. I think of the few dollars I have in the bank, and of how they'll grow now that I face no more major expenses.

There's a knock on the door. My wife calls, "Who is it, Mike?" from the kitchen, and I tell her, as I always do, "I don't know, I haven't answered it yet." I sense, of course, the kind of visitor it is—the therapy persona isn't strong enough to blank out all knowledge of what's happening. But it does override my anxieties, and make me step across the bottle-green rug and swing the door open.

There are three of them, all in their twenties, and the first one jabs the barrel of his revolver into my stomach. My pained grunt brings Nancy from the kitchen, still drying her hands on a dish towel. She gasps, and the towel flutters to the floor like a duck shot out of the sky. The last intruder closes the door and smiles. He has bad teeth.

"What do you want?" I mutter from my doubled-over stance.

"For starters," says their leader, smoothing his greasy black hair, "all the cash you got would be nice."

I give them that, naturally, and also a suitcase into which they load all our liquor. They remember that my wife might have jewelry. They're very patient, and don't make fun of her for crying while she tugs her wedding ring off her pudgy finger. After unplugging the TV, they decide it's too big to carry away, so one of them hurls the marble ashtray into the glass and it implodes. Like a starter's gun, the noise sets them off. Five minutes later, my apartment is a shambles. I'm neither excited nor outraged; I'm too stunned. My mind won't behave. It looks at the splintered dining room table and computes how many salesmanly smiles will be needed before I can replace it. It measures the pile of shattered china and tells me how many sweaty feet I'll smell before we can eat off something like it. It weighs the rubbish that used to give ease to our lives, and balances it against my remaining years. I start to shake my head in sorrow, but the pistol barrel cuts across my temple and drops me to the floor. I'm only vaguely aware that they're pushing my wife into the bedroom.

The Takser home dissolves into a picture of the street. Therapy is over for the day, but I'm still shaking. I always shake after empathy treatment: that's why they do it to me. But at least I don't go into bleak despair, as I do when I'm reminded of the pleasures from which my crime has cut me off. The freedom scenes, with their blue skies and wide worlds waiting for me, are plenty bad, as the ones featuring my buddies in the neighborhood bar. When the shrinks make cuddly little children smile at me, it's like they're tearing my heart out. And when they put me in bed with a woman who loves me, I cry for days.

A wobbly figure is stumbling from shadow to light to shadow. With the infrareds and the parabolic, I recognize her. She's a divorced junior executive who lives across the street. I could pick her up for a D & D, but that's only two points, and besides, she's not making a nuisance of herself. I think I'll wait. She's going to enter that lobby. The guy who's lurking there will take her purse, and then waltz out onto the street.

But he won't get past me. Uh-uh. He's at least fifteen points, twenty if he's got a gun.

And I only need five thousand two hundred eleven points before they'll give me back my body.

GOING DOWN

If the past does not exist, is it necessary to invent it?

Eleanor Arnason

"Do you ever wonder," I said to Aurelian after we finished the Great Sow, "what the point of all this is?"

Aurelian, who exactly fitted his golden name—his hair was pale yellow and his eyes were a shade of brown so light it seemed almost yellow—shook his head.

"I envy you your certitude or stupidity or whatever it is," I said.

We were standing high on Peak 32, looking across the valley at Peak 33, where the Sow was, a pictograph cut with lasers in the rock of a mountainside we'd scraped clean and sheared flat. There was a wind blowing, cold and wet, and grey clouds were moving quickly across the sky. The enormous sow lay on her side, her gross bulk covering an entire mountainside, while her piglets sucked on her rows of tits.

"Skipped your pill, didn't you?" Aurelian said.

I nodded and pulled up the collar of my jacket. It was cold up

210

there above the treeline, with nothing around to break the wind. I'd known for several days I was going into a depression, but I couldn't make myself take one of the little blue pills out of their bottle and pop it into my mouth. The doctors told me it was all chemical, my ups and downs, a cyclical imbalance of something or other in my brain. All I had to do was take the blue pills when I was down and the orange pills when I was up, and I'd be as sane and happy as the next person, who was probably popping pills too.

"What's so difficult about taking a pill?" Aurelian asked me. "You must be crazy or something to make a problem out of that."

That remark, of course, was to reassure me: there was nothing really wrong with being crazy, nothing we couldn't joke about. I said, "Uh-huh. Come on, let's go somewhere warm."

We went back to the helicopter and Aurelian flew us out of there, over the grey mountains and down over the green plain. The sky had cleared in the west, so we could see the sun setting. Its color at sunset was darker than Sol's, an almost purple red; its red light glinted on the rivers and rice paddies below us. I lit a cigar. Aurelian said, "Do you have to?"

"Okay," I said, and put the cigar out. In a normal state, I'd have been angry with him, but I have only one emotion when I'm going down, a kind of numb despair. Ahead of us was the first thing we had done on this planet, the Ring of Heaven. We had cut a circle in the plain and run the Maison River into it, bringing the river in and out through long tunnels so that all you could see from above was the ring of water, encircling a smooth, green lawn with a huge standing-stone at its center. I could remember how excited I had been the first time I saw it after it was done. Aurelian and I had gone up in a helicopter with a couple of bottles of rice wine and someone to fly the chopper while we got drunk: a Meshniri, since they got sick not drunk on our booze and we knew he/she wouldn't drink even if we got drunk enough to try passing the bottle. Now the Ring bored me. A cheap trick, I thought as we passed over it.

Ville-Maison was a little way beyond it, spread out on both sides of the Maison River, a few of its lights already on. The city was two grids at a thirty-degree angle to each other. The great bow curve of the river separated them, and they were joined by the five bridges. The sun had set and the city's colors had all turned to grey, but I could imagine them: the dark reddish-brown of the river, the pale grey of the streets and buildings and the bright summer green of the trees and the lawns. Not bad, not bad, I thought, and it had been done more or less by accident, the basic plan laid out by a couple of engineers in the settlement days and modified by almost everyone since then. I looked at Aurelian, who was busy talking to the control tower. An engineer, a stupid engineer. I got the ideas and he figured out how to make them work. If I were not around, he would probably do as good a job as the guys who had laid out Ville-Maison. So what was the point of having me around?

The runway lights were on, and we dropped slowly into the center of a circle of white light. When we had landed, Aurelian said, "Look, you go home and take a pill."

"Maybe." I retrieved the cigar from the ashtray, figuring I would light it as soon as I got out of the helicopter.

Aurelian turned to look at me. "If you were diabetic, you'd take insulin, wouldn't you?"

"In my present mood, maybe not."

"Listen, every time we do a job, you get more and more manic, till finally you're kiting so high you're barely in sight. Then, as soon as we're done, you come crashing down. And you're not easy to get along with either up or down, so I wish you'd take the pills."

"Okay," I said, and climbed out of the helicopter. It was pretty cold even on the plain, but that was normal. They had had to develop a new kind of rice to grow here, because the regular kinds couldn't take the cold. I walked across the wet grass into the terminal and out again, just in time to catch the bus downtown. I still had the cigar, unlit because they won't let you smoke cigars on any kind of public transport. We ought to organize, I thought, looking out at the wet streets, the dark trees moving in the wind, the houses set back behind little gardens, light shining out their windows. Cigar smokers, arise.

I went to the office instead of home. There was nothing at home except the pills. I lived alone in a one-room apartment, its windows looking out at the windows of another house. All I had there was a bed and bookcases full of books, and more books that I had to stack on the floor or put in the kitchen cabinets, because there was no more room in the bookcases. I didn't do much there except sleep. Even my reading I did elsewhere, usually at one of the cafés you found on every other sidewalk like cafés in Paris; but here they were glassed in for protection against the cold and wet, and the windows were opened only on bright days in summer. I liked them best in winter. I'd sit by a window and drink hot tea, looking out through the rain-streaked glass at people with umbrellas hurrying down the street. If the spectacle of other people getting wet began to bore me, I could read or order something to eat. I always ate out. I didn't even own any kitchenware.

Our office had two rooms, one for me and one for Aurelian, and the windows opened out on a canal lined with trees. It was dark enough out there so that I could see the pale, glimmering lights that were ghost moths flying among the trees. I opened the window in my office and smelled the weedy canal smell, then sat in the dark to watch the ghost moths and smoke my cigar. When I had finished the cigar, I turned on the lights and looked around. I had three big blowups that covered most of three walls: aerial photos of Stonehenge and a five- or six-level interchange somewhere in North America and bomb craters in Vietnam, almost a century old and still visible. They didn't know, the guys who dropped the bombs, that they were creating an enduring work of art. Under the grass or whatever was growing there, you could still see the faint lines that had been the boundaries of rice paddies. Scattered across the uneven grid the paddies made were

deep pocks left by the bombs. It's all art, if you get high enough.
Remember that Italian pilot—you won't unless you've read a lot
of history books—who dropped bombs on the Ethiopians and
saw the explosions as red roses blooming below him? But that,
as they say, was long ago and in another country and all those
people are dead.

On my drawing board was a sketch of the next project: the
Serpent. It was going to be a mound like the ones built by the
North American Indians: a wide, low, grass-covered ridge that
began with a series of hummocks—the rattle—and went spiraling
out till finally it straightened and ran due north for two or three
hundred meters, and ended in a diamond-shaped hill that was the
snake's head. I didn't like the way the sketch was coming along,
so I fiddled with it for a while, wrecked it and tore it up. Forget
that, I thought, and turned off the lights. It must have been
raining, though the only sign of it I could see was a mistiness
around the street light across the canal. The ghost moths were
gone, all except one that gleamed, then vanished, then gleamed
again in the dark beneath a tree.

We had been brought out here, Aurelian and I, because they
had found out—years ago when we first began to settle other
planets—that people were so used to living surrounded by their
own artifacts, living on top of the debris of millennia, that a bare
planet made them uneasy. They felt exposed and vulnerable,
somehow, without mounds, dolmens, Roman roads, arrowheads
in the earth that turned up when they plowed. So we came and
made a past for them. Your friendly neighborhood history-mak-
ers. Give us a month and we'll make you a century. They could
have got the result they wanted by dropping bombs all over a new
planet. The craters would have marked the land sufficiently, said
"This is ours" to all comers.

There was a Meshniri bar down the street, and I needed a
drink. I closed up the office and went downstairs. As I had suspected, it was raining, a light drizzle that was barely more than
a mist. Somebody had their windows open and a recording on:

a Chinese opera. Almost all the planet's settlers were East Asians, Chinese mostly. The climate was too cold for the Indochinese, the Thais, or the Indonesians. I walked to the corner where the bar was, orange light shining out its tiny windows, orange being the color of Meshnir's sun. Their sun was visible from this planet, a dim star in the Dragon constellation. People told me it had a definite orange tinge. But I've never been able to see the colors of stars; they all look white to me.

Inside, the air was hot and full of the sweet smell of Meshniri bodies. The jukebox was playing old-time Meshniri music, which used a lot of percussion instruments made out of wood. This particular piece had a lot of rattling and clicking in it, along with the clear sound of a wooden drum. The jukebox screen was blank, since the Meshniri didn't combine pictures with their music. But the screen had not been disconnected. A grey-white flickering light filled it. It was bright enough to be irritating, and I didn't know how the Meshniri could stand it. The Meshniri looked at me, not really wanting me there, but too polite to tell me to get out. I went to the bar and asked the bartender for *ansit*. He/she poured me a glass. For some reason we can drink Meshniri booze, though they can't drink our stuff. I sipped a little. At first you taste the sweetness. It's as sweet as a liqueur. Then it starts burning. You feel as if you've just stuffed your mouth full of hot peppers. You choke and gasp and drink the water chaser and then try another sip. The Chinese from Szechwan, where they cook with hot pepper, love the stuff. It was a Szechwanese who first got me drinking *ansit* and going to Meshniri bars, getting used to the Meshniri watching me—wishing I would go and leave them in peace.

I sat down at a table. The jukebox was playing a modern piece, an electric flute from Earth replacing a Meshniri wooden flute. If I hadn't been there, they would probably have danced, all of them in a row, their long, thin arms and legs moving slowly and stiffly. I sipped more *ansit*, listening to the sound of the wooden pipe-gongs. They loved wood and trees, the Meshniri. They sculpted

trees the way the Japanese did, but the trees they bent and
pruned were enormous. They had whole gardens full of sculptured trees, all centuries old. The sculptors must have been very
patient and very determined; I envied them those qualities. I
didn't have the discipline to bend a branch and wait for the tree
to learn to grow that way. If I were working with trees, I would
probably have Aurelian bulldoze them all down and put in plastic
substitutes whose branches went the way I wanted.

I drank slowly, which is the only way to drink *ansit,* and went
through four or five glasses of water. I felt myself sliding deeper
into depression, sitting in the dim room, surrounded by the
black-brown shiny bodies of the Meshniri, their sweet smell so
thick I thought I could taste it. Soon, I knew, the floor beneath
me would collapse, and I'd be falling through black space for
hours or days. I had to get out before that happened, get back
to my place and take a pill. I left my drink unfinished, got up and
walked out, looking straight ahead so I couldn't see the Meshniri
watching me. Their eyes were large and so pale they seemed
colorless.

Outside it was still raining, a fine, misty rain. Burrowing beetles
were everywhere, driven out of their burrows by the water. They
scurried across the sidewalk, their black, scaly bodies glittering in
the light from the street lights. I had to watch my feet to avoid
stepping on one. They crunched underfoot the way really big
roaches did. Sometimes when I went down, something funny
happened to my vision: things seemed to recede and get very
distinct, both at the same time. Those beetles on the sidewalk
were a long, long way below me, but I saw them so clearly I could
almost count the scales on their backs.

I hurried, thinking my apartment was only four or five blocks
away; I'd be there in a few minutes; all I had to do was take a pill
and hold on an hour or so till it took effect.

The rain started coming down hard. The beetles scurried for
shelter, and I ran the rest of the way home, up the front steps and
in the front door. Ms. Li opened her apartment door and looked

out when I came slamming in. I could hear her 3D: the evening
news giving the body count for a border skirmish somewhere
light-years away.

"Oh. It's you," she said.

Right, I thought, going up the stairs. It was me. The mad
genius was home. But where were the flowers, the red carpet, the
band? The hall upstairs was bare except for a piece of silk embroi-
dered with flowers and birds, framed and glassed, hung by Ms.
Li. It had come with her all the way from China, and it was
hideous. I could smell marijuana smoke coming from the room
across from mine, where a girl lived who, Ms. Li had told me,
worked as a systems analyst for the Statistical Center. I would
come up the stairs sometimes and hear her hurrying to get inside
before I appeared; or open my door and see her door open then
shut again, when she realized I was coming out. As careful as she
had been, I had seen her a couple of times. She was a perfectly
ordinary-looking girl, from North China probably, since she was
tall and very fair-skinned.

My phone was going *meep-meep-meep*. I unlocked my door, got
inside, turned on the phone and said, "History Unlimited. If you
don't like your old past, let us build you a new one."

"Just checking," Aurelian said. "You weren't home earlier."

"I was out drinking. I'm going to take my medicine, so you can
stop worrying."

"Why don't you take it right now and come back and tell me
you've done it?"

"Okay." I went and took a pill. When I got back to the phone,
I said, "Your good deed is now done. The ghosts of dead Boy
Scouts can rest easy."

"I'll see you at the office. Okay?"

"Uh-huh," I said and turned the phone off. I got out my last
bottle of rice wine and took a big swallow to get the metallic taste
of the pill out of my mouth. I had only one picture in my apartment: a blown-up aerial photo of Manhattan, the spiky towers
thrusting up like trees in a forest, blurred by the thick pollution

haze. What an amazing artifact, I thought, looking at it. The photo had been taken from so high up, all you could see was the towers. The people who scurried like beetles between them were invisible. I opened a window and sat on the ledge, wine bottle in my hand. The rain had become a downpour. I swallowed more wine, watching the rain come down, shining like silver where the street lights lit it, filling the gutters, swirling down the drains. All I had to do was wait an hour till the pill went to work, and then I'd be fine.

THE DISGUISE

I do glory
That thou, which stood'st like a huge pyramid
Begun upon a large and ample base,
Shalt end in a little point, a kind of nothing.

Kim Stanley Robinson

I pulled open the theater door and stuck my foot against it to keep the wind that swirled in the street from slamming it shut. I swung my duffel bag through the doorway and followed it inside. The door closed with a forced hiss and the bright lights of the street were replaced by dim greys. The air was still.

My eyes adjusted, and slowly, as if candles were being lit, I perceived the narrow high room which was the foyer of the Rose Theatre. I crossed the room and peered in the ticket window. A thin young man, with eye-sockets blacked, and white hair cropped close to his head, looked up at me. I dropped my bag, pulled my card from my pocket and handed it to him.

"Pallio," I said.

"Very good," he said, and looked at the card. "Now when Velasquo arrives we'll have everyone." He picked up a cast list and put a check beside my name. After slotting my card into the register, he touched some keys, and the square of plastic disappeared. "The charge is twelve per cent higher now," he murmured. "They're trying to tax us to death." The card reappeared and he handed it back to me. "Let me take you to your room."

I picked up my bag. The cashier appeared through a doorway beside the window and led me down the hall, looking back over his shoulder to talk: "I don't trust this *Guise* play, I think that whole Aylsebury Collection is a Collier forgery. . . ." I ignored him and watched the footprints he left in the thick blue-black carpet. Dull bronze-flake wallpaper shattered the light from a half-dozen gas jets. The Rose was in its full Regency splendor, for the first time in months. The halls felt as subterranean as before, however; the Rose occupied only a few bottom floors in the Barnard Tower, an eighty-story complex.

The cashier stopped at one of a series of doors and opened it for me. Light flooded over us. We went in and were on a different set; snapping Jacob's ladders and colored liquids bubbling up tubes made me look for a mad scientist. But it was only a white-coated technician, at the computer terminal. He turned around, revealing a scrubbed, precisely shaved face. "Whom have you brought us?" he said.

"Pallio," replied the cashier. I dropped my bag.

"We're ready to give you your part," the technician said.

The chair was dressed up like a chrome-and-glass version of the table Frankenstein's monster was born on. "Does Bloomsman have to do this," I said.

"You know our director."

"Last time I was here it was a dentist's chair."

"Not many liked it that way, as I recall."

I got into the chair while he tapped keys at the terminal, calling up from that artificial mind a detailed description of my brain's structure. When he was done he wrapped the pharmaceutical band around my neck. "Ready?" he asked. He tapped a key on the chair's console and I felt the odd sensation, like flexing a stiff muscle, of the injection—a tiny witch's brew of L-dopa, bufontenin, and norepinephrine. As always my heart began hammering immediately: not because of the introduced chemicals, but because of my own adrenaline, flooding through me to combat the imagined danger of a primal violation.

We waited. The room enlarged and flattened out into a painted cylinder. "Now for the hood," said the technician, his voice like tin. The hood descended and it was dark. The goggles were cold against my face, and my scalp prickled as filaments touched it.

"Time for the implant," the technician said. "Let's have alpha waves if you please." I started the stillness behind my nose. "Fine. Here we go."

In my vision a blue field flickered at around ten cycles per second, and voices chattered in both ears, creating counterpoints of blank verse. In those connected clumps known as the limbic system, scattered across the bottom of my cerebral cortex, new neural activity began. Electrical charges skipped through the precise network of neurons until they reached the edge of the familiar; synapses fired in new directions, and were forever changed. I was growing. I felt none of it.

Memories came before me in confusing abundance, passing before I could fix on them. An afternoon by the window in an Essex library, watching green hills become invisible in the grey rain. In the colony off Jamaica just after the earthquake, when everyone was silent, feeling the pressure of the hundred fathoms of water above. The run of basses in the scherzo of Beethoven's *Fifth*. A strong smell of disinfectant—hospital smell—and the voice of Carlos, droning quietly: "It was in the fourth act of *Hamlet*, when I as Claudius was on my knees, attempting to pray. Hamlet was above and to one side, on the balcony, and in my peripheral vision his face distorted into a mask of fang and snout. As he finished his soliloquy he turned away from the balustrade, but his head stayed fixed, twisted entirely over one shoulder, and he continued to glare down at me. My memory flooded. The moment I understood he was the Hieronomo, he jumped the balustrade, and I leaped to my feet only to meet the falling epée blade directly in the chest. I heard the cries of shock, but nothing more. . . ."

Blackness. Then the suction pulling at my eyes as the eyepieces withdrew. The hood rose and the white room reappeared. I twisted my head back and forth.

"Got it?" asked the technician. I paused and thought. Pallio . . . yes. A series of exclamations marked his entrance in the first scene, a conference with Velasquo. I knew only my first few lines, plus cue lines, and Bloomsman's laconic blocking, appropriate to the improvisational nature of the art: "Confront Velasquo center stage." The rest of my part would come to me throughout the course of the play, irregularly, recalled by unknown cues. This was the minimum script that Bloomsman allowed one to receive; it was the preferred preparation among seasoned actors.

"Backstage is that way," the technician said. He helped me up. I swayed unsteadily. "Break a leg," he said brightly, and returned to his terminal. I picked up my costume bag and left the room.

The hall expanded near the gas jets and contracted in the dimmer sections. I stopped and leaned against the wall, concentrating to recover from the dissociation of the implant. The wallpaper was not actually flake—it had once been a smooth sheen, but had cracked and peeled away into thousands of bronze shavings. Chips broke off under me and floated to the carpet. I strode down the hall, uncertain how long I had stopped. My sense of estrangement was stronger than usual, as if I had learned more than a play.

The hall ended in a T and I could not remember which way to go. Acting on a dim intuition I turned right and found myself in a veritable maze of T-connections. I alternated turns, going first right, then left. One hall I followed dropped several steps, then turned and became a flight of stairs, which I descended. At the bottom of this stairway were three long, dim halls, all furnished (like the stairway) with the same dark carpet, bronze wallpaper, and gas jets. I chose the right-hand one and ventured on. Just as

I began to think my self inextricably lost there was a door, recessed into the right wall. I opened it and was at the back of the
theater, looking across the audience to the curtain.

The audience was large, about forty or fifty people. Many times
I had acted in plays which no one had come to see; in those the
imaginary fourth wall had become real, and we had played for
ourselves, aware only of the internal universe of the play. Most
actors preferred it that way. But I liked the idea of an audience
watching. And it was not surprising, with this play. It wasn't often
that one got to see the first performance of a play four hundred
years old.

An usher appeared and propped the door open for me. Behind
him a fully-armed security guard looked me over. He was there,
I supposed, because of the Hieronomo. The usher offered me a
program and I took it. "I need to get backstage," I whispered. He
smiled. "Just go through the door by the stage," he said. "It's
easier."

Backstage I stopped and looked at the program in my hand.
The first page listed the *dramatis personae:*

THE GUISE

Pallio, Duke of Naples
Velasquo, his younger brother
Donado, a Cardinal
Sanguinetto, a Sicilian count
Orcanes
Hamond } gentlemen: followers of Donado
Mura, a priest: attendant to Donado
Ursini
Ferrando } friends to Sanguinetto
Elazar, a supposed doctor
Caropia, sister to Pallio and Velasquo
Leontia, wife to Donado, and sister to Orcanes
Carmen, servant to Caropia

Courtiers, Masquers, Officers and Guards, Pages, Seer.

Director: Eunice Bloomsman

The opposite page was almost filled by one of Bloomsman's learned program notes:

The Guise is one of the four previously lost plays in the Aylsebury Collection, twenty-four plays and hundreds of miscellaneous papers discovered in 2052. The invaluable books and manuscripts, found at Aylsebury Manor near Oxford, had been locked in a storage trunk for over three hundred years.

The copy of *The Guise* in the collection is a quarto volume, published in 1628 "by N.O. for Thomas Archer." Stage directions have been added by an unknown 17th century hand.

The text is anonymous. It was presumed that the play was by John Webster, who mentioned a work of his by the same title in the dedication to *The Devil's Law Case* (1623). But this has been questioned. Earlier references to a *Guise* play—variously spelled *The Gwuisse,* or *The Guesse* —indicate that there was probably more than one play so named. Most of these presumably concern the de Guise family, but the plot of our play was taken from an Italian novella, *Il Travestimento di Pallio.*

Critics have made cases for the authorship of Middleton, Tourneur, and Massinger. The debates continue—even the authenticity of the entire Collection has been questioned recently. While this state of uncertainty remains we at the Rose have thought it best not to attribute authorship.

This is the first Vancouver performance of *The Guise.*

It was less than I already knew from talking to Bloomsman. I had been one of many requesting a part; it had been worse than trying to get reservations to play Hamlet. Everyone who performed Jacobean drama had inquired, fascinated by the prospect of a new and unknown play. It had been a surprise when Bloomsman called and said, "You'll be Pallio."

I made my way through backstage corridors to the dressing room, found the cubicle with my name on it. My first costume— grey britches, white ruffled shirt-front, long blue coat—felt as familiar to me as my street clothes. The other costumes went on hooks. I sat down before the mirror, turned on its lights, and pulled my makeup kit from the bottom of the bag. My face was damp; the white powder stuck to it. I darkened my eyelids, exaggerated the curve of my upper lip. The sight of the stranger in the mirror, face white as a mask, quickened my pulse. I considered the many layers of his character, and played over his archaic language.

A small crystal perfume bottle rolled against my foot. I reached down, picked it up; still seated, I stuck my head around the partition separating me from the next cubicle. There was no one there. Dresses, white and scarlet and black, hung from the walls, making the cubicle seem smaller. Crystal bottles like the one in my hand reflected the blue light from the makeup mirror behind them.

Within the mirror there was movement. I turned my head and looked up at an auburn-haired actress, one I had never seen before. Her face was a narrow oval. Her eyes, grey as slate and flecked with black, surveyed me calmly. She looked into her cubicle and back, clearly framing her question. I lifted the bottle in explanation, and her mouth, which curved down sharply in repose, lifted as if propelled by the same motion, into a warm smile.

"Caropia?" I asked.

Her head turned aside. She walked past me into her cubicle without responding. A strand of her hair spiraled down; her slim back was splashed with tiny streaks of the powder that whitened her shoulders. I noticed that the grey eyes were still observing me from the mirror, and I quickly withdrew. Pallio's face mocked me in my own glass. Remember where you are, he said. . . . By and large, acting was as congenial an art form as any other; friends often performed plays together. But those of us who gravitated to the world of Jacobean tragedy were not a very communicative bunch. Strangers came in, played their parts, and went their separate ways into the city, remaining strangers to each other. The Hieronomo was one of us.

The stage set was large and uncluttered. The bedroom at the
rear had wide black staircases bracketing it, and a narrow balcony
above, so that it was deeply recessed, like a cave. I experienced
the familiar wash of *déjà vu* as I viewed it; a false one, in that I
had truly *already seen* the set, as part of the implanting. Without
that knowledge it would have been an uncanny feeling, I was
sure; but in a world of memory implants it was as common as
recollection itself. (Still, there were people addicted to the sensation. They would implant in their memory the remembrance of
a world tour and then take that very tour, in a continuous state
of *déjà vu*, pulse high, adrenaline running in their arteries. . . .)

In the large prop room directly behind the stage the director,
Eunice Bloomsman, was holding the first and final cast meeting.
Bloomsman was quite short, and very calm. Many of the players
were ignoring her, expressing the common belief among them
that directors were powerless lackeys, no more than the stage
managers of old. But they were mistaken—directors programmed the information to be implanted in the players, and that
gave them the chance to exert much subtle influence.

Bloomsman looked up at me, then continued. "All of you but
one chose minimum text, so you'll have to stay alert to keep up.
I've made the cues two and sometimes three lines long, so you'll
have plenty of warning. In case you get lost there will be prompters in the usual places.

"This play has an extraordinary history, as you know, and
there's a large audience here to see us, so let's try to do a good
job. That means an absolute ban on interpolations—agreed?"
There were nods from several. "Good. Now introduce yourselves
so you'll know who's who."

A tall man stood, dressed in the rich red robes of stage clergy.
"I'm Cardinal Donado," he said.

Two men then rose and introduced themselves as Hamond and
Orcanes, followers of Donado. I had played with them before;
they always performed together.

The actor next to them tugged at his black waistcoat and
looked about the chamber. "Sanguinetto," he said in a harsh,

low voice. I had played with him before also. He always took
the part of the most deranged villain the work had to offer,
which in revenge tragedy was saying a great deal. I had watched
him play Iago with the most chilling bitterness; and in *Edward II*
he had laughed his way through the ugly part of the murderer
Lightborn. This actor took the backstage convention of silence
to its limit, and never said anything but his lines. Between
scenes he stood wordlessly near his next entrance. This was too
much for some. Once a young actor had drawn me aside and
asked me if I thought he was the Hieronomo—I had laughed.
No, I told him, the Hieronomo always takes the part of the
hero. Besides, he always returns with a different face, and I've
seen this man before.

The others rose and identified themselves. I didn't recognize
any of them. Latecomers from the dressing room arrived, and the
diverse mix of costumes now included every color, creating a
confusion much more plausible than any coordinated costuming
could be. This was Bloomsman's idea, another of her innovations
that seemed to give the players more freedom.

When the auburn-haired actress stood, she looked directly at
me. Behind the mask of cosmetics (her mouth was a dangerous
sickle of dark red) her grey eyes seemed colorless. "Caropia," she
said. I remained expressionless, and she smiled.

Then there was a rustle and a man stepped out of a dim back
corner of the room. He was dressed in black, and his short hair
was a light, dull blond. He had thin lips, and a wide jaw that made
his face look square.

My heart was thumping rapidly. Bloomsman turned to him.
"And you are?" she inquired.

"I am Velasquo," the man said, and at that moment I felt
extreme cold, as if suddenly probability had relaxed, and all the
air had left my side of the room. Something about the man—the
turn of his nose—told me I should know him, and in my brain
thoughtless energy ran through neural corridors, struggling in
vain for recognition.

"That's very good," Bloomsman was saying. Everyone else was

attending to their appearance, each of them preparing for his or her five thousandth, ten thousandth entrance. . . . I felt isolated. "The whole cast is here. Is everyone familiar with the stage?" The question was ignored. Bloomsman pursed her lips into an expression of contempt. "Let's begin."

The curtain rose. Lights dimmed, and the audience was nothing but rows of white faces, which slowly became indistinct, like blobs of dough, then faded away in the deeper gloom. Small rustlings ended, and the little room was perfectly silent, perfectly dark.

A shaft of blue light, so faint that it first appeared to be only a seam in the blackness, gained strength and defined center stage. Into this conjuration of blue walked Velasquo, who stopped as if snared by it. He turned to face the audience, and from my vantage point at stage right I could see his sharp profile, and the light hair, now glazed blue, and a suddenly raised hand, in which a sheet of paper fluttered. He spoke, in a nasal tenor:

"This note commands me: I must have revenge!"

He read the note aloud. It was a garbled, nearly incoherent document, which informed him that his father the old Duke had been murdered, "poison'd by a spider in his bed," and exhorted him to vengeance. It made only obscure references to the identity of the killer—"What now seems finest is most ill"—and Velasquo threw it down in disgust.

He explained to the audience that his father's death had been unexpected and mysterious; it had been attributed to overeating by Elazar, a doctor of doubtful reputation. He saw now that the foul play had been obvious. Bitterly he described the corrupt court of Naples, which, under the "dull and amiable" hand of his elder brother Pallio, now the Duke, had become the plaything of riotous sycophants. Pallio was too stupid to want to search for a murderer. (I listened with great interest.) The rest of the court was too evil, and probably somehow implicated in the deed. Only his sister Caropia remained untainted. As he described the rest of us, one by one, my mind reverberated with the memory of the play, which hovered just on the edge of consciousness. Suddenly I knew the end of the play; the tangled plots that led to it were still a blank, but there were tendrils of association that linked each character with his final fate, and I saw the culmination, the vivid murders, my own death, the bloody, corpse-littered stage.

Shaken, I watched Velasquo walk toward me. I had never divined the end of the play so soon before— Velasquo raised his voice, and my attention was drawn back to him. He vowed to look for the note's author, who clearly knew more than he had written, and then search for the killer:

> "I'll seek him out—to do it I'll dissemble:
> And if there be a murderer, let him tremble."

That was my cue.

I walked on stage and an aura of blue light surrounded me. Velasquo greeted me and I replied, a bit too loudly, I thought, for the size of the room. I began concentrating, working to express naturally lines I had never spoken, doing that improvisation of stance and gesture which makes ours so much different from the acting in any previous tradition.

His eyes never leaving me, Velasquo suddenly told me of the contents of the note—"Our poor father has been most foully murdered!" My mouth fell open. "But nay," I objected, "he's dead." Velasquo ignored me and proceeded to describe the deed, in much more elaborate detail than the mysterious letter had, as if the bald mention of the crime had brought the scene up full-bloom in his imagination. At the end of the gruesome tale I said, "That's not so well done, brother!" and continued to make exclamations of shock as Velasquo listed the rest of the potential assassins at court. Finally he exhorted me to vengeance, and I eagerly agreed to help him. "I'll be your constant aid. But now, what shall we tell our holy sister?" "Nothing."

With an audible snap the stage was flooded in white and yellow light, and nearly the entire cast paraded on. Velasquo moved away from me and drifted off through the colorful throng. The Cardinal led his retinue on, and I performed my function as Duke by calling, in a clear falsetto, for order amongst the revellers. One of the Cardinal's men proposed a masque, to be held two days hence, and I gave the idea my ducal approval. At the other side of the stage Sanguinetto voiced caustic, railing asides, that were making the audience laugh; in my peripheral vision I could see their mouths opening, faint in the wash of light from the stage. The Cardinal lost several lines by speaking too soon. I had no idea what he had said, and wondered if I had been cued. It was always at this point, in the first crowd scene, that confusions were most likely to occur. . . .

Caropia entered in a white gown, holding a cross at her breast. By the obsequious gestures of the others it was clear she was revered by all. Even Sanguinetto was silent. I went to her and she held out the cross; I kissed it. Velasquo did the same, and the Cardinal bowed deeply. She went to him and they began a quick exchange that the rest of us were supposed to ignore. I remembered my blocking, voiced in Bloomsman's dry tones— "Mime dialogue with Velasquo, far stage left."

Velasquo grabbed my arm and pulled me there. I mouthed words and he stared at my forehad. His mustard-brown eyes were nearly crossed in their intensity. Again I had the overpowering sensation of *presque vu* which told me I *almost knew* him. He mouthed words and as my memory supplied his high, rasp-like voice, the sensation of recognition grew to something like panic. Abruptly he turned and began his exit, yet he looked back at me, as if in response to my inner turmoil; his head swiveled almost completely over his right shoulder. At once I knew him.

I stepped back. He squinted slightly, surprised by the move. I turned and crossed the stage, unable to face him, and halted only

when I was alone in the narrow corridor between the wings and
the prop room.

He was the Hieronomo, I was certain of it. Was he?

Hieronomo is the hero of Thomas Kyd's *The Spanish Tragedy*,
the first and most influential of English revenge dramas. In it
Hieronomo's son is killed by noblemen of the Spanish court.
Hieronomo feigns insanity to facilitate his revenge, but despair
pushes the imitation into reality, and by the time he completes
his vengeance he is mad.

Someone playing this role had apparently experienced a similar breakdown: the previous December, in a performance at the
Kean Theatre, the actor playing Hieronomo's foe, the old Duke,
had actually died, killed by a knife with a loose button-tip. By the
time this was discovered, the Hieronomo had disappeared.

In the months following he had appeared six more times, perhaps ten, depending on how many rumors you believed; each
time with a different face, and a different name, but the same
deadly blade. In *Women Beware Women*, and *Antonio's Revenge*, and
in three different *Hamlet*s, the end had been disrupted by the
villain's death. It was said that once he had stayed to finish *Hamlet*,
and had taken a round of applause before slipping away. Others
reported that another Claudius had been killed at his prayers, in
act four, providing a surprise ending; I knew that one to be true,
I had known the actor. The rest was hearsay and rumor, spreading at differing speeds through the strange community, so that
undoubtedly each of us had heard a different selection of stories,
whispered to us in dressing room or lavatory.

I was sure Velasquo was he. I scoffed at the notion, aware of
the power the new legend had gained among those who played
in these dramas. But once the suspicion had appeared, it was
impossible to expel—it was more *certainty* than suspicion, yet I
resisted it. It was as likely as not that he was just another actor,
doing an excellent job. In such company, how could I tell otherwise? How could I tell anything in this theater? I knew each player

only as his part. It was impossible to know anything for sure—
or if not, it would have to be cleverly learned.

Someone tapped my arm and I jumped. It was one of the
prompters. "You're on," he said. I hurried to the stage, afraid I
would have to ask him where we were, but the sight of Caropia,
standing alone by the bed in the inner chamber, brought the
scene to me. It was late in the act. I composed myself and walked
on.

Her slim face was a shadowed mask of contemplation, and in
the weak blue light she was nothing but modulations of grey. We
stood frozen for long moments, until white light splashed across
center stage. Then Caropia looked up. "Who's there?" she
asked. "Your brother Pallio," I said, in a lower voice than I had
used before, and then we rushed at each other and crashed together, to embrace and kiss with abandon. She bit at me, and I
pulled my head back and laughed directly at the audience, aware
of their collective gasp, which marked the pleasure of suspicions
confirmed.

We desisted and I told Caropia, with suitable contempt, how
Velasquo had come to me to confide that he suspected foul play
in our father's death. At this her mouth set in its sharp downward
curve. "You play the fool," she said, "he *is* one. Make your
Sanguinetto kill him, as you had him kill our odious father.
. . ." I explained that this was impractical, since clearly someone
at the court already knew what had happened. We had to dissem-
ble, and find that person out, before we could deal with Velasquo.
Caropia shrugged; it was my problem, I was to solve it as I would.
I reminded her that I had had the old duke killed at her instiga-
tion—she alone had feared his discovery of our incest—but the
reminder was a mistake. In harsh and dangerous tones she asked
me not to mention the matter again. I agreed, but begged her to
help me find the informer, and as she walked offstage she replied
that she would if it pleased her. Out of the audience's sight she
turned and the faintest trace of a smile lifted her mouth. She
nodded at me with approval. But I still had a short soliloquy:

"Damned bitch!" I said, "I'd kill you too did I not lust for you."
Then I looked to the audience.

"I love her as a man holds a wolf by the ears," I said, and
launched myself with vigor into the soliloquy of the villain, the
stage-Machiavel: glorying in my crimes, gleefully listing my sub-
terfuges, basking in my own cleverness, wittily seducing the audience to my side. "To lie upon my sister I have laid my father
under earth—grave crimes," I informed them, and their laughter
was an approval of sorts. I voiced the final couplet as a close
confidence:

> ". . . there's no one knows me.
> An honest simpleton still be my guise—
> Who does not seem a fool cannot be wise."

The theater blacked out and I made my way to the staccato roll
of applause. The first act was over.

I sat down on a stool just offstage and watched the second act
begin. Caropia stood before the bed. She was dressed in red, a
muted crimson with gold thread in it. In the sharp white-yellow
light it seemed the same color as her hair, and her mouth.

Sanguinetto entered from above. He stepped down soundlessly, choosing the stairs to the right. His black doublet comple-
mented black hair and beard; his face was powder-white. He
greeted her and told her of the arrival of the seer. "Does he read
dreams?" she asked, and looked pleased when Sanguinetto answered that he did.

Sanguinetto reached the stage and crossed in front of Caropia.
When he came between her and the audience it was like an
eclipse; the light shifted to blue, and when she reappeared it
seemed she was dressed in grey. Offstage in the wings opposite
me, Velasquo leaned against a wall and watched.

With contemptuous amusement, Sanguinetto was blackmailing
her. His references were vague to me; apparently he referred to
something I had missed in the first act. Something that Caropia
had done, or was doing, had been discovered by Sanguinetto.

Now he was using the information as a lever to extract sexual favors. "Thy painted visage will be naught but candied flesh," he told her, "if you lie not with me." He circled her briskly and balked her attempts to turn her back on him. She tried to forestall him by denying his accusation, but he ran his hand over her hair and mocked her; and slowly, bitterly, she acquiesced.

As they moved back to the bed, continuing the macabre dance of thrust and parry, I marveled at their skill, at the absolute verisimilitude of their every movement and intonation. This was acting of the highest order; it was impossible for me to imagine them as anyone but Caropia and Sanguinetto.

Velasquo watched the scene without expression.

With Sanguinetto's hand at her throat, Caropia sank back on the bed. The lights dimmed with her descent and the theater was black before Sanguinetto joined her.

I sat in the dark, and considered tests.

I was startled to attention by my cue lines. The next scene had already begun. I strode on stage and spoke to the audience:

"O excellent! By that he'll conquer Rome!"

The audience roared. I had no idea what I had referred to, having forgotten the cue. I retreated to the left staircase, in my confusion aware only of my blocking.

More characters arrived and the scene became complex. Everyone was involved in the central event (which I had not yet deciphered), but many were making covert conversation, or uttering malicious asides. The Cardinal spoke, and suddenly I understood the import of the scene: he was asking Caropia to take holy orders, to become a nun. He persisted with an icy calm that I couldn't interpret, and her refusals became increasingly strident. Sanguinetto, Hamond and Orcanes, Ferrando and Ursini, all publicly encouraged her while privately vilifying her. Only Velasquo actually meant his praise. I could see the dim white faces of the audience breaking into laughter, and I felt Caropia's humilia-

tion keenly. We could make her comic for the rest of the play, if
we wanted to (I recalled once playing in a *Revenger's Tragedy* in
which the cast had nearly killed themselves with mirth). Finally
my cue lines arrived and it was easy for me to feign Pallio's anger:

> "They that mock her soon will lie in heaps
> Of rotting flesh, all broken open to
> The sun and flies and maggots,
> And their half-empty eye sockets will stare
> At naught but Pallio, astonish'd still by his
> Abrupt revenge . . ."

The scene continued, but the laughter was greatly diminished.

Velasquo grasped me by the arm. "Brother, I must speak to
you anon," he said, staring at me curiously. I agreed, averting my
gaze, and he slipped offstage behind me, leaving me with my
heart knocking. He would have to be tested. . . .

Now Caropia approached me, ostensibly to consult in private
about the question of holy orders. She drew me out on the apron
just above the audience, and in a voice tight with rage demanded
that I kill Sanguinetto. I asked why, and she told me a near-truth,
the best sort of lie; Sanguinetto was blackmailing her, demanding
sexual favors in exchange for silence concerning *my* guilt in the
old duke's death. I reacted with a lover's anger, and as I railed
against Sanguinetto she stroked my arm, the softness of her
hands belying the absolute implacability of her intentions.

She left with a last velvet command, and I found myself alone
—the rest had exited during our dialogue. Blue light surrounded
me, as tangible as if the gel covering the bulb had poured down
into the cone of light. I collected myself and tried to project an
assured, amused control:

> "The brother that I hate, and the sister
> That I hate and love (for there's
> Two feelings closer each to other than
> The minds of any pair of us) both press
> Me now like halves of a garotte,

Yet I'll slip out and let them gnash together;
I have a plot—yet soft—Velasquo—"

He entered. My back to him, and face to the audience, I let my features slacken into those of the Pallio he knew. There was laughter, and with a sudden leer I encouraged it, for it was directed at Velasquo. I turned and greeted him. He began by complaining that he had found no clue to the murderer's identity. I informed him that I had some news that might help him, then answered his questions so foolishly that it took him some time to deduce that if Sanguinetto kept spiders, and was blackmailing Caropia, he must indeed be the villain we were searching for. I expressed amazement at his intelligence.

While the audience laughed at my duplicity, Velasquo's face darkened, his jaw muscles bunched. The laughter died away completely before he spoke: "I'd have this be vengeance all will remember," he said, in a voice so harsh that it enforced belief, made one wonder, with squeamish anticipation, what forms revenge might take. . . . He spoke no more of it, however, which made me suspect he was omitting lines; he sent me on my way, then stalked aimlessly around the stage. Suddenly he stopped and laughed, first quietly, then in a sharp howl. In the midst of this nerve-shattering mirth the blackout snapped down and terminated both light and sound.

I was conscious of a plan that had formulated itself sometime during Velasquo's ominous drunkard's walk. I had a test, one that would leave me concealed; he would know he had been tested, of course—it was an unusual test that did not reveal that—but he would not know by whom.

In the prop room Ferrando and Ursini were running over an exchange of dialogue in double-time. A prompter at the rear entrance raised a hand; they filed on, allowing two brief bursts of yellow into the dark, grainy green of the room. I went to the prop table and casually scanned the small pile of stage-notes.

The top one was the one that would betray Pallio. I picked it up, and, holding it against me, went into the lavatory. Inside a stall I took a pencil stub from my vest pocket (my ribs were sticky with sweat), and flattened the vellum against the wall with my other hand. In a clumsy, rounded imitation of Bloomsman's Italianate lettering, I listed all the plays I had ever heard connected with the Hieronomo:

> *The Spanish Tragedy*
> *Hamlet*
> *Hamlet, Act Four*
> *Antonio's Revenge*
> *Women Beware Women*
> *The Atheist's Tragedy*

I couldn't think of a fully appropriate tag, and so finally added *manet alta mente repostum*; it remains deep in my mind. That would do.

I had just quietly replaced the note, and was turning from the prop table, when Sanguinetto appeared from the left hallway. He watched me as he picked up the sheet of vellum and put it inside his black doublet; I couldn't tell if he had seen me return it or not. His beard, rising almost to his eyes, hid all expression, and his steady stare revealed nothing but interest. He went to the curtained opening and paused for a moment. He pushed the curtain aside, allowing blue light to wash over him, and made his final entrance.

From the rear I could see only a portion of center stage, and I feared Velasquo would be out of my sight at the crucial moment, aborting the test and leaving me with my uncertainties. Hastily I made my way through the dark to stage right, to the vantage point where I had observed most of the play.

Caropia was there; noticing my appearance, she gestured me to her and with a lift of her head directed my attention to the stage. I stood beside her and looked out, feeling her hand's pressure against my arm.

Velasquo was in disguise, wearing a black hooded cape. He was establishing his credentials—he was, he said to Sanguinetto, Pinon d'Alsquove, a fellow-Sicilian, who had been forced to flee their native island because he had unfortunately murdered a gentleman of importance. Sanguinetto accepted this, exhibiting the usual Jacobean inability to see through even the simplest of disguises. They seated themselves at a dining table set out on the apron, and proceeded to drink and regale each other with tales. Strange revelers they were, both dressed in black, presented in a brilliant white-violet light that illuminated every face in the audience. They traded bloody stories, and it became clear that Pinon d'Alsquove had much in common with his fellow-country-man. (There was a certain logic to this Jacobean thinking: since all Italians were depraved, it made sense that the farther south one went, the worse they became.) The crime that caused Pinon's exile had been the last in a long and gruesome series. Sanguinetto became unnaturally gay as Pinon described the various methods he had used to dispatch his enemies back in Sicily, and they quickly finished a tall, slim bottle of wine. As Sanguinetto uncorked another one Pinon spoke to the audience, in Velasquo's high voice: "In midst of all his mirth he will meet death." Then they were roaring with laughter again, at the champagne cascading from the bottle Sanguinetto held in his lap. As he drank and bit huge chunks from a turkey leg, Pinon described one of his weapons:

> ". . . a most ingenious toy,
> A tiny spring with rapier-pointed ends,
> Held tight by threads of lightest leather; which
> Then hidden in thy victim's food, and ate,
> The threads are quick digested, and the spring
> Jumps to its fullest length, ripping great holes
> Within thy rival's guts. Thus do Moors
> Kill dogs . . ."

Sanguinetto chewed on obliviously, and everyone in the theater watched him eat. "Aye," Pinon concluded,

> "Methinks I know all of the finest ways
> To end th' existence of a foe—"

Sanguinetto swallowed and struggled to his feet. He leaned over Pinon:

> "Thou say'st not a way that should be known
> To all Sicilians—I will show thee."

He hurried to the rear exit in long strides, knocked the curtain aside and disappeared. Pinon spoke in Velasquo's voice:

> "Now I suspect I've drawn him out like snail
> From shell, into the light where I may crush him."

Sanguinetto reappeared, holding at arm's length a tall glass box, like a candle-lantern. Within it a thick-bodied, long-legged spider—a cane spider, I guessed—scrabbled up the walls and slid down again. Pinon leaped up, knocking his chair over. Sanguinetto pointed at the spider and leered proudly.

> "This spider's of a kind known but in Sicily.
> 'Tis said they come out of the sides
> Of fiery Aetna, as if escaped from hell.
> They live i' the fumes, feed on the fruit that's killed
> By ash, and are most poisonous."

"Tell me," Pinon said, his voice rising uncontrollably up to Velasquo's high tenor,

> ". . . might I buy that beauty
> From thee? I have a murder would be done
> Most fitting thus, most artful . . ."

Sanguinetto considered it, cocking his head drunkenly to one side.

> "I've more of these, they breed by hundreds—aye.
> Done, if you pay me well enough."

Pinon: "I'll pay you."

They made the exchange, Sanguinetto accepting a small pouch. He looked in it and grinned. Pinon was staring with an intense frown at the spider within the glass. Sanguinetto returned to the table and sat down, his back to Velasquo.

Sanguin: "We'll celebrate this sale with more revelry."
Pinon: "Indeed it is a glad occasion."
Sanguin: "I give you my assurance, the man
            You set that tiny demon on will die
            Most painful—"

Pinon: "You'd know best, I'm certain . . ."

Now Pinon was standing right behind Sanguinetto, caped arms high so that he appeared a huge shadow, holding the glass box directly over the seated man's head. (Caropia's fingers were digging into my arm.) The spider's legs struck at the glass soundlessly. Sanguinetto reached forward and grabbed the foam-streaked bottle, raised it to his lips, tilted his head back; they froze:

Pinon pulled the floor of the box away and the spider dropped onto Sanguinetto's face. He struck at it with his free hand and it jumped to the table. As it skittered across, he smashed the bottle on it, scattering green glass everywhere. He staggered to his feet and arched back; his scream and Velasquo's high staccato laugh began simultaneously. The laughter continued longer.

On the table three or four spindly legs flailed at the air, their fine articulation destroyed. With stiff, awkward movements, Sanguinetto pulled his dagger from his belt and stabbed at the legs of the beast until they were still. He left the dagger in the table and collapsed over his chair. His voice, guttural as a rasp over metal, rose from near the floor.

        "Stranger, I would thy heart were that black corse
        Upon the table: surely it resembles nothing closer.
        You had no cause to murder me . . ."

Velasquo pushed the hood from his head, and his face, gleaming with sweat, suffused with exhilaration, shifted as he looked about the room. He circled the table, leaning over Sanguinetto to shout at him, interspersing his lines with bursts of strained laughter:

> "I did have cause; I am Velasquo, see you?
> My father's murder made me seek revenge!
> You murdered him, 'gainst you I had revenge!
> Now all that's sweet is nothing to revenge!"

"Wrong," croaked Sanguinetto.

> ". . . As well might I commend myself
> For vengeance 'gainst you, having killed that spider,
> As you to gloat o'er me, who was no more
> Than insect used to slay your father—"

Vel: "What's this?"

Sanguin: "I was hired, hired by Pallio—here's my commission—"

He pulled the note from his doublet and tossed it on the floor, then twisted as spasms racked him.

> "A cauldron churns and bubbles within my skull—
> I see hell waiting; Death will have its fill—"

After a while he moved no more.

Velasquo kneeled at the sheet of vellum, smoothed it on his leg, read. I could feel my heart knocking at the back of my throat—

His head snapped up, his eyes, ablaze with a vicious, yellow intensity, searched from exit to exit, *looking at actors:* his expression was absolutely murderous. I wanted to flatten myself against the wall, to hide; it was difficult indeed to stand beside Caropia and feign unconcerned interest. For *his* was no acting, he had understood, he was the Hieronomo! I felt a surge of relief at the certainty of it, replaced by fear when I recalled what I was certain of. I was in mortal danger. But I *knew.*

Finally he broke the silence, in a voice that filled the room like cold air.

> "Pallio. Pallio, the simpleton, the fool.
> That mask conceal'd a parricide most cruel.
> Though first deceiv'd by his quick cloak of lies—"

He paused then, so that the next line would contain his private reference, unaware how accurate it already was:

> "I'll use his blood to wash away *his* guise."

The blackout allowed me to flee to my cubicle.

Act four began, and with it the gradual acceleration and disintegration typical of revenge tragedy. Plots skipped and jumped and ran afoul of each other, twisting without evident logic to their conclusion; characters died. . . . From my cubicle I listened to the first scenes emerging tinnily from a speaker placed in the partition. Leontia, the Cardinal's wife, whom I hadn't seen since before the play began, was being strangled by the Cardinal's men. The Cardinal entreated Caropia to leave Naples, and, perfectly aware of the danger at the court, she agreed. I felt pained at that; foolishly, I had hoped we would remain lovers until the end. Caropia was then confronted by Carmen, her maid, who had been eavesdropping. Carmen demanded payment to keep her from informing me of the Cardinal's plan—I laughed at that—it was a strange world we existed in, where some plotted against others, who listened as they did it. Caropia agreed, and then promptly poisoned her. The maid's screams brought guards, and the doctor Elazar, who declared it a natural death. He too had blackmail in mind, and after the guards left, Caropia was forced to stab him and hide his body under the bed.

I stopped listening, and attempted to decide what I should do next. Nothing occurred to me. *Nothing,* I thought, remembering with disgust the century or two of experience I had to draw on: I recalled canoeing down the Amazon, fighting in the streets of

New York, a thousand other like events . . .

But what I actually had done was difficult to distinguish from all the things I remembered doing. All I was sure of was that I had spent a lot of time in a chair, living in words; and on stages. It was as if I were driving a vehicle, and the rear-view mirror had expanded to fill the windshield. Or as if I were the Angel of Time, flying backward into the future! Metaphors came up to me like bowling balls out of an automatic return; but no plans, nothing like a decision. Who was I to decide? Who was I?

"Pallio," said the speaker loudly. It was a prompter, calling for me. I returned to the prop room, reluctant to take to the stage again. I could no longer remember what attraction I had ever had to it.

Bloomsman herself waved at me: I was on. I stepped out upon a dark stage. There was just enough grainy, purple light leaking down to enable me to perceive the silhouettes of three men, pulling something from beneath the bed. Something about the scene—the lithe, long-limbed black figures, crouching—lacked all familiarity—*jamais vu* swept over me like nausea. I no longer understood what I saw. The dark room was a dimensionless field, and the black figures were nameless objects, ominous because they moved. Meaningless sounds rang in my ears.

I came to and found myself confronted by Ferrando and Ursini, on a brightly lit apron. Their blades were out and pointed at my throat. My first thought was that I'd left my epée in my costume bag, and was defenseless; then synapses fired, for what reason I knew not, and my lines came to me. I was safe from them.

They accused me of Sanguinetto's murder, and in a rather weak imitation of the ingenuous public Pallio I informed them that Velasquo had been the last person seen with their late master. With trembling voice I quickly shifted their suspicions to Velasquo, feeling thankful that it made sense to play Pallio as a distracted man. I left the stage, and then had to watch while Velasquo surprised them and knifed them both in the back. He did it with a verve and accuracy that left me chilled; surely their

improvised blocking couldn't be so well-done: had he begun
already? But in the darkness between scenes Ferrando and Ursini
brushed by me, muttering and giggling together. I shook my
head in hopes of clearing it, inhaled sharply, and moved back
onstage.

Again the light was a deep crevasse-blue. Caropia was already
there: we embraced. This was to be one of our last scenes together, I knew. Surely everyone knew. I moved to the apron and
saw below me, in the front row, Ferrando, Ursini, Elazar, Carmen, Leontia, and Sanguinetto. It was the custom for actors
whose work was done to join the audience, but it made me uncomfortable. Given the traditions of the genre it always seemed
to me that they were still in the play as ghosts, who might speak
at any time. I resisted the impulse to move to the other side of
the apron.

My attention shifted back to Caropia. In her slim face the
pebble-grey eyes were large, and filled with pain. I had so many
disparate images of her to link . . . and yet, within the play and
without, I knew nothing real about her. Our backstage silence
augmented the Jacobean notion that the other sex was unknow-
able, a different species, an alien intelligence. Still, watching her
bowed head, her slender arms moving nervously, I felt Pallio's
emotions as my own, and I wanted to break into the play and
experience that incestuous closeness. I spoke, infusing my lines
with all these illusory feelings, to the invisible actress inside her,
the one who made them both a mystery. I spoke tenderly of our
love, and lamented our situation: "We are so far in blood . . ."
" 'Tis payment," Caropia cried, and railed against the sequence
of unchangeable events she found herself trapped in. Bitterly she
blamed our incest: "Our sin of lust has webbed these plots
around us, so I've dreamt—" I interrupted:

> "Why shouldst thou not love best the one known best?
> It is no crime, and were it, it has gain'd
> Us more than lost . . ."

She spoke of the church and we argued religion. Finally I interrupted again:

> "In this world all are quite alone,
> All efforts grasp for union. Who's succeeded
> More than thou and I? We shar'd the womb,
> The universe of childhood; lov'd
> As lovers in the lust of youth—"

And Caropia, thinking no doubt of her pact with the Cardinal, replied:

> "Thou know'st me well as one can know another."

I smiled, a tremendous effort, and continued:

> "Thus be calm—thy dreams are naught but visions
> Of thine other self, beheld while in
> The timeless void of sleep. We've fears enough
> In this world."

I turned from her and the tone of reassurance left me. I voiced my real concern:

> "... I fear Velasquo's
> Found me out; his eyes shout 'murderer'
> With all the brutal energy of horror.
> He greets me mornings, dines with me at noon,
> And stalks the palace grounds at night,
> As if he were a hungry wolf, and I
> A man alone on the trackless waste—"

Velasquo entered, several lines too early. Unable to finish in his presence, I moved to the other side of the apron and returned his baleful glare. Below me Sanguinetto was smiling.

There was silence. It was the first time the three of us had been on stage by ourselves, and the triangle we formed was the focus of all the tension we had managed to create. Beneath our polite exchange (Velasquo was inquiring if Caropia would accompany him to the masque), were layers of meaning: the reality of the play, the reality of the players ... Velasquo's crafted jests probed at me with an intensity I alone could understand, although all that he did made perfect sense in the context of the play; indeed it must have appeared that he was doing a superb job. Only small stresses in his intonation revealed the danger, like swirls in a river, indicating swift undercurrents. I replied with a brittle hostility that had little acting in it, and we snapped at each other like the two poles of a Jacob's ladder:

Pallio: "She goes with me, keep you away from her—"

Velasquo: "Would you be kicked?"

Pallio: "Would you have your neck broke?"

The audience's silence was a measure of their absorption. Despite my earlier revulsion, and the blank nausea of the *jamais vu,* I felt growing within me, insidiously, the pleasure of acting, the chill tingling one feels when a scene is going very well.

This pleasure in the scene's success was soon overwhelmed by the fear which was making it succeed; Velasquo's thinly veiled attack was strengthening. His pale eyes glared at me intently, looking for some involuntary movement or expression that would show me to be the one who had recognized him. I struggled to keep only Pallio's wariness on my face, but it was a delicate distinction, one becoming more and more difficult to make. . . . I exited to the sound of his high laughter.

Once off, I hurried around toward the dressing room. Caropia's was the only voice emerging from the wall-speakers in the narrow corridor, and footsteps were padding behind me. I almost ran, remembering the early death in *Hamlet.* But it was only the Cardinal, completing errands of his own.

The dressing room was momentarily empty. I took my epée from my costume bag and once again locked myself in a lavatory stall. The steel of the blade gleamed as I pulled away the leather scabbard.

It was an old epée, once used in competitive electric fencing. I had polished the half-sphere bell, and removed the plug socket

from inside it, to convert it to a theater sword. The wire running
down a slot in the blade was still there, as was the tip, a small
spring-loaded cylinder. The blade was stiff, and curved down
slightly. At the bell it was triangular in cross-section, a short,
wide-based triangle, with the base uppermost. It narrowed to a
short cylindrical section at the end, which screwed into the tip.

I tried to unscrew the tip, certain that what I was doing was not
real, that I was acting for myself. Surely the thing to do was to
stop the play (I winced) and proclaim Velasquo's identity to all.
Or to slip away, out the back, and escape him entirely.

Yet naming him before all would not do—where was my proof?
Even my own conviction was shaken by the question of evidence.
There wasn't any. The first real *proof* I would get would be a
sudden hard lunge for my throat, with a sharp blade. . . .

The tip wouldn't unscrew. I twisted until my fingers and hands
were imprinted with red bars and semicircles, but it felt as if tip
and blade were a solid piece. I clamped the tip between two
molars and turned, but succeeded only in hurting my teeth. I
needed pliers. I stared at the tip.

And if I were to escape, the Hieronomo would also. Surgery
would change his face and voice, and he would return. I knew that
in that case I would never be able to perform again without
wondering if it were he again, playing opposite me . . .

I put the tip on the floor under my boot sole. Holding it flat
against the floor, I pulled up on the blade. When I lifted my foot,
the tip stuck out at right angles from the blade. I put it back on
the floor, and carefully stepped on the new bend until it was
straight again. I repeated the operation delicately; I knew, from
years of fencing, how easily the blades would snap. Presently
there appeared behind the tip a ripple, a weak spot that would
break when struck hard enough. I slipped the scabbard back on,
satisfied that the epée could be swiftly transformed into a weapon
that would kill.

At some level unknown to me I had decided. I left the stall and
stared at the white face in the mirror, feeling a stranger to myself.

Back in the dressing room, Caropia and Velasquo were in earnest conference. When they saw me, Caropia returned to her cubicle and Velasquo, looking angry, crossed to the other side of the room.

I sat down beside Caropia and listened to the speaker above us. The Cardinal was arranging, with whom I could not tell, to have Hamond and Orcanes poisoned at the masque. Apparently the masque was to take place very soon. As I changed my coat I could feel my pulse throbbing in my arms.

"Disguise," said a voice in my ear. I jumped and turned to see Velasquo, his square face set close to mine.

"It's an odd word," he continued. "Shouldn't it be enguise, or beguise? Doesn't *dis*guise imply the opposite of what you want it to mean?"

I stared at him, in an agony of apprehension that he might go on, that he might reveal (disguise?) himself openly, and dare me to act—"*Dis* can also be used to intensify a verb," I finally stammered.

"You are disguised," he said, and scrutinized me closely. Then he walked away.

In my brain a chemical typhoon whirled. The exchange had been so—dramatic . . . suddenly I was stunned by the horrible suspicion that all our words were lines, all the events backstage part of a larger play . . . Bloomsman, Bloomsman . . . By coincidence (or perhaps not) Caropia appeared to sense this thought. She stuck her head around the partition and said, with a sardonic smile, "You learnt it of no fencer to shake thus," a line from a play that I myself had once spoken. I picked up my epée and strode away in agitation, all my certainties shattered.

Caropia caught up with me just outside the prop room, and touched my hand. I watched her and tried to conceal the fact that I was still trembling. She smiled and slipped her arm under mine. The archaic gesture seemed fraught with emotion. For the first time I understood that it was not just another dominant/submis-

sive signal from the past, that it had been able to express one
human's support for another. My confusion lessened. One way
or other I would know, soon enough.

The prop room was filled with actors getting ready for the
masque. Bloomsman had done her usual meticulous prop work;
the masks were bright animal heads that covered one to the
shoulders. A menagerie composed chiefly of pigs, tigers, and
horses, we stared at each other and whispered with excitement.
Bloomsman handed us our masks and smiled—a smile that now
seemed to be filled with ominous possibility. "It's going fine,"
she said. "Let's do this last scene right." She put on a mask
herself, a remorselessly grinning gargoyle.

I looked at my mask: a red fox. I could guess what Velasquo's
would be. Caropia's was an exact model of her own head, with
holes cut out for her eyes and mouth. The result, once on, was
grotesque. She looked in a wall-mirror and laughed. "I'm animal
enough already," she said. The gargoyle shrugged and said, in
Bloomsman's calm voice, "I thought it the right thing."

Velasquo was already on stage, announcing his plans to the
audience. Somehow he had learned of the relationship between
Caropia and me. Long after everyone else in the theater, he had
seen through her guise. His desire for vengeance now focused as
much on her as me. She was to die of poison placed in her
drinking cup. Beside me, she watched the cup, still on the prop
table, and shivered. I felt fear for her then, and great affection,
and heedlessly I whispered to her, "Don't drink from it."

She stared at me, and began to laugh. But I did not and she
stopped. Her grey eyes surveyed me and slowly widened, as if in
fear of me. "I won't," she whispered in a soothing voice. She
disengaged her arm and moved away, glancing back once with an
expression I could not read, but which could have been one of
. . . terror.

The stage was divided by two long tables, both laden with silver
and gold, fruits and meat, candles and flasks of liqueurs. As the

stage filled with masquers, servants—in masks that were faceless
white blanks—continued to load the tables. The fantastic menagerie milled about, slowly and randomly seating themselves. Lines
were shouted simultaneously, creating a cacophony that could
only have been Bloomsman's doing.

I stood behind Caropia, at one end of the front table, peering
through the eyeholes of my fox-face in search of Velasquo. My
black, shiny nose protruded far before me. I saw that the Cardinal
was not masked—he was still in his red robes, but a papal coronet
was tilted back on his head. He viewed the uproar with an indul-
gent smile. Around him goats in formal dress drank wine.

My eye was caught by a movement above. A tall figure dressed
in black leaned over the balcony and observed the activity; his
mask was a skull. I glanced into the audience, and the backwash
from the multicolored glare was enough illumination to confirm
my suspicion. Sanguinetto was gone. It was he on the balcony,
playing the medieval death-figure. He began to descend the
stairs, pausing for several seconds after each step.

The masque gained energy. A plate piled high with meat was
tipped over; people rose from their seats, shouting witticisms. A
long body of glittering red liquid flashed through the air and
drenched one of the Cardinal's goats. There was still no sign of
Velasquo. An orange-fight started between tables, and the noise
reached a frantic pitch, timed by the metronome of Sanguinetto's
steps. Two women, both with tiger masks, began to claw at each
other.

At the height of the cacophony a long scream cut through the
sound, making its ragged descant. When it ended there was silence and the company was still, forming a bizarre tableau. A man
with a pig's head and red doublet staggered to the apron. He tore
at his snout and pulled the mask off, to reveal Orcanes. His face
was bloated and purple. He clutched his throat, sank to his knees.
As he collapsed another scream ripped the air. Another player,
also in pig mask, fell to the floor and drummed out his death.
Sanguinetto, now on the stage, paced between tables.

The Cardinal stood, his face grim. "Who can account for these untimely deaths?" he demanded.

"Pallio," a voice behind me called. I spun around and saw the wolf's face, fangs protruding, yellow eyes agleam. I tore off my mask and stepped back to increase the distance between us.

"Who is this man?" I asked, my voice preternaturally calm. "He must be mad."

"Your brother I," he said, and pulled off his mask. "Velasquo."

"Velasquo!" I cried, and spoke to the Cardinal:

> "Why, he kill'd Sanguinetto, Ferrando
> And Ursini; yea, perhaps the old Duke too.
> These new deaths without doubt are also his devise—"

Velasquo: "He's false; he is the murd'rer of our father.
> Here's proof—"

Velasquo threw Sanguinetto's note down. I picked it up and looked at it. Penciled beneath my Latin tag, in a fine imitation of Bloomsman's hand, was another title: *The Guise.* Proof indeed.

I crumpled the sheet and tossed it to the floor. "A forgery," I said, voice still calm. "He tries usurping me."

I pulled my epée from my scabbard. Velasquo did the same. The company drew back, pulling the front table with them to make room. The Cardinal made his way forward. Sanguinetto stood beside him. The two of them linked arms, and the Cardinal spoke:

> "The truth is in Fate's hands. Let them fence."

And in my mind I heard the blocking instruction, in Bloomsman's dry voice: "Fence."

Finally, finally the light became red, a bright crimson glare that bathed us both in blood. We circled each other warily. I watched his wrist, his stance, and in my concentration the world contracted to the two of us. Adrenaline flooded through me and my pulse was triphammer fast.

His blade had a tip on it, but that meant nothing; I knew it would slide back on contact, releasing the sharp point. The Hieronomo had used it before.

We began tentatively. He lunged, I parried, and we established a simple parry-riposte pattern, often used in practice, at very high speed. The flashing blades and the rapid clicking of clean parries were highly dramatic, but meant little.

After a short pause to regain balance, Velasquo lunged again, more fully this time, and we bouted with increased speed, using the full variety of tactics. The scrape and ring of steel against steel, the wooden thumping of our footwork, our hoarse breathing were the only sounds in the theater.

The exchange ended and we stared at each other, breathing heavily. A wrinkle of concentration appeared between his eyes. I was sure he now realized that my knowledge of fencing was not implanted, that it was learned from actual experience. Implanted fencing was adequate for theatrics, but it consisted entirely of conscious moves and strategies, it was a verbal memory. Fencing learned by experience was remembered to a large extent in the cerebellum, where movement and balance are controlled, and thus reactions were nearly reflex-fast. Velasquo was certainly aware of this, and now he knew that he had been discovered by someone capable of besting him.

Suddenly he lunged with great violence. The thrust avoided my parry and I had to leap back to dodge his blade. The real fight had begun. He lunged in straightforward attacks that were easy enough to parry, but when I did so he remised, continued to attack. He was ignoring my tipped weapon, which was clearly harmless. When I understood this, I jumped back and slapped my epée against the floor. The tip stayed on. I had to retreat and parry for my life, watching nothing but his blade, and striking it aside desperately each time it thrust at me.

My heel hit the bottom of the left stairway and I nearly stumbled. I stepped up backward, and Velasquo followed, negating my height advantage with the energy of his attack. I turned and ran up to the balcony, swinging my epée against the bannister all the way. The tip stayed on. I turned and lunged fiercely at my pursuer. He halted, lead foot three steps above his hind foot, and we engaged in a grim slashing battle, as if we were fighting with sabers. I didn't want him to reach the balcony. It was hopeless; still unafraid of my epée, he drove me back by degrees and managed, step by step, to make his way up to my level. When he reached the balcony I turned and sprinted down the other staircase four steps at a time, spinning and slashing once to impede his pursuit, and slamming my blade viciously against the side wall all the way down.

When I got to the stage, I saw that my tip had snapped off and disappeared. Exultantly I turned, parried Velasquo's running attack, and riposted straight at his chest. He leaped to one side to avoid the thrust. Several feet separated us; we stood panting.

He saw the change in my blade, invisible from more than a few feet away, and his expression became one of alarm—the idea struck him, perhaps, that tonight we had reversed roles; tonight I had become the Hieronomo. He looked up to my face, and I smiled.

Instinctively he lunged and in a fury of desperate motion drove me back across the stage. But now we were armed evenly, he had to respect my blade, and I wasn't forced to retreat for long. We battled with a sweaty, intense, total concentration.

He stopped and our blades circled each other: mine jagged and blunt, but slender; his still tipped by the treacherous false button. He started a complicated, deceptive attack. I stole the offensive from him with a stop thrust, lunged for his chest and hit just below the sternum. Amazingly, the blade did not bend and push my hand back, as it always had before: *it slid right in.*

Velasquo dropped his epée, stumbled back and fell, tugging free of my blade. I lifted it; the steel was streaked with blood, unnaturally red in the light. It dripped like water. Velasquo rolled onto his belly.

I looked up and surveyed the stage. Most of the cast had moved into the wings, which were blocked.

Caropia stepped forward, her tall cup still in her hands. Her

eyes and mouth were black holes in a face as white as the mask
she had long since removed. She appeared confused, but spoke
her lines nevertheless, in a dry, airy voice:

> "There lies he, chok'd in his own blood,
> A ravenous wolf whom all the world thought good."

Velasquo rolled over. Caropia's cup toppled to the floor. Sanguinetto, his mask still on, stepped toward me. I swung my epée
in his direction and he stopped. I walked toward the rear exit,
keeping the blade pointed at him.

Above me on the balcony, the gargoyle waved an arm, and the
curtain jerked downward. The audience leaped to their feet, and
I thought *They're after me, I'm caught;* but they were clapping,
cheering, it was an ovation—the gargoyle bowed—I fled.

An unfamiliar door in the dressing room gave me access to a
dark storage room. I crossed it, entered another hallway. It
turned and almost immediately I was lost, running without plan
down hallways and through dark rooms. Muffled shouts of pursuit reverberated through the walls from time to time, spurring
me on. I tried to work my way in a single direction. A short set
of stairs led me up to a little closet theater, stage no bigger than
a sitting room. Hearing voices backstage, I crouched down between two rows of seats. I looked through the slot between two
seat backs and watched a red-coated guard, one of the extras
from our play, run on stage and halt. I held my breath. He
surveyed the room quickly, then left as quickly as he had entered.
The voices receded like echoes and I got up and ran again, out
the back of the theater.

I was in a long white hallway with a very high ceiling. Green
light poured from long strips in the wall. To my left, at the end
of the hall, was a door. I ran for it. As I approached I saw words
printed on the door, above the horizontal bar that opened it:
EMERGENCY EXIT—ALARM WILL SOUND.

The moment I comprehended the words, the dry, ineffable
presence of *déjà vu* filled me: *this had happened before.* In a flash I

knew everything, I understood all that had occurred in the theater, it stood before me in my mind like a crystalline sphere. But just as quickly the entire matrix of thought collapsed, leaving no trace except the memory of its existence: *presque vu,* almost seen.

I slammed into the bar crossing the door, and it flew open. To the sharp blast of a siren I leaped out into the chill air, and back into the world.

Arcs & Secants

JOHN VARLEY ("Lollipop and the Tar Baby") has written and sold a novel and more than twenty stories since he began in 1974. He lives in Eugene, Oregon, with his wife, three children, several dogs, and an opossum named Raspberry. This is his second story for *Orbit.*

Persons who are curious about what goes on at the Clarion Workshop in East Lansing, Michigan, may get a partial clue from a letter we wrote to an ex-Clarionite in 1975: "We had a good group at Clarion this year—Katie bought eight stories for the anthology. Lenny [Dr. Leonard N. Isaacs] took a water gun away from a student and stomped it into pieces no larger than 1 mm²."

KATE WILHELM ("State of Grace") has appeared in every *Orbit* but two. A collection of her stories, *The Infinity Box,* was published by Harper & Row in 1976.

We wrote to Craig Strete, the author of "Who Was the First Oscar to Win a Negro?" *(Orbit 18),* "I showed your bio thing to a professor of linguistics at Clarion, and he said he thought it was a put-on, I forget whether it was because of the capital letters or the *b*'s and *p*'s, or what. I was afraid to run the whole thing in Arcs & Secants because it might be obscene or libelous, but I did run parts of it—probably the obscene & libelous parts. It blends in pretty well."

GENE WOLFE ("Many Mansions" and "To the Dark Tower Came") wrote on Boxing Day, 1975, "When I was a very little boy, at the beginning of the dark ages, I used to memorize all the rules and regulations in the stories that were read to me. I knew with a divine perfection of knowledge that if I were given a mysterious box and told not to open it I should not open it; I knew that whenever I discovered a corpse in a private library I ought on no account to get my fingerprints on the gun; I knew that the foreman of any ranch owned by a pretty girl (that was what we called them then—the charming creatures are extinct now) was a man to be wary of. . . .

"The realities are something else again. The realities are two hundred and ninety-three sheets of paper lying beside my typewriter, the aggregation making up perhaps one third of a novel in which it is possible next to no one will be interested. People (so I imagine) are already beginning to ask one another, 'What is Wolfe doing? Has he dropped out?' 'Writes mostly for *New York,* I think.' 'Not him, the other one.' 'Oh, *him.* He died back in the thirties.' "

We wrote to a writer we esteem, "You have two terrible habits which you should discontinue instantly, even if it takes self-flagellation or aversion therapy. One is using an apostrophe for a French accent (an accent leans left or right; an apostrophe is neither one nor the other, & just gets in the way when the copyeditor has to correct it); the other is using an *X* to delete letters. No copyeditor is going to believe that a printer is bright enough not to set that *X;* so he's got to cross out your mark and add the correct one, making a real mess in the process. No marks at all would be better than wrongo marks."

FELIX C. GOTSCHALK ("The Veil Over the River") told us recently, "I'm about half through a Southern gothic, and the story is told by the hero, who is 100 years old. The tennis bug has hooked me, I've been playing daily, and have a 137 mph service, and an 8% first-serve accuracy. The coach has been discouraging my cannonball service, but I think he is just jealous. I have lost interest in cars, but big money would revive that."

We wrote to Brian Aldiss in September, "Thank you for your letter after [James Blish's] death. I've only been to two funerals in my life; after the second I was so outraged that I wrote an essay suggesting an alternate procedure. . . . The bastards had made the corpse up like a Byzantine whore, and the preacher alluded to Jesus in favorable terms but had nothing to say about the deceased. My idea in brief was that the remains ought to be cremated without ceremony, & then the guy's friends ought to get together of an evening, drink wine and eat bread & cheese, and remember what a good old boy he was."

R. A. LAFFERTY ("Fall of Pebble-Stones"), one of our favorite authors, first appeared in *Orbit* in 1967, and since then has contributed sixteen more stories. We meet him only at science fiction conventions, where he smiles inscrutably.

To a promising young writer we said in October, "This has its poetic moments, but there is a misty & vague feeling about it throughout and particularly in the opening, and I think that's a mistake. Stories using mythical material should be as hard-edged & specific as possible, to keep the whole thing from turning into Jell-O."

STEPHEN ROBINETT ("Tomus") told us recently, "I spent time bumming around Europe, time in the army, time collecting a couple of academic degrees (neither of them, fortunately, having anything to do with writing) and getting a license to practice law, which currently hangs unused on my wall, though it represents reasonably good job training in case writing for a living—the only thing I've ever really wanted to do—proves a financial mistake."

MICHAEL W. MCCLINTOCK ("Under Jupiter") teaches English at the University of Montana. He is thirty-four, married; three cats, no children. Except for a story which appeared five or six years ago in the *Carleton Miscellany*, this is his first published fiction. Recently we wrote to Mr. McClintock, "Thirty years ago the dominant s.f. writers were engineers or scientists, & the problem was to get them to write literate prose; now they are English teachers and the problem is to get them to keep their science straight, but there are a few people like you who can do both, & I think there is hope for us yet."

Dave Skal, a frequent contributor, wrote in December, "It is a little known fact that the distinguished English illustrator John Tenniel visited the United States in the late 1800's and while touring the West filled several notebooks with sketches of the fast-dwindling buffalo herds. The drawings were eventually collected in a volume entitled *The First American Bison Tenniel*."

MICHAEL CONNER ("Vamp") spent some time in a garment factory, being cursed at in six languages. After that he paid a visit to his alma mater, San Francisco State, where he was surprised to find the students neatly dressed and well-groomed. "When I went there, the situation was something like the oily residue of the sixties left in the bottom of a giant Mr. Coffee filter. Hayakawa was still around, and the old guard SDS, dressed in rumpled field gear, still were passing out mimeo'd communiques. (Though, in truth, Jews for Jesus were a more potent political force on campus.)"

PHILLIP TEICH ("Beings of Game P-U") is a marketing manager who lives in California; this is his first story. He would like it to be known that although he is a member of MENSA, he is not now and has never been a Scientologist.

In March we wrote to Charles and Dena Brown, editors of the science fiction newsletter *Locus*, "*Orbit* requirements are the same as before, any length to 30,000—no space opera, no conventional fantasy (i.e. no werewolves, shuggoths, kobolds, etc.)." We have been saying the same thing for ten years, but it has yet to do any good.

KEVIN O'DONNELL, JR. ("Night Shift"), not to be confused with K. M. O'Donnell, who is a pseudonym of Barry Malzberg's, got a degree in Chinese Studies from Yale, then spent two years teaching English in Hong Kong and Taiwan. His first story appeared in the October 1973 issue of *Analog*.

ELEANOR ARNASON ("Going Down") wrote us a long time ago: "I now live by Lake Calhoun—a pretty busy place, today. I took a walk around it after breakfast. Besides the usual swimmers, joggers, bicyclists, and sunbathers, I discovered a civic fish fry, a gymnastics display, and milk carton boat races. I never realized you could make boats out of milk cartons—big boats, I mean, twenty feet long and more."

Eugene, Oregon, where we have been living since January 1976, turns out to be a hotbed of science fiction. Besides ourselves, five s.f. writers live in Eugene—Paul Novitski, Duane Ackerson, Glenn Chang, Tony Sarowitz, and John Varley. We see more people here in a week than we did in six months in Florida. So much for the idea that Oregon is a remote backwater.

The drift of s.f. writers and editors westward in the last decade is one of those lemminglike phenomena for which science has no explanation. Three of the four surviving s.f. anthology series are now edited on the west coast—*Orbit, New Dimensions,* and *Universe.* California has more SFWA members than any other state, and New York, once populous, is now a desert. If we were inclined to give in to our latent Lamarckism we would say that Americans have a genetic urge to move west. Luckily there is nothing to this, or the continent would tilt.

KIM STANLEY ROBINSON ("The Disguise") is teaching a freshman writing course and working on a study of the novels of Philip K. Dick. This is his fourth published story; the first two appeared in *Orbit 18*, and the third in *Clarion*.

To our dismay, most readers who sent lists of words for the Little Lexicon for Personality Changers *(Orbit 18)* completely missed the point: some contributed time-words appropriate to the Little Lexicon for Time Travelers *(Orbit 16)*; others seem to have thought that any scrambled word would do. Five dollars and a copy of this volume go to Carter Scholz, 180 Power Street, Providence, Rhode Island 02906, for "Panama Coral," to Caroline L. Evans, Box 131, Concord, VA 24558, for "on asty," and to Carol Springs, Route 9, Box 168, Monroe, North Carolina, for "Hetero sapiens," the only three entries that seemed to us worthy of awards.

For the benefit of readers who came in late, we had better explain that each of the Lexicon words was made by substituting some personality trait for its opposite: e.g., "Linda Hatelace," "Lake Excitable," "Victor Immature," etc. Some others that would have won prizes if any reader had thought of them are "Chicken New World," "Busytame," "Sly Herbert," "depressiveotti," and "Arrogant Oil." Is it all clear now? We hope so.

In an effort to make up for this debacle, we offer still another Little Lexicon (see page 143), and this time we will take care to spell out the rules.

It is assumed that the imaginary Martian described in the Lexicon words has all the same parts and organs as a human being, but in different places. The rule of opposites does not apply, but parts and organs should be substituted in some logical way, e.g., "arm" for "leg," or "eye" for "ear."

As before, we offer five dollars and a copy of the next *Orbit* for each of the five most outrageous words submitted; in addition, we will pay twenty-five dollars for the best drawing or other representation of a scrambled Martian. Entries may be in any medium except pencil—pen and ink, wash, oil, etc. All entries become our property (but we will return them if a stamped self-addressed envelope is enclosed); we ourself are the judge, and all decisions are final, etc. Entries should be sent to Damon Knight, 1645 Horn Lane, Eugene, Oregon 97404, and must be received before January 1, 1978.